TRUMPET OF DEATH

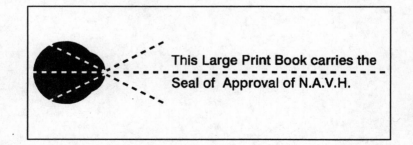

This Large Print Book carries the
Seal of Approval of N.A.V.H.

A MARTHA'S VINEYARD MYSTERY

TRUMPET OF DEATH

CYNTHIA RIGGS

THORNDIKE PRESS
A part of Gale, a Cengage Company

Farmington Hills, Mich • San Francisco • New York • Waterville, Maine
Meriden, Conn • Mason, Ohio • Chicago

Copyright © 2017 by Cynthia Riggs.
Thorndike Press, a part of Gale, a Cengage Company.

ALL RIGHTS RESERVED
This is a work of fiction. All of the characters, organizations, and events portrayed in this novel are either products of the author's imagination or are used fictitiously.
Thorndike Press® Large Print Mystery.
The text of this Large Print edition is unabridged.
Other aspects of the book may vary from the original edition.
Set in 16 pt. Plantin.

LIBRARY OF CONGRESS CIP DATA ON FILE.
CATALOGUING IN PUBLICATION FOR THIS BOOK
IS AVAILABLE FROM THE LIBRARY OF CONGRESS

ISBN-13: 978-1-4328-4394-6 (hardcover)
ISBN-10: 1-4328-4394-x (hardcover)

Published in 2018 by arrangement with Macmillan Publishing Group, LLC/St. Martin's Press

Printed in the United States of America
1 2 3 4 5 6 7 22 21 20 19 18

FOR
DIONIS COFFIN RIGGS
POET
1898–1997

CHAPTER 1

Victoria Trumbull rapped on the door to the stairway that led up to the small attic room above the kitchen. She'd rented the room to a nice young man from off-Island named Zack Zeller. She heard a sleepy grunt. The bed groaned, footsteps shuffled across the squeaky old floorboards, and he trudged down the steep stairs, scratching his bare chest with one hand, and rubbing sleep out of his eyes with the other.

"Ma'am?" he asked, politely covering a yawn. He was carrying his cell phone.

"Can you give me a ride to Sachem's Rock, Zack?"

He glanced at his phone. "Now?" He covered another yawn. "It's not even six."

"We won't have many more days like this," said Victoria.

Zack looked at his watch again. "I got to be at work by noon."

"We'll be back before then." Victoria

glanced at him. She couldn't fathom why Elizabeth, her granddaughter, had been so negative about him. Elizabeth was usually a good judge of people.

"Well, sure, Mrs. Trumbull." Zack yawned again, too polite to protest further. "It'll take me a couple minutes to get dressed." He stumbled back up the stairs to his room.

It was a perfect day for a walk, and ninety-two-year-old Victoria Trumbull had set a goal of walking one of the Island's trails every week. Her problem today had been transportation. Casey, as the village police chief was known, wasn't available to give her a ride today.

By the time she'd packed a modest breakfast picnic in a brown paper bag, Zack was back down, ducking his head under the low doorway.

He helped her into his car, a typical Island car held together with duct tape, its frayed ends drooping in the still morning air.

"Do you know the way?" Victoria asked.

He shook his head. "You'll have to show me. I been meaning to get there one of these days." He backed out of his spot under the great Norway maple at the end of the drive and turned onto the Edgartown Road.

To their left, the early fall crop of hay lay drying in Doane's pasture. The air smelled of fallen leaves and plants settling them-selves in for winter.

In the Mill Pond next to the police station, a pair of swans fed. Three of their cygnets had survived the depredations of the snapping turtles and sailed along close to their parents, almost full-grown now.

The entrance to Sachem's Rock, the two-hundred-acre conservation area, was about four miles from Victoria's house. Zack parked. The sun was almost above the treetops now and the morning was beginning to warm. Victoria slipped off her heavy sweater.

They started out on the path that lay next to the marsh, where the grasses, stirred by a light breeze, were russet and tan waves.

"September is so rich and productive," Victoria said when they stopped the first time to let her catch her breath. "A good time of year to find mushrooms."

Zack nodded.

They set off again quietly, listening to the rustle of chewinks in the underbrush, the cawing of crows in the distance.

"I guess you know mushrooms pretty well," he said after a while. They'd stopped again.

"I know which ones not to eat." Victoria smiled at him.

"I guess so," said Zack.

The path wound up a gentle slope that led to a growth of tall oaks and beech. They paused at the top of the hill. Victoria leaned on her lilac wood stick.

"I don't know anything about mushrooms," said Zack.

"The Island is a mushroom hunter's paradise. We have more than two hundred different species."

"Wow," said Zack.

"We'll probably see some common ones today. Maybe chanterelles, boletes, amanitas. Amanitas are deadly."

"You mean, they kill you?"

"Yes, if you're foolish enough to eat them."

"South Boston, where I come from, Mrs. Trumbull, the only mushrooms I seen come in blue cardboard boxes."

"When you gather wild mushrooms you do need to be careful." Victoria nudged an acorn out of the path with her stick. "Several species are quite poisonous."

"Yeah?" asked Zack. "Several kinds?"

"Yes, indeed. You need to know what you're looking for." She leaned on her stick. "If we're lucky, we may find black trumpets."

"Black trumpets?"

"They're also called trumpets of death,"

10

said Victoria. "Old-timers thought the trumpet-shaped mushrooms were played by dead people buried beneath them."

Zack bent down, picked a grass stem, and stuck it into his mouth. "Creepy."

"They're difficult to spot unless you're knowledgeable, and, of course, I never pick them."

"Why not?" asked Zack.

"They're quite rare." Victoria leaned on her stick. "If you can find them in a specialty store, they're very expensive."

"I guess so," said Zack.

"Elizabeth doesn't care much for mushrooms."

In the silence that followed, they heard the occasional croak of a frog in the marsh below. Another acorn dropped onto the ground. Under a pine tree Victoria pointed out a patch of chubby mushrooms that looked like miniature hamburger buns on fat stems.

"Boletes," she said. "Delicious."

"I don't much like mushrooms," said Zack. "Me and Elizabeth agree on that."

They continued walking. Exposed roots knotted the path. Victoria stopped every once in a while to poke through the vegetation below the oaks with her stick.

At one of their stops, Zack asked, "Are

you looking for those black ones?"

Victoria was glad to have an excuse to rest. The day was quite warm. "They usually grow under oak or beech trees."

"Death trumpets." Zack scratched his stubbly beard. "I guess you want to be careful if you find them."

"Yes, indeed," said Victoria. "You don't want people picking them."

They walked on, Victoria stopped to run her stick through the fallen oak leaves. Zack watched, hands in his pockets.

"How's your girlfriend?" Victoria asked at one point when they'd stopped. "Samantha, isn't it?"

Zack pulled the grass stem he'd been chewing away from his mouth and tossed it aside. "It's over, far as I'm concerned."

"What a shame. She seems like a nice girl."

"She seemed nice to me, too, at first." Zack took a deep breath. "It's over. She don't think so, though."

"I'm sorry," said Victoria.

"There's other girls around," said Zack.

The next time they stopped, Victoria bent down. "Look! There they are." She pointed to a dark patch among the oak leaves.

Zack stared at what she was pointing to. "All I see is dried-up brown leaves."

"Look straight down. See? They look a bit like black flowers." She pushed the leaves aside.

Zack leaned down, hands on his knees.

Nestled in a clump of leaves was a bouquet of black, ruffled, trumpet-shaped mushrooms, each one only a couple of inches tall.

He looked up at Victoria. "Those are black trumpets?"

Victoria nodded. "Yes. This is a wonderful find."

"Black trumpets of death?" He stared at them.

"An evil-sounding name for such delightful mushrooms," said Victoria.

Zack stood up straight. "I sure won't let people know what we found. Wow! Trumpets of death."

After supper, Elizabeth lit the fire, their first of the season. Earlier, in anticipation of a cool evening, she'd laid the fire with twists of newspaper, scraps of shingles, and topped with seasoned logs. When she touched a match to the paper, it caught with a satisfying blaze. Soon the dry wood snapped with a comfortable sound, sending up showers of sparks. She replaced the fire screen and hung the tongs on the hook below the mantel.

"It's really too warm for a fire," she said to her grandmother. "I'd better open the window."

"I've always liked a fire on the hearth," Victoria replied. "Even on a warm night."

Elizabeth propped the window sash open with a beach stone kept on the sill for that purpose and settled on the sofa near Victoria, who was in her usual mouse-colored wing chair.

The evening breeze blew through the west window, billowing out the sheer curtains.

Two glasses of cranberry juice and rum were on the coffee table. Victoria reached for one and took a sip.

"That hits the spot."

"How was your walk this morning with my friend Zack?" Elizabeth asked.

"We had a lovely time." Victoria set her glass down. "I found a patch of black trumpets of death. Despite their name, they're a delicacy and have a pleasing, rich flavor, something like truffles. Zack seemed quite interested."

Elizabeth said nothing. She picked up her glass.

"I don't know why you have such an aversion to him," said Victoria. "He has nice manners."

"That's about all."

"What is it that you don't like about him?"

Elizabeth set down the glass. "He's either awfully stupid or is high on something." She shifted around on the sofa with its prickly horsehair stuffing. "Probably both."

"You're not being fair to him."

"Much as I love you, Gram, I think you are blind when it comes to nice-looking bad boys."

Victoria laughed. "Bad boys have always appealed to me."

The sound of intermittent traffic on the Edgartown Road was interrupted by the distinctive low rumble of the town's fire truck. Elizabeth stood up and looked out the window. "It's heading west, up Island."

"It's likely a chimney fire," said Victoria. "People forget to have their chimneys cleaned before they light the season's first fire."

Elizabeth returned to her seat. "Did you find anything interesting on your walk besides the trumpets of death? I'd never think of those as being edible. I hope you didn't bring any home with you."

A siren sounded in the distance, coming toward them from the direction of Edgartown. In moments, a fire engine passed and the sound of the siren receded.

"A second engine. More than a chimney

fire," said Elizabeth.

"We'll find out soon enough," said Victoria.

McCavity, Victoria's marmalade cat, strode into the room, stretched, front paws out, hind quarters up, yawned, and lay down, soft belly fur to the warmth.

"I hope it's not serious, although with a second engine responding it doesn't sound good." Elizabeth got up and added another log to the fire. "Was Zack interested in the mushrooms?"

"He was interested in the trumpets of death, but otherwise didn't seem to care much about mushrooms in general," Victoria answered.

"The only smart thing I've ever heard about him."

CHAPTER 2

The next morning when Victoria was eating breakfast the police car pulled up and Casey slid out of the driver's seat, rumpled and exhausted looking.

Victoria greeted her. "You look as though you could use a cup of coffee."

Casey yawned. "I don't think I can stand another cup. I've been up all night."

"Oh?"

Casey slumped into a seat in the cookroom, a pleasant room with windows on two sides. It had served as a summer kitchen in Victoria's childhood. An oval table took up most of the room, and baskets and pots of ivy hung from overhead beams.

"What happened?" asked Victoria.

"A fire last night."

"We heard engines. I gather it was more than a chimney fire."

"All six towns sent engines." Casey looked down at her hands. "The old parsonage burned." She glanced up at Victoria. "They found a body."

"No!"

Casey nodded.

"Who?"

"Burned beyond recognition. They'll have to go by dental records."

"I didn't think there was anyone living in the old parsonage."

"It's been vacant for close to a year." Casey yawned. "My guys check occasionally. No sign of anyone staying there. At least not regularly."

"Was it destroyed?"

"The chimneys are still standing. That's about all."

"Where was the body?"

"Near what was the back door." Casey set her elbows on the table and rested her head on her hands.

Victoria stood. "How about a sandwich, something to settle all that coffee."

"Thanks. I never got supper last night."

"How did the fire start?"

"We don't know. It's still too hot to investigate."

Victoria made a bacon and egg sandwich, thinking as she worked, who could have been in the parsonage? How horrible to be trapped by fire. And what was someone doing there?

The old parsonage had been one of the oldest buildings in town. When she was a child, every year starting around Thanksgiving she skated on the parsonage pond. Now, entire winters passed without the pond freezing. Her hands would get so cold her fingers would stiffen and have no feeling. Sometimes the minister's wife would invite skaters into the parsonage for hot cider. In the warmth of the parsonage her fingers would thaw and burn with pain. The tingling pain of thawing fingers was a good memory.

How insensitive I'm being, she thought, recalling fond memories of the parsonage when someone died there last night. It could be a neighbor. If so, who?

She glanced toward the cookroom. Casey was asleep, her head resting on her folded arms. Her coppery hair formed a bright halo around her head.

Victoria put the sandwich on a plate and carried it and a napkin into the cookroom. Casey stirred and looked up.

"Thanks." She reached for the sandwich and ate hungrily.

"I was wondering why you were on the scene." Victoria sat again.

"The fire chief called me. Suspected arson." Casey wiped her mouth on the napkin. "Patrick stayed with the neighbors. They have a nine-year-old who's in the same grade." She took another bite. "This is good. Thanks, Victoria. The state police were there all night. They're still there."

"I don't suppose you have any details yet?"

"The arson team is coming from off-Island this morning. I gotta grab a couple hours of sleep before they get here, but I wanted to let you know."

Victoria nodded.

Casey carried her plate into the kitchen and rinsed it before she left. Victoria watched her go. The vision of the old parsonage was clear in her mind. So was the vision of a person trapped by a fire inadvertently set, perhaps by a dropped cigarette.

Thursday, the day after his walk with Mrs. Trumbull, Zack was bent over a sink full of dirty pots at the Beetlebung Café. The luncheon crowd had left.

He looked up from the sink, where he was elbow-deep in hot suds. Will Osborne, his co-dishwasher, was balancing a load of five or six pots, the outsides festooned with runners of boiled-over crud in shades of tomato sauce, burned milk, and baked-on grease.

"Where'd those come from?" asked Zack, shaking the suds off his hands. He pointed to the full sink. "I thought this took care of all the lunch pots."

"Yeah, that does," said Will, unloading the pots onto the drain board next to Zack. "These are from last night. Asshole cooked for a catered party. After supper. Late. Didn't think to warn us."

"Didn't it occur to him to soak the pots?"

Will snorted. "Phil? You're kidding. He's not going to dirty his hands putting pots in the sink."

"Well, shit." Zack shook the suds off his hands. "I figured I was done for the day." He stood up and pointed at the pots. "Those are gonna have to soak."

"Nope." Will shook his head. "He wants them for dinner tonight."

"Look at that stuff cooked onto them."

"Yeah, yeah." Will pulled up a stool to the prep table and sat.

"I was hoping to get out of here early," said Zack. "Any chance you . . . ?" He glanced at Will.

"Don't even think about it. I'm on lunch break. You in a hurry this afternoon? I thought the farm job wasn't until later."

"I gotta talk to my girlfriend."

21

"Sam? You mean she knows how to talk?" Will snorted.

Zack turned back to the pots in the sink. "I'm breaking up with her." He turned on the hot water and steam rose from the sink.

"About time. Surprised you stuck it out this long. She's a piece of work."

Zack said nothing. He immersed his hands into the full sink, fished around for the scrubber and went back to work.

"I warned you about her," said Will. "Didn't I."

Zack scoured a sauce pan. He rinsed it and set it upside down on the drain board opposite the one with the dirty pots.

When Zack continued to ignore him, Will said, "She hit you up for money?"

Zack turned his head. "Leave me alone, okay?"

"She did, didn't she. She's got plenty of money from her old man. But she doesn't want her old man to know about the stuff she sticks up her nose. So she likes to play, 'poor lil' ole me,' to suckers like you." His voice rose in imitation of a three-year-old. " 'I don't have any money. Lend me fifty dollars, and I'll pay you back.' Right? That what she said? How much did she get you for?"

Zack said nothing. He rinsed a fry pan

and set it on the drain board.

Will pushed the stool back and stood. "Well, good luck with getting rid of her. She sticks like Gorilla Glue." He zipped up his jacket and as he turned to leave, asked, "You met Daddy yet?"

Zack looked up, puzzled.

"Her old man. Daddy." Will pushed the swinging door and held it for a moment. "She's sure to invoke him. I gotta warn you, beware of Daddy." With that, Will went through the door, and it swung shut behind him.

Zack finished washing the lunch pots and put them away, then moved last night's dirty pots into the relatively clean water. All he could think about was his meeting with Sam when he got off work. Everyone had told him Samantha Eberhardt was bad news. He hadn't listened. She was this beautiful girl who came on to him, like a dream. Dark, shiny hair, so clean it had blue highlights. Really stacked. She was clean-cut looking, kind of innocent. A sort of red-blooded American girl look that was really sexy. And she liked him. He'd thought she did. Well, Will was right. She'd borrowed money and more money. She'd pay him back. Yeah, sure.

It had taken him a while to realize she was smoking it up or shooting it up. He knew how that went. He should have recognized it sooner.

He finished scrubbing last night's pots. He dried them and put them on their hooks, took off his apron, and headed out the swinging door into the empty restaurant.

A man, as tall as Zack, but heavier, stopped him. "You cleaned those pots from last night?" He was near the swinging doors to the kitchen.

"Yes, sir, Mr. Smith," said Zack.

"Phil. About time you called me Phil." He rested a hand on the left door.

"Yes, sir," said Zack.

"Sorry about that, letting them sit all night. Food dried on them. I apologize."

"No problem, Mr. Smith. Phil."

Phil Smith pushed the door slightly, but before going through turned to Zack. "Going to the farm job now? You're a hard worker."

"Yes, sir."

"Saving up for something? College?"

"No, sir. I been hoping to get a better car."

"You've already got a great Vineyard car. Nothing like duct tape to hold a car together." He chuckled. "See you tomorrow. And thanks, again." He pushed the door

24

open and it swung shut behind him.

Zack got into his car, only halfway listening to his car radio, which was blaring out static along with the local news. He finally switched it off.

With the static halted, he thought about his walk yesterday with Mrs. Trumbull. She sure knew a lot about plants. Amazing that she found those mushrooms. Trumpets of death. Scary what's growing out there in the wild. They're rare, she said. Probably why you didn't hear about people dying from eating them.

He knew nothing about the wild stuff that grew here that you'd better not eat or it would kill you. He'd met up with poison ivy in May, the first week he was here. Peed off in the bushes by the side of the road and got the stuff all over his legs and worse. Then there were those floating pink and blue balloon-like jellyfish, Portuguese man o' wars, that washed up on the beach, and he'd almost picked one up this summer thinking it was a balloon before an Islander shouted at him that they had poisonous tentacles that could send you to the hospital. Sharks. They'd filmed that horror movie, *Jaws*, here.

He was almost at Sam's place, and for the first time he began to have qualms about this parting talk with her. What did Will mean about Daddy? According to Sam, her father was a real softy.

Well, Zack thought, sitting up straight, in a half hour, the talk will be over, and I'll be able to get to the farm job by three o'clock.

CHAPTER 3

That afternoon, while Zack was on his way to his talk with Samantha, Victoria was typing her weekly column for the *Island Enquirer* when she heard the squeal of bicycle brakes. A young boy, a neighbor and friend, leaned his bike against the handrail and was climbing the stone steps. She got to her feet and met him as he came in the entry.

She held out her arms. "Robin! I didn't realize how late it is. Is school out for the day?"

"Yup." He squirmed out from her embrace. "It lets out at two thirty."

He was about eleven years old, small and fragile looking, wearing a faded red baseball cap turned backward so the band was across his forehead almost touching his glasses. Above the band a tuft of sandy-red hair stuck out in several directions. He wore jeans with knees frayed to horizontal threads and a gray sweatshirt.

"I haven't seen you for several weeks. What brings you to this part of West Tisbury?"

"Softball practice."

"Do you have time for a cup of hot chocolate?"

"I guess." He nodded and followed her in. Victoria set the teakettle on the stove. "Are you practicing in the field next to the fire station? I thought you usually played at the school." She opened packets of hot chocolate mix and dumped them into mugs.

Robin sat in one of the gray painted chairs. "It's just for this one big game. The fire department's sponsoring it."

"Well, I'm delighted to see you." When the water boiled, she poured it into mugs and handed one to Robin along with a spoon.

"Thanks." He took the mug and held it in both hands.

She seated herself at the kitchen table across from him. "You must have started sixth grade this year."

"Yup." He took a cautious sip. "We're having a cookout next week. Friday. Really late. After dark."

"That sounds like fun. After practice?"

He shook his head. "It's a pep rally for the game Saturday morning. We're having a bonfire and all."

Victoria, too, took a cautious sip. "Who are you playing?"

"The Charter School." He made a face.

She got up, took down the box of graham crackers and put several in front of him and one in front of herself. "Have you played the Charter School before?"

"Not softball." He reached for a cracker, broke it in half, and dipped it into his chocolate. He lifted the soggy end of the cracker to his mouth just as it was disintegrating.

"If you're playing a week from Saturday and the public is invited, I'd like to watch."

He looked up. "You would?"

"Of course. I'd like to see your team win."

He grinned and dipped the other half of the cracker.

"I need to get more exercise." Victoria watched and then dipped her own cracker, too. "I'll walk there along the bicycle path." As she lifted it to her mouth, the sodden half of the cracker dropped into her lap. "Oh, bother!"

Robin laughed. "You have to catch it quick."

Victoria wiped up the mess in her lap with her paper napkin and set the wadded-up napkin beside her place. "I don't think the ball field is more than a half-mile from here."

"I'll walk with you, then," said Robin. "I can leave my bike here."

And so it was decided.

Zack turned onto the dirt road that led up to Samantha's, a gray-shingled shack perched on a grassy hill. The house was what he'd heard Islanders call a "camp," a tiny place consisting of one room that was living room, bedroom, and kitchen combined, with a mini bathroom added on who knows how many years ago. One wall of the room had been opened up to provide a window with a wide-screen view of Vineyard Sound. Every time Zack opened the door to Sammy's place, he was faced with first her godawful mess, and beyond it that million-dollar view spread out below. Every time he went there, he marveled that his girl lived in a place that, despite its size, must rent for a thousand dollars a week during the summer. Probably more than that.

He eased up on the gas as he passed through the grove of stunted oak trees and reached an open field, the approach to Sam's place.

This will be simple, he thought. She'll probably be relieved to part company. No hard feelings.

He parked his ratty convertible next to hers, a Mini Cooper her father had given her. A birthday present. From everything Sam said about him, he sounded like a pretty nice guy.

The view from her hill was partially blocked by trees on the other side of the field. Once inside her house, though, the view was something else, especially on a clear day like today.

He got out of his car. Kind of slowly.

This talk with Sammy was going to be okay.

Three big flat stones with grass encroaching around the edges led to a fourth big stone that formed her front step. Now that he was almost at that front step he suddenly thought he should have brought her a parting gift. Well, he couldn't turn back now.

He mounted the big step and rapped on the weathered front door. In South Boston, where he came from, the peeling paint and splintered wood meant poverty. Not here in Chilmark.

"That you, Zack? Come on in."

Her voice was high and lispy like a little girl's. When he'd first heard her speak, the lisp seemed pretty sexy. But now it grated on his nerves.

31

He lifted the old-fashioned latch on the door and pushed it open. "Yeah, Sammy. It's me."

She was lying on the unmade sofa bed that partially blocked the view. Looking past her he could see the sound spread out below, and beyond it a chain of islands. Today, it was so clear he could even see hills on the far distant mainland.

He looked down at her. "Sorry I'm late."

"No problem." She sat up and muted the TV volume with the remote. As he took a step toward her, she wrinkled her nose and tossed the remote onto the bed. "Didn't you wash up? You smell like cooking grease."

"Yeah, I did. But I had a bunch of pots to clean. Left over from last night. Stuff stuck on them, and —"

"I don't want to hear about your job." Samantha shuddered. "Honest, Zack, you oughta change before you come here."

Zack was about to defend himself. After all, he was going from the dishwashing job to the farm job. The smell of manure didn't conflict with cooking grease. He kept his mouth shut.

Samantha slid off the bed and stood, tossing that mane of shiny blue-black hair over her shoulder like a wave you could ride. She nodded toward the bathroom. "Go in the loo and wash up." She'd started calling it "the loo" after watching too many British TV shows. She was pretty tall, but not as tall as he was. Her bathrobe opened when she stood, showing off an extremely small orange bathing suit he hadn't seen before.

"Stop staring and clean up, will you?"

"You look good."

"Go!" She fastened the belt around her robe.

He did the best he could, knowing that the kitchen smell was coming from his clothes, not from him. He dried his hands and face and went to confront her, feeling as though he'd already lost the first round.

"Sammy, I need to talk to you."

"You don't smell much better." She'd closed up the bed while he was in the bathroom and was standing in front of the TV switching channels, the sound still muted. She didn't look up.

"You want to sit?" he asked.

She looked up. "Why?"

"I don't know. Just that we need to talk." This was not going to be as easy as he'd thought. "Want to go outside? Sit on the grass?"

"What's the matter with you? You want to talk, then talk." She turned back to the TV and fixed it on some channel he couldn't see from where he stood.

"I've been thinking, Sammy —"

"Glad to hear that."

There was a chair next to the bathroom door. He reached for it, but didn't sit. "I mean, you know, we've had some good times together." He stopped. This wasn't the way to begin.

She looked up from the TV. "Oh?"

"Don't you want to sit down?"

"No."

He needed to sit for this discussion. But as long as she was on her feet he should stand. Besides, if he sat and she stood, she'd tower over him and he didn't need that.

"Well. Okay. I think maybe it's time to call it quits. Go our own ways, you know?"

"No, I don't know." She jammed her hands into the pockets of her bathrobe.

He held on to the back of the chair. "I mean, my jobs . . . I don't have any more money I can lend you . . ."

She stood there, no response, silhouetted against the view so he couldn't see her face.

"No hard feelings, Sammy. I got to, you know, go my own way. You been real good to me . . ."

She still said nothing, stood like a statue.

"Well . . . I guess this is, like, goodbye, then." He let go of the chair back. He thought about turning to leave.

Samantha spoke. Her voice was no longer babyish. "If that's what you think, you've got another think coming."

"You don't . . . you don't need to pay back the money I loaned you." He grabbed the seat back again. "I figured you feel the same, you know. About me. We seen enough of each other."

Samantha laughed, not a nice laugh. "Backing out of responsibility, *Zack*?" She emphasized his name.

"What do you mean?" She was the one who owed him money. "I said *you* don't owe *me* a thing."

"Is that right." Not a question. "You forget all those afternoons and evenings we spent together."

"What are you talking about?"

"If you recall, we did more than a little fooling around, *Zack*."

Zack paled. "We were, you know, real careful."

She laughed again. "Not careful enough."

"We were. Both of us. Real careful."

"Oh?" said Sam. "Think again."

"You're not . . . ?"

"Think not?"

"Jeezus!" He lifted his hands from the back of the chair and immediately set them back, a helpless gesture.

"You think you're dropping me? Just try."

Zack didn't know what to think. He couldn't speak. Didn't know what to say even if he could.

"Drop me and I tell Daddy about those times we spent together."

Zack's mind spun. He couldn't think the word *pregnant*. What did it mean, anyway? An abortion? A baby? Marriage? Beware of Daddy, Will had said.

"Daddy will just *love* having you for a son-in-law." Her little-girl voice was turned on again.

Zack backed away. He bumped into the counter that held the sink. Felt behind himself for the door. Pushed it. Latched. Turned. Pushed down the thumb-hold that unlatched the door, and the door flew open.

And he fled. Down the big step, across the three flat rocks with the grass growing in on them. To his car, so crummy looking next to her flashy new Mini convertible.

Samantha slammed the door behind him and watched from the many-paned window as Zack stumbled across the field toward his car, wrenched the car door open, backed carefully away from her convertible, and drove off with the scritching sound of sand under spinning tires.

"The nerve of him." She turned away from the window. "No goddamned loser is going to ditch me first." Sam undid the belt of her bathrobe and shucked it off. She grabbed the remote and flicked away the images on the TV screen. "I'll show him who gets to call it quits first." She retrieved her jeans from under the sofa bed and tugged them on over her orange thong. "Just you wait, Mr. Zack Zeller. Just you wait."

While Zack fled from Samantha's, the regulars at Alley's Store were in their usual positions, early today because of time off in respect of the death at the old parsonage. Joe the plumber leaned against the post that held up the roof, Sarah Germain sat on the bench next to the rusty Coca-Cola cooler, and Lincoln Sibert, tall and lanky, leaned against the frame of a door that led into the store.

"What's the matter, Linc?" asked Joe. "Something bugging you?"

"Yeah."

"That son of yours?"

Lincoln said nothing.

"He still seeing that Eberhardt girl?"

"That's what's bugging me," snapped Lincoln.

"Cheer up," said Sarah. "She's been hanging out with that kid who lives at Mrs. Trumbull's. She's probably ready to drop Sebastian."

"Zack Zeller," said Joe. "She hangs out with him and Sebastian and a few others besides."

"Cut it out, will you?" Lincoln turned and smacked the door frame with his fist. He brought his fist up to his mouth and sucked it.

Joe took a package of Red Man out of a pocket. "This too shall pass." He took his penknife out of another pocket and carved off a chunk of tobacco.

"Thanks." Lincoln lowered his hand. "Just what I need. You and your philosophizing."

"Not me," said Joe, stuffing the tobacco into his jaw. "Some dead Persian wrote that."

"Where's Sebastian now?" asked Sarah.

"He didn't come home last night."

"Doesn't sound like a big deal to me," said Joe.

"Of course he comes home at night. He's only sixteen."

"Not me when I was sixteen," said Joe.

"You'd be home in bed asleep by ten, if you were my son," Lincoln snapped.

"Don't worry about him," said Sarah.

"He's a good kid."

Joe said, "Not to change the subject, but that was some fire last night."

Lincoln turned away.

"Have they identified the body yet?" asked Sarah.

"Cops don't share nothin' with us," replied Joe.

"They think it's arson," said Sarah.

"I coulda told 'em that." Joe looked over at Lincoln, who was slumped against the doorframe. "C'mon, Linc, lighten up."

"I've got to go." Lincoln straightened and, without another word, left his spot next to the door, stepped off onto the asphalt parking lot, got into his truck, and steamed off. Joe and Sarah watched his truck disappear, heading toward Chilmark.

"That Eberhardt bitch is trouble," said Joe. "Someone's gonna take care of her one of these days."

CHAPTER 4

Zack headed toward his farm job, scarcely noticing the scenery around him. Twenty minutes later he was almost at the airport before he'd calmed down enough to think straight after that meeting with Sam.

Yesterday he'd felt like telling Mrs. Trumbull that his girlfriend was getting weird, like the stuff she was snorting was frying her brain or something.

Now telling him she's pregnant. If she really was pregnant, it wasn't him. Was this her idea of a joke? She was probably getting even with him because he broke up first. Marriage to her was definitely not in his plans. He couldn't imagine it in her plans, either.

This summer was the first time he'd had a job away from his familiar haunts in South Boston, where he'd worked as busboy in a crummy restaurant. He'd come to the Island to earn some money. With two jobs, he'd end the summer with a chunk of cash. But then he met Samantha. Didn't take long before he could tell she was snorting or shooting up or smoking his money. Like it belonged to her.

He hit the steering wheel with the palm of his hand. Exactly how much time did he have? He knew nothing about having babies. How long would it be until she showed, if she really was pregnant. How long did he have if she had to get an abortion?

How did he get out of this mess?

He'd passed the airport and was almost at the big windmill by Morning Glory Farm before he thought of his walk with Victoria Trumbull yesterday. Those black trumpets of death had been sort of in the back of his mind all morning. Amazing how the mind works.

He'd go to Sam, apologize, offer to patch things up. A friendly meal together. Those nice black mushrooms would make her sick and that would end the pregnancy.

But he for sure couldn't have dinner with her and not eat them.

He was thinking so hard, he passed Meeting House Road, the shortcut to the farm. Well, he had time and the long way wouldn't delay him that much.

He was still thinking as he came to where

41

the road ended in a *T.* He'd only just learned the nice-looking captain's house in front of him was the county jail. Not a place he'd like to stay, nice as it looked on the outside.

He turned right onto Main Street.

He'd present her with some of the black trumpets. Tell her they were a delicacy. He'd be shocked when she got sick. For sure lose the baby, if there even was one. Why, he had no idea they were poisonous, he'd say. Mrs. Trumbull never said they were.

As he headed toward Katama and the farm job, he flipped on his radio with a lighter heart. Never say die, he told himself.

This will be easy.

The following day, Friday, Zack got up early, even before Victoria was awake. He borrowed one of her baskets, drove to Sachem's Rock, and retraced his steps to the place they'd walked two mornings before. It took him a lot less time to find the death trumpets because he didn't have to stop every few minutes while Mrs. Trumbull examined something on the ground or in the trees or in the sky. He picked every one of the little trumpet shaped mushrooms and they half-filled the basket.

He drove to work leaving the basket in the

car, the mushrooms covered with one of Mrs. Trumbull's red-checked napkins.

Will greeted him at the door of the restaurant. He'd parked his bicycle in the rack next to the hedge. "How'd the meeting with Samantha go?"

"Fine," said Zack with a bright smile, not wanting to hint that he felt ready to kill the bitch.

"I don't believe you," said Will, grinning.

"No, really, fine. Everything was, like, friendly."

Will shook his head. "You're shitting me. Samantha has never, and I mean never, let a guy walk away from her first. She's a control freak." They headed toward the kitchen. "But okay. Believe what you want. Vampires turn into vegetarians. Samantha turns into the Sugar Plum Fairy." He pushed the swinging door open and they both went into the kitchen.

"What's the luncheon crowd look like?" asked Zack.

"We got a lot of reservations. More than usual. Plus the usual walk-ins. Means plenty of dirty dishes."

"He cooking anything messy this noon?"

Will laughed. "Doesn't he always?"

They laid out detergent and scouring pads.

Zack said, "You know anything about mushrooms, Will? I mean, like how long they keep?"

Will looked up. He'd been kneeling by the sink looking for a brush. "Where'd that come from?"

"Just curious."

"One kind turns black and slimy almost right away," said Will. "I think most kinds keep for a week, maybe more. They dry pretty good."

Zack was thinking of the black trumpets. It would be just his luck to have them be the ones to turn black and slimy. He changed the subject. "I hope the mess is not too bad today. I want to leave early."

"A parting with sweet Sam?"

"Ex-Zack-ly," said Zack, and grinned at his own cleverness.

The morning had a feel to it that Victoria loved, a sort of closing in. Sounds were clearer. The atmosphere seemed to magnify them. She could hear foghorns as far away as the distant North Shore. She would go for a walk this afternoon and let beads of moisture collect in her hair, just as she'd done when she was a child.

After lunch, she hiked the short distance to the tiny police station next to the Mill

Pond. She carried a paper sack of stale bread in her cloth bag for the ducks, geese, and swans that inhabited the pond. When they saw her coming, they flocked around, honking and quacking. She emptied the sack of crumbs and made her way up the steps to the station house door, which she knew would be unlocked.

She knocked. "Anybody home?"

Casey looked up from her paperwork. "Yeah, but not for long. Got to go back to the fire site. You want to come with me?"

"Yes. I'd like to see what's there."

"Have a seat, Victoria. I have to finish up this stuff." She pointed to the pile of papers in front of her. "Paperwork," she said in disgust. "Well, it's not as bad as it looks. I won't be a minute."

While she waited, sitting in the wooden armchair in front of Casey's desk, Victoria watched the swans immerse their heads and long necks into the water to nibble on morsels in the bottom muck. How perfectly they were designed for the job of foraging in shallow water.

Casey tossed down her pen, straightened the pile of papers on her desk, and stood. "That's it. Let's go."

"Any word on the victim's identification?" Victoria followed Casey down the steps.

"They sent what information they could about the victim's teeth to Island dentists, and if that doesn't yield any IDs they'll widen the search to dentists on the Cape. Maybe as far as Boston."

"How long is that likely to take?"

Casey shrugged. "No idea."

Victoria seated herself next to Casey. "We'll have fog later this afternoon."

"Looks to me like nice sunny weather in the works."

"There'll be fog." Victoria took her blue hat out of her cloth bag. Gold lettering on the hat read WEST TISBURY POLICE, DEPUTY.

"You're usually right about weather." Casey backed out onto the main road. "You seem to have a sixth sense about it."

Victoria settled her hat on her head and pulled down the sun visor to peer into the small mirror.

By the time she'd finished, they had gone the short distance to Brandy Brow and the triangle where State Road, South Road, and the Edgartown Road joined. And where, straight ahead, Victoria could see two chimneys and the ruins of the parsonage. Thin trails of smoke drifted with the breeze.

"Have you had any reports of missing people?"

Casey shook her head. "Nope."

They turned into the drive next to what was once the parsonage and parked near an array of vehicles, all with insignias on their door. The entire charred area was cordoned off with yellow tape that fluttered in the light breeze. White-suited, booted, and hooded investigators poked through the rubble. Radios crackled with static and voices.

Tears stung Victoria's eyes. A tragedy. The death of a human being as yet unknown and the death of a fine old building.

Someone must miss that person. Who? Surely, somebody must be worried.

When Zack finished the lunchtime dish-washing and cleanup that afternoon, he went out to his car to check the condition of the black mushrooms. He lifted the napkin that covered them to make sure they weren't the kind that turned into slime. They looked as fresh as when he'd picked them this morning. He replaced the napkin and headed for Sam's place.

Thin tendrils of mist drifted in from the Sound. When he drove up to her place, the tendrils were snaking up the hill. He shivered. Summer was over and once he got rid of Samantha he'd go back to South Boston where life was normal.

He parked next to her Mini and reached into the backseat of his car for the basket. He gathered up his jacket from the front seat and tossed it over his shoulders.

He knocked on her door and, when there was no answer, walked around to the back of the house. Thin fog was beginning to mask the sun. Samantha had gotten up from her lounge chair. She was wearing that same tiny orange bathing suit, earbuds in, listening to something on her iPhone. She didn't notice him at first, and he watched her shrug into her white terry cloth robe, tossing her body around in time to music he couldn't hear. The view out over the water was blotted out. A seagull flew overhead mewling.

She turned, saw him, and pulled off the earbuds. "What are you doing here?"

"I came to, like, apologize."

"Is that right?" She tightened the belt of her robe. "Aren't you supposed to be at the farm right now?"

He held up the basket. "I brought you a present."

"It's freezing out here." She shivered and ignored the basket. "I'm going inside. Bye!" She stepped up onto the back deck and opened the door.

He followed.

She turned. "You still here? You're blocking the door."

He followed her inside. Why did he let her make him feel so stupid? Well, Samantha Eberhardt, we'll see. He held up the basket again.

She glanced at it. "What did you bring me?"

He went over to the kitchen counter and set the basket on it. "Something really special." He removed the napkin with a flourish, but it caught in the handle, ruining the effect. He grabbed the basket before it fell.

She peered into it. "What's that?" She looked up at him. "What are they supposed to be?" She tossed her head, and her hair flew over her shoulder in a blue-black cascade.

"Mrs. Trumbull took me mushroom hunting." Zack stroked the stubble on his chin. "They're black trumpet mushrooms."

"What am I supposed to do with them?"

"Victoria Trumbull says they're a delicacy," said Zack, stretching the truth a bit.

"I'm not about to eat something that grows wild in the woods. They're probably poisonous."

Zack flinched. "Mrs. Trumbull's word is

good enough for me."

Samantha picked up the basket. "Well, then, thank you soooo much. I'll put them in the fridge and sauté them for our supper. You will be here for supper, won't you?"

"I can't." Zack assumed a stricken look. "There's a potluck supper at the farm."

"Tomorrow, then?"

"No, you go ahead. Anyway, I picked them for you. Will you forgive me?" He leaned toward her about to kiss her.

She pushed him away. "That beard of yours scratches." She pursed her mouth. "Now we're friends again, maybe we should keep the baby. Wouldn't you like that?"

The fog closed in quickly. A thick fog that swirled around him like a cape, drifting around his feet. He could barely see his way back to his car.

Would she eat the mushrooms? Didn't sound as though she was real excited about them.

Maybe the whole thing was a waste of time. What if she did eat them and got really sick or even died?

He didn't really hate her. He just didn't want to marry her. Or, my God, have a baby with her.

Almost the worst thing was the basket,

one of Mrs. Trumbull's favorites. And the red checked napkin. He'd taken them without asking her. He'd have to get them back before she missed them.

He had time to go back and retrieve the basket, the napkin, and the mushrooms. He'd march in and tell Sammy that since she didn't want them, he was taking them back to Mrs. Trumbull.

But he didn't want to face Mrs. Trumbull with the rare mushrooms. She'd told him not to pick them.

He didn't want to face Samantha, either. She wouldn't eat them.

He got into his car, started it up, and inched his way slowly down the dirt road he could barely make out toward the main road and his farm job.

It would serve her right if she ate them. They weren't going to kill her, after all.

Those black trumpets of death loomed up in front of him, a giant basket the size of the restaurant's sink. Black mushrooms, like grease-caked saucepans, danced before his eyes.

Go back?

No. She won't eat them.

He slammed his hands on the steering wheel.

He'd fucked up again.

CHAPTER 5

The minute Zack left, Samantha tossed off her robe, slipped buttercup-yellow sweats over her bathing suit, took the basket of black trumpets out to her Mini Cooper, and set it on the front seat. She switched on the headlights, but that simply made the fog close in. She turned the lights off and drove slowly down her road. At the main road, the fog was thinner, and she went straight to her father's house overlooking Quitsa Pond. She glanced back toward her little house on the bluff, but it was hidden in a dense cloud.

Her father was having his post-lunch martini on the deck. He was sprawled out on a teak bench, feet up on a coffee table. The once-bright sunlight had become watery and cool. He stood as she came up the steps onto the deck.

"Sweetie pie, what brings you here?" He set the martini glass down on the coffee table. He was several inches taller than she, built like an ex–football player. His thinning silver hair was cut short.

Samantha nodded at the sliding door. "Where's the bitch?"

"I like those yellow sweats," said Daddy. "Good color for you."

"She inside?"

"You don't mean Isabella, do you?"

"You got someone else?"

"Now, now," he said, patting her shoulder. "Be a good girl. Isabella and I are having a few people over for supper next Friday. Care to join us?"

"No thanks, Daddy."

"Got other plans?"

"I'm going off-Island for, maybe, a week. Maybe more."

"Doing something special?"

"Not really. Shopping. Take in a couple shows. More shopping. Dinner with friends." She held out the basket. "That stupid Zack, the guy who has the hots for me, gave me these."

He looked into the basket. "Black trumpets. Well. Where did he find them?"

"Who knows. He went someplace with Victoria Trumbull and he claims she said they're good to eat. I don't trust him."

He picked one of the mushrooms out of the basket. "One of the choicest mushrooms there is, sweetie pie. Like truffles."

"Black mushrooms?"

"I'll get Cook to prepare something special with them for our dinner Friday. Sorry you won't be here."

"Thanks, but I'm not sorry," said Samantha. "Besides, she gives me indigestion."

"Not Cook, surely?"

Samantha gave him her look. "How much longer are you going to let her live off of you?"

"Now, now," said Daddy.

Samantha headed for home down the long drive and turned onto South Road. She hadn't gone far when a deer leaped out of the undergrowth to her right. She jammed on the brakes, skidded on the moisture-slick surface, and the car stalled. An oncoming pickup materialized out of the fog and narrowly missed her. The horn blared and the high-pitched blast faded off into the distance.

"What did you expect me to do, asshole?" she shouted at the disappearing taillights. She started up the engine, pulled over to the side of the road and sat, calming her nerves. What an idiot. God, she was lucky he didn't crush the Mini. He probably wouldn't have noticed.

Once she calmed down she thought about Zack and his black mushrooms. She had an idea. She fished her cell phone out of the pocket of her sweatpants and punched in Number 1.

"Sweetie," Daddy answered. "Where are you? Driving's tricky. You be careful."

"You're not just kidding. I almost got creamed by some freak in a pickup."

"Hope you're not driving and talking on the phone."

"No, Daddy. I'm parked." She switched the phone to her other ear.

"You get his license number?" He sounded concerned.

"He was going too fast."

"Anything at all?"

"How am I supposed to know? He went past me in a blur. Anyway, I'm almost home." She paused. "Daddy, would you do me a big little favor?"

"Of course. Anything my sweetums wants."

"You're serving those black mushrooms Friday, aren't you?"

"They're in the fridge. Cook's got her recipes spread out over the kitchen table now, as we speak. Isabella informed her she's to serve the black trumpets Friday. Pièce de résistance."

"How much longer is that *bitch* going to be around?"

"You keep asking me that, darlin'." Daddy laughed. "We'll see. Now, what's my little girl's big little favor? Another car? Your Mini too small for you?"

"You're so silly, Daddy. I want you to invite Zack to dinner."

"Is that all? When?"

"Friday, of course. When you have guests and serve those mushrooms he gave me."

"That would be a nice gesture, sweetie. Will do. Haven't met my darlin' girl's boyfriend yet."

"He thinks they're poisonous."

A pause. "What's that?"

"You heard me."

"I don't think I did."

"He thinks they're poisonous. He does, Daddy."

"And he gave them to you?" his voice rose. "Thinking they're poisonous?"

"He gave them to me and when I invited him to stay for supper — I said I'd cook them — he refused."

"I'd say that says something about your culinary skills. Doesn't mean he's trying to poison you."

"Stop it, Daddy. Believe me. He thinks they're poisonous."

"And you want me to invite him to supper Friday." Her father paused. "And he thinks those mushrooms of his are poisonous." After another long pause he barked out a short laugh. "They *are* called trumpets of death, you know."

"I don't know anything about mushrooms."

"Right up there with truffles, eighty bucks a pound."

"Daaaddy! I don't care about mushrooms."

"Clever little girl. Chip off the old block. Give me his number before you leave town. How long did you say you'll be gone?"

"A week or so."

"Have a good time, then. Don't forget to call." He lowered his voice. "I'm going to enjoy meeting your boy. What did you say his name is?"

"Zack."

"Fine, fine. I look forward to this meeting."

Samantha started up her car again. By now all her landmarks were obscured and she had trouble finding her drive. When she reached her house she opened the bottle of wine she'd had in the fridge and poured herself a full glass.

Fog eddied around outside her house,

closing everything in. The view below her was gone. Somewhere a foghorn moaned, unusually loud. Mournful. Every sound was magnified. Somewhere close, a vehicle engine whined then stopped. Eerie how sounds carried. Condensation dripped from the eaves, sounding like footsteps, and she shivered.

This kind of weather could drive people crazy, if they let it. Creeping on little cat feet, for sure. She sank onto her sofa bed, switched on the TV, surfed channels until she found a soap she could tolerate, and turned up the volume to block out the sounds outside.

"I'm not letting that stupid weather dictate to me." She reached for her wineglass and held it up. "Let's see how Mr. Asshole deals with Daddy and his ugly black mushrooms." She swallowed a mouthful, hardly tasting it. "Sorry I won't be here to see him react to Daddy's dinner invite."

Someone knocked on the door, and Samantha started out of her reverie. "Come in!" she called out.

The door creaked opened and she glanced up. At first she couldn't see who it was in the large yellow slicker. Then she laughed. "Come on in. You're just the person I want to be with on this creepy afternoon."

She reached for the remote and switched the TV off.

"How about a glass of wine? Or two. I've already started."

"I wonder if Sebastian's home yet," Sarah said to Joe later that afternoon at Alley's. Lincoln still hadn't shown up.

"He's probably with Samantha." Joe spit off to one side.

"You know, Joe, that's disgusting."

"Want me to swallow it?"

"Stop!"

"It kills bugs. Good pesticide."

"It's going to kill you, too," said Sarah. "Sebastian's a good kid. He'll probably come home all apologies."

"When he does, Linc better give him a good whaling."

"Not Lincoln. You shouldn't be so mean to him, Joe."

Joe carved off another chunk of tobacco and stuck it in his cheek. "Only way to shake him outta it."

"You know, I do wonder where Sebastian is," said Sarah. "It's not like him to worry his dad like this."

CHAPTER 6

On Sunday morning the sky was the brightest blue possible, a fluorescent blue so brilliant it sparkled.

Victoria greeted the morning as though this day was prepared just for her. She put on her Sunday-go-to-meeting clothes, her green plaid suit, a soft white blouse with bow tie at the neck, and her everyday shoes with a hole cut in one to relieve her sore toe. No one ever noticed that she wasn't wearing something more stylish. She clipped on the green earrings that Jonathan, her husband, had made for her out of jadeite stones he'd found washed up on the beach.

The leaves, still unchanged, still on the trees, were fresh with moisture from two days of fog. Spiderwebs of the finest silk spread like drying linen on the bright green grass. Mourning doves called. A *V* of Canada geese flew overhead.

Not many years ago the geese would head

south this time of year to spend winter in far places like Chesapeake Bay. Now they wintered on the Island. But the far places must still be calling them, for they circled overhead, honking with that nostalgic sound she recalled from childhood, a sound that meant approaching autumn.

The church bell began to ring. She could hear it clearly from the kitchen, the half-hour warning before service would begin.

"Ready, Gram?" Elizabeth, looking quite spiffy with her short sun-bleached hair and becoming tan, was wearing a light gray pantsuit with black turtleneck shirt.

At the church door they greeted friends and neighbors, and once inside sat in their usual pew in the fourth row left of the center aisle. The organ music and choir were as joyful as the day, a good day to be alive. Vases of brilliant flowers flanked the altar. Sunlight poured through the tall windows touching them and they glowed as though they had an inner light. Victoria sat quietly, the way she'd been brought up, soaking up the calmness and peace of the simple church with its plain wooden pews and clean, white-painted walls.

The music ended. The service began.

Time for the Reverend Milton Jackson to launch into his sermon. He spoke about the fire at the parsonage and about death and loss, and the day seemed less bright. He talked about the inhumanity of mankind. About the destruction of priceless treasures by senseless mobs abroad. About human thoughtlessness and cruelty. About the selfishness of politicians. About people's abandonment of God.

The day dimmed for Victoria. She thought of the joy she'd felt an hour earlier, when the world seemed so bright, so hopeful, so innocent, and she'd believed such magnificence had been created just for her. She felt a wash of selfishness.

The final hymn. The benediction.

The congregation filed out.

"Wonderful sermon, Jack."

Hand shaking.

"A lot to think about, Reverend."

"Inspirational."

Victoria slipped past.

"Are you okay, Gram?" asked Elizabeth as they went down the steps of the church.

Victoria shook her head.

Elizabeth said, "That sermon was kind of a downer, wasn't it?"

Victoria nodded.

"Cheer up, Gram. We have a lot to be thankful for. Sunday dinner is in the oven, ham and scalloped potatoes, ready to heat up."

Victoria smiled.

On Monday, Lincoln Sibert made a formal report to the West Tisbury police that his sixteen-year-old son, Sebastian, was missing.

By Wednesday, there was still no identification of the body in the parsonage.

Lincoln had feared from the very beginning that the victim was his son. On Wednesday he drove to the West Tisbury police station and gave Casey the name of Sebastian's off-Island dentist and his office telephone number in Falmouth.

"I hope we can rule out Sebastian, Lincoln," said Casey.

"There's nowhere else he can be." Lincoln wore his usual plaid shirt, jeans, and scuffed boots. "I need to know, Chief."

"I'll call over there right now." Casey put the paper with name, address, and phone number next to her computer. "How long has it been since his mother . . ." She couldn't finish.

"Five years," said Lincoln. "Sebastian was eleven."

"Oh, God," said Casey. She stood.

"Drunk driver on State Road." Lincoln

was standing in front of Casey's desk.

"I remember." She looked down at her desk. "I remember too well. I'm sorry, Lincoln." She came from behind her desk to Lincoln and put her arms around him. He stiffened.

Casey backed off.

"I know it's Sebastian," he said. "And I know who's responsible." Lincoln turned and stumbled out of the station.

Casey watched the tall, lanky man with his almost caved-in chest, until he'd driven away. She went back to her desk and called the Falmouth number for Sebastian's dentist.

Before she left for the harbor the following morning, Elizabeth was having a second mug of coffee. "Has there been any word on the fire victim yet, Gram?"

"I should hear from Casey any minute," said Victoria. "She told me she'd call as soon as she heard from the dentist."

The phone rang.

"I'll get it." Elizabeth answered and handed the phone to Victoria. "It's Casey."

Victoria listened, her face solemn. Without another word, she passed the phone back to Elizabeth, who put it in its cradle.

"Anyone we know, Gram?" Elizabeth

picked up the coffee mug again.

"Lincoln Sibert's son, Sebastian."

Elizabeth held her mug tightly. "I don't know what to say."

That same evening, Zack's phone barked like a dog. He checked the number, didn't recognize it, but answered.

"Zack, my man," said a hearty male voice. "This is Samantha's daddy. How're you doin'?"

"Ah . . ." Zack paused ever so slightly. "Fine, sir, thank you."

"The girlfriend and I were just saying how we'd like to meet you, get to know you. Meet little Sammy's boyfriend, you know. About time you got to know her old man, we were saying. Sammy's off-Island, you know. Shopping. Girly get-together."

"Yes, sir," said Zack.

"Want you to come to dinner tomorrow night, Friday. Nothing formal." He laughed. "A command appearance, you might say."

Before Zack had a chance to finish swallowing the bile that suddenly rose in his throat, Daddy went on. "Tomorrow. See you at seven."

"I'm afraid I . . ." stammered Zack.

"Won't take no for an answer. According to my Sammy you're quite a fellow. No need to dress up. We're having a few friends over. You know where my place is, of course. Tomorrow at seven."

"Thank you, sir, but . . ." he had already disconnected.

What had she told Daddy? Zack thought. I don't want to meet him. Or his girlfriend. I don't want to go to dinner at his house. There's no way I'm going. I've gotta get out of this somehow.

He staggered down the narrow stairs and barely made it to Mrs. Trumbull's bathroom before he threw up. Maybe he could cancel last minute. The thought made him feel sicker. Maybe he was coming down with something.

As he came out of the bathroom and into the kitchen, Victoria looked up with a smile that instantly turned to a look of concern. "Are you all right?"

"Thank you for asking," said Zack, blotting his lips with a pad of toilet paper. "Just a little upset."

"I'll fix you some tea and cinnamon toast. That always helps."

"Yes, ma'am."

"Sit down." Victoria pointed to a gray-painted kitchen chair. She put two slices of bread into the toaster. "What has upset you?"

"Not exactly upset," said Zack. "I mean
. . . ," he paused. "Yes." He looked down at
the pad of toilet paper he still held.

"Do you care to talk about it?" Victoria
took the glass jar of cinnamon and sugar
from the cabinet over the sink and set it
next to the toaster along with the butter
dish. Then filled the teakettle and put it on
the stove.

"Mr. Eberhardt invited me to dinner."

Victoria looked up and laughed. "Why,
that's wonderful. When?"

"Tomorrow."

"You don't need to be nervous about your
girlfriend's father inviting you to dinner."

Zack looked up. "I told Sammy we're
breaking up."

"Oh?" said Victoria. "How did she re-
spond?"

"It wasn't good," said Zack.

The toast popped up and Victoria buttered it and sprinkled the cinnamon mixture
on it. The kettle whistled. She rinsed out
the teapot with boiling water, then added
tea and water.

Zack watched her in silence. Then he said,
quite suddenly, "She was gonna tell her
father she's pregnant."

Victoria turned. "Are you responsible?"

He shook his head. "No, ma'am. No way.

Definitely not."

She went back to her tea-making. "Then you have nothing to worry about. It's Samantha's problem, not yours."

"Yeah, but she said . . ." He didn't finish.

Victoria set the cinnamon toast and tea in front of him. "I don't think you have a thing to worry about, Zack. From what I've heard, Samantha has a number of male friends."

Zack bit into his toast. "You don't understand, Mrs. Trumbull."

Victoria flushed. "Yes I do, Zack."

She fixed her own tea and turned to him. "If you're not the father, it's not your problem. Go to dinner tomorrow night. Don't let him intimidate you. And you have a good time." She sat down and helped herself to a piece of toast. "The best defense is a good offense."

"Yes, ma'am." Zack set the uneaten portion of his toast on his plate. The one bite he'd taken was still dry and crumbly in his mouth and he couldn't swallow it.

"Get a good night's sleep, Zack. Things will look better in the morning." She glanced at him. "Perhaps you're coming down with something."

Zack looked down at his uneaten toast. "I hope so."

CHAPTER 7

On Friday morning, Zack hadn't appeared at eight o'clock, the time he usually got up. At eight thirty, Victoria knocked on the door at the foot of the steps and opened it. "Zack? It's getting late," she called up.

The bed frame squeaked, she heard his feet thud onto the floor, and a sleepy voice called down. "What time is it?"

"Half-past eight. I've made coffee for you and an egg sandwich. You can take it with you."

"Omigod, thank you, Mrs. Trumbull. Be right down."

A few minutes later he stumbled down the stairs into the kitchen. "Thank you for waking me up." He rubbed his eyes with the back of his hand. "I didn't get to sleep until the birds started singing." He rubbed his stubbly chin.

"If you're worrying about dinner tonight, stop, this very minute." Victoria was wondering as she spoke to him, how he had managed to keep the unkempt growth on his chin the same length for the entire four months he had lived here. "You're worrying about nothing. Dinner will be delicious and you'll enjoy meeting the people."

"Thanks again." Zack picked up the thermos of coffee and the sandwich bag. "I'll wash the thermos and bring it back."

He darted out the door just as Elizabeth appeared, dressed for work in her uniform of tan slacks and a white, short-sleeved shirt.

"What's his problem?" she asked.

"He overslept."

"One thing I'll say in his favor, he's conscientious about that dishwasher job." Elizabeth went over to the coffeepot and poured herself a cup.

"I'm glad you found something redeemable about him."

Elizabeth joined her grandmother at the kitchen table. "Was he out late last night with that girlfriend of his?"

"Samantha? No. He's broken up with her."

"He told you that?"

Victoria nodded.

Elizabeth took a sip of coffee. "I didn't think he had the guts."

"Apparently she didn't take the news

70

well." Victoria got up and poured herself more coffee. "He told me he'd gone back and apologized to her, and she said something about their being friends again." She returned to her seat. "I don't think he's happy about the situation. He's been invited to dinner tonight at her father's."

"That would be enough to cause anyone a sleepless night. Dinner with Samantha's father? Brrr."

"Have you met him?" Victoria sipped her coffee, her eyes half-closed in the steam.

"No, but I've heard enough about him."

Sunlight poured through the east door, creating a warm path on the wood floor. McCavity stalked in, stopped in the sunlit area, turned around several times, and laid down.

Elizabeth watched. "What a soft life cats lead."

"I'm going to walk over to the police station and talk to Casey." Victoria took a deep breath and stood.

"I'll give you a ride," said Elizabeth.

The station house door was open and Casey was sitting at her desk, staring out the window, when Victoria entered. The police chief was focused on something other than the waterfowl on the pond.

"Casey?" Victoria interrupted her thoughts.

Casey turned to her. "Sebastian was a nice kid. What was he doing in the parsonage? He wouldn't break into an unoccupied building."

Victoria took her seat in front of Casey's desk. "He was smitten by the Eberhardt girl."

"Samantha. You know anything about her?"

"Not really." Victoria rested her hands on her lilac wood stick. "The boy who's renting that room from me, Zack Zeller, is, or was, dating her."

"What are you thinking, Victoria?"

"I don't know what to think." Victoria glanced up.

Casey picked up her beach stone paperweight and tossed it from one hand to another.

"Yesterday afternoon," Victoria continued, "her father called and invited Zack to dinner tonight. Zack is so apprehensive, he's sick to his stomach."

"I don't suppose he can very well decline." Casey dropped the stone back on top of a pile of papers and sat back. "Why I asked about Samantha is because of what Lincoln

Sibert, Sebastian's dad, said to me yesterday."

"About Samantha?"

Casey nodded. "He didn't actually use her name, but it was clear he believes she's responsible for Sebastian's death."

"That's extraordinary," said Victoria.

Casey picked up the stone again and tossed it back and forth, over and over.

"Was the parsonage locked?" asked Victoria.

Casey snorted. "As I discovered when I first got to this crazy island, nobody locks doors. People leave keys in their car's ignition while they go shopping." She swiveled in her chair. "The police station didn't have a lock until I asked at Town Meeting to have a lock installed. Even then, a lot of villagers thought that was an unnecessary expense."

"It's a public building," said Victoria. "It should be available to the public."

"Sure, Victoria, with all the records and forms and . . . oh, forget it." She tossed the stone down. "Yeah, the parsonage was locked, but a two-year-old could have broken in. The lock dated from seventeen-something."

"It would be an attractive secret meeting place, on a slight rise with the back door facing the pond, not the road," said Victoria.

"The arson team is going over the remains of the building now. They can deduce amazing stuff just from the ashes." Casey turned to look at the pond. "Sebastian was a decent kid. And his father is crushed. Something he'll never get over."

"I'd like to talk to Samantha and hear what she has to say," said Victoria.

"All we can do, Victoria, is give the state cops all the information we have, all our suppositions, suspicions, everything. We can't get involved."

Victoria said, "But —"

Casey held up her hand. "I mean it, Victoria. It's not our jurisdiction. We have to give Lincoln all the support we can. He's going to need it."

CHAPTER 8

Although it was a beautiful, clear evening with the sun just beginning to set, Zack felt as though the entire world was, enveloped in a dense soup.

Was he crazy? Why was he heading toward Samantha's father's house? Furthermore, it was Friday the thirteenth. Why didn't he have the guts to say no to this dinner invitation? Mrs. Trumbull had noticed how sick he was.

Did Samantha tell her father she was pregnant?

He didn't want to think about that.

He slowed down to make a U-turn back to the safety of Mrs. Trumbull's, when the dump truck that was on his tail blasted its air horn at him, startling him. He sped up.

The next dirt road was her father's driveway, and he flipped on the right turn signal. The dump truck's horn blasted at him again. The sound trailed off as the truck passed.

The long unmarked road led up a hill to the house. A sprinkler was soaking the manicured grass in the center strip for a natural rutted-road Island look. When he reached the end of the road Zack parked in a wide area paved with crushed white shell and opened his door. Before him and below him was a view overlooking a pond that was full of small boats.

He felt a sour rush in his stomach. How come other people were messing around in their boats with not a care in the world, and here he was, about to have dinner with Samantha's father. And his guests.

He swiveled in his seat and set both feet on the crushed shell. He groaned and stood up. His first meeting with Samantha's father. He straightened his pant legs, which had ridden up above his ankles. He took a step in the direction of Daddy's house. His feet sank into the crushed shell and slowed him. The walk to the house was up an incline that was broken into steps with old railroad ties. The steps were higher than he expected. He stumbled and caught himself before he fell.

He straightened his shirt. He should have changed it. Mrs. Trumbull said it looked fine, but how many times did she go calling on someone like Samantha's father?

He coughed and felt in his pocket for a used paper towel.

He climbed the second step. And the third step.

In what seemed to be the far distance there was a level area and stairs that led up to a wide porch where people were gathered.

Somehow he climbed the fourth and last step and crossed the level area. The sound of cocktail chatter got louder and he could make out individual words. All seemed to be about money or boats or horses.

A huge, hearty man with a glowing tan and short silver hair greeted him. He was dressed in tan slacks with a knitted white collared shirt, identical to Zack's.

"Zack, my boy! Nice to meet you. Where's Sammy been hiding you?" Daddy slapped him on the back and Zack staggered. "Come meet my friends. Can't tell you how delighted we are you provided us with our supper." He slapped Zack's back again.

"Sir?" Zack was dumbfounded. What was he talking about?

"My guests look forward to this meal. When they heard you are the one responsible for what promises to be a memorable treat, well, they can hardly wait to shake your hand."

Zack felt sweat trickling down the back of his shirt, the one exactly like Daddy's. "I . . ." said Zack. "I . . . I . . . I . . . ?"

"That's okay, boy. I don't want to embarrass you. But I have to compliment you on your generosity."

"Generosity?" Zack finally blurted out. "Sir . . . ?"

"Why, black trumpets, of course," he said. "Don't think I've ever eaten one. You know they're also called trumpets of death. Odd name for a mushroom we're about to dine on. Have to tell you, this meal is going to be memorable." He whispered in Zack's ear, "Only invited a half-dozen close friends. Don't want the whole world to know what we're having for dinner." They were standing on a deck of some kind of expensively oiled wood. Daddy held up his hand and the chatter ceased. "Folks, meet Sammy's fiancé. The man who brought us the black trumpets."

There was a smattering of applause. In the midst of it, Zack felt the porch tilt and the people began to swirl around him in a ghastly dance. Sick people. Hospitalized people. Maybe someone would die? Their sepulchral voices merged together in a cacophony of guffawing and mocking

78

sounds. Zack reached for the porch railing to steady himself.

"You okay, boy?" Daddy's concerned voice broke through the chorus. He placed a large hand on Zack's shoulder. "You look like death warmed over. Hunger, that's what it is. Growing boy. Need to get some food into that stomach of yours."

Zack shook his head. "I'm fine, thank you, sir." An idea hit him. "Must be coming down with something. Better get on home. Don't want anyone to catch whatever . . ." His voice trailed off.

"Nonsense. Double shot of bourbon, perk you right up." He raised a finger. "Kill whatever's bothering you."

Out of his haze Zack saw a white-coated figure approach. The figure was holding over its head a white-napkin-covered tray topped by a squarish bottle of some golden liquor and a glass full of presumably the same stuff. He shut his eyes briefly and when he opened them things had cleared. In front of him stood Will Osborne, his fellow dishwasher at the Beetlebung Cafe.

"How's it going, Zack? Double shot of bourbon coming up."

Daddy had turned away and was conferring with a bosomy blonde.

Zack shook his head and held up a hand.

"No, thanks, Will."

"Boss's orders." Will held a hand up to his mouth so only Zack could hear. "Drink it and smile. The stuff ain't cheap."

He turned away from the blonde and back to Zack. He waved at the glass Zack held in trembling hands. "Fourteen-year-old Wild Turkey you're holding there. Fix you right up, boy." He took hold of Zack's upper arm. "Want you to meet the GF. Girlfriend, you know." He gestured to a tall dark-haired woman in a form-fitting red satin dress with spaghetti straps. "Isabella, meet our Sammy's fiancé." He turned to Zack.

"How lovely." She smiled. "What did you say your name was?"

"Zack, ma'am."

"Isabella's an Indian from Gay Head, son."

Isabella's smile was forced. "He meant to say, 'Wampanoag from Aquinnah.' " She offered Zack her hand. "How do you do."

After they shook, she discreetly withdrew a tissue from a pocket, wiped her hand of Zack's cold sweat, and smiled at Daddy. "It's not called Gay Head anymore, darling." She crumpled the tissue and turned away from Zack. "If you'll excuse me. My guests."

Daddy turned to the blonde he'd been

80

talking to. "Leah Littlefield, this is my little girl's fiancé, Zack . . ." He turned to Zack. "Never did get your last name, son."

"Zeller, sir," said Zack.

"How appropriate," cooed Leah. She reached into the neck of her blouse and tugged at a hidden shoulder strap. "You know, of course, I'm sure you know about Zeller's bolete."

"Um, no ma'am." Zack was confused.

"The mushroom. Zeller's bolete." She sipped a bit of wine and said, "We're so thrilled about the black trumpets you've brought us. I don't believe any of us have ever tasted them."

Maybe this was an opening. Zack said, "I understand you have to be careful about wild mushrooms."

"Oh, yes!" breathed Leah. "There's one perfectly delicious mushroom that you'd better not eat if you drink. A few drinks too many, and it will kill you." She smiled and with a wave of her hand moved on, murmuring over her shoulder, "Lovely to meet you." A silvery bell rang, and Samantha's father led his six guests and Zack to a polished wood table set with tall lighted candles and a centerpiece of white orchids. Isabella directed guests to their seats. Each place setting had a hand-woven white linen place mat, two wineglasses, one short and fat, one tall, and a variety of knives, forks, and spoons that Zack puzzled over during a brief moment when he wasn't worried about the black trumpets.

There was a small bowl of cold white soup with a sprinkling of green stuff in front of Zack. He stared down at it, waiting for someone to be the first to pick up a spoon and let him know which one.

Guests bowed their heads, and Zack did too.

"Bless us, O Lord," said Daddy, "and bless this fine food we are about to partake of."

The grace went on and on and Zack, too, prayed. "Please, dear God, save me this one time. I promise I'll go to church. I'll even marry Sammy . . ."

He finished with a hearty "Eat up, folks. You may never have another meal like this."

Zack lifted a spoonful of soup but couldn't open his mouth. He laid the spoon down on the saucer. Conversation buzzed around him. He felt as though he were somewhere else, maybe floating around the ceiling watching the dinner party from above.

Someone was talking to him. The woman to his left.

"I'm sorry, my mind was somewhere else."

Zack turned to her, politely tilting his head toward her.

"I asked where you'd found the black trumpets. They're quite rare, I understand." The woman, a plump person with white hair, blue eyes, and a pink embroidered jacket, paused briefly, then went on. "I don't suppose you want to give away your secrets, do you?"

"Ah . . ." Zack was interrupted by a smattering of applause.

The cook had entered carrying a large serving dish of something smothered in a white sauce with black lumps floating in it.

"Black trumpets over wild rice," murmured someone. "How lovely!"

Zack pushed his chair back and stumbled to his feet. "Sir," he mumbled to Daddy, who sat at the head of the table to his right. "I don't feel so good. I'm afraid I'm going to be ill . . ." and he rushed out of the dining room, staggered across the porch and down the flight of stairs, made it across and down the railroad-tie steps, wrenched open his car door, somehow despite violently shaking hands, got the key in the ignition, started the car up, and fled.

Hell's fiends pursued him as he drove back along the rutted dirt road. The sprinkler system that kept the grass green in the center started up again suddenly and dashed water against the underside of his car, startling him. A bird of some kind screeched. The road was endless. He wondered briefly how much money it took to keep the center of the dirt road looking unnaturally natural like that. Then he thought of Samantha's father, his girlfriend, Isabella, and their six guests sitting around that polished wood table dining on death's trumpets. He stopped the car, opened the door, leaned out, and emptied his stomach of nothing but bile.

He had to leave the Island. Now. He certainly couldn't return to Victoria Trumbull's upstairs room. But he had to go up to his room to pick up his clothes. The trip to West Tisbury was endless.

As he turned into Victoria's drive he saw lights were already on in the kitchen, though it wasn't dark yet. He backed out and drove around the corner to New Lane, where he could see the lights. He'd wait until they went out. Then he would slip in and gather up his stuff.

CHAPTER 9

While Zack was escaping from what he had convinced himself would be eight seriously sick people at Daddy's dinner, Victoria and Elizabeth were in the kitchen shelling dried beans. Victoria had harvested them from the garden that afternoon. In late summer, after they'd had their fill of green beans, Victoria let the remaining crop dry on the vine until the pods were crisp and papery and individual bean seeds rattled inside.

Elizabeth picked a dried pod out of the basket on the table, slit it open with her thumbnail, and nudged five perfectly formed yellow-eyed beans into the bowl between them.

"I wonder how Zack is coping with dinner at Daddy's." Elizabeth slit another pod and shook out four rock-hard beans.

"He was terribly nervous," replied Victoria.

Elizabeth indicated the basket a quarter

full of the papery-shelled bean pods. "Are those the last that need to be shelled?"

Victoria nodded. "We'll have enough to get us through the winter." She reached for a full pod. "We had Boston baked beans every Saturday night when I was a child. Always made with yellow-eyes."

They worked quietly for a while, each thinking her own thoughts.

After a few minutes, Elizabeth tossed an empty shell at the compost bucket. It missed and fell on the floor. She pushed her chair back and stood. "Samantha's father wants to show ex-wifey, Samantha's mother, that Samantha loves him better than she loves her."

Victoria looked up again. "That does happen."

"Whatever Samantha wants, Samantha gets."

"You've had some dealings with her?"

"I've seen her around." Elizabeth bent down and picked up the dropped empty shell.

"I've never known you to be so upset about someone, Elizabeth. What's the trouble?"

"The trouble is, Gram, that she's toying with Zack, and he's not bright enough to understand."

"I thought you didn't care much for him."

Elizabeth pulled her chair closer to the table and sat again. "I don't." She reached for a handful of bean pods. "But I hate to see someone with money and power tease someone who has neither money nor brains." She looked up with anger in her eyes at her grandmother. "It's like those nasty children who torment cats."

"I see."

"When he wakes up, something unpleasant is going to happen, believe me," said Elizabeth.

"He doesn't plan to be here much longer now the season is over."

"He can't leave soon enough for me. I can't stand seeing the drama unfold."

Victoria checked her watch. "It's getting late. He should be home soon."

Elizabeth glanced up. "Maybe this is Zack. A car just stopped in the drive."

Victoria eased herself out of the chair with a sigh. "I've been sitting too long." She straightened her back and went to the kitchen door.

From where he was parked, Zack saw the police car pull up in front of Victoria's. All he could think was, The police are looking for me. The guests. Someone must have died. I gotta get out of here. And now. He needed to get his clothes and stuff. He'd have to wait somewhere until it was safe to go back to Mrs. Trumbull's.

The ball field. He could walk to her house from there on the bike path.

He started up his car, turned on his lights, made a careful U-turn, drove to the field, and left the car behind the fire house, where it was partially hidden from the road. He grabbed his flashlight out of the glove compartment. He'd slip into Victoria's house, get his belongings when it was quiet, then leave the Island on the next boat.

The bike path curved around behind the ball field before it paralleled the Edgartown Road. He slammed the car door and headed off to Mrs. Trumbull's. Twilight was turning into night.

On the path, trees on either side arched over him. The wind was blowing, and the trees cast eerie shadows. He watched his step, careful not to trip over a rough spot camouflaged by moving shadows. On either side the bushes were almost waist high. He'd heard that a lot of the underbrush on the Island was huckleberry and you could eat the berries.

No way.

His stomach ached. The hand holding his

flashlight trembled.

He'd touched those death trumpets. He'd picked them and put them in the basket. Maybe they poisoned you by touch, like poison ivy or those Portuguese man-o'-wars. All he knew about stuff that grew in the wild was you'd better not eat anything you found, especially mushrooms, unless you were dead sure what it was. He shivered. Mushrooms could kill.

With that thought, hot acid rose up in his throat, again, and he spit into the under-brush. Something rustled, and when a small shape scurried across the path, he yelled out. A skunk. That was all he needed, to startle a skunk.

He waited until his heart slowed down, then walked on.

How long after eating those black trumpets before Samantha's father and his guests got sick? Probably not right away. They'd finish dinner, say good night, go home, and in the middle of the night . . .

Would they wake up with a horrible pain in the gut? Would they know what caused it?

That police car showing up at Mrs. Trumbull's . . .

He heard voices back at the fire house. The town ambulance was kept there. Maybe the EMTs were coming for it.

Something screeched above him. Or was it the sound of sirens rushing to the scene? Sweat trickled down his back. Tree branches were rubbing together in the wind.

He'd walked almost halfway to Mrs. Trumbull's. Why had he been so stupid as to think of feeding poisonous mushrooms to Samantha? Dumb, dumb, dumb.

He stumbled over a shadow and caught himself. Weird how a shadow can trip you up. He bent down to catch his breath and when he did he thought he heard footsteps in the dry leaves beside the path.

Was someone following him? Maybe it was a deer. Or a skunk. This Island was full of things that lurked in the dark. He walked faster, stepping high over the shadows that might hide roots and stones.

Did he really have to go back for his clothes and stuff? All the money he owned was in his wallet, a hundred bucks or so. That would get him off-Island and on his way to freedom. He could write to Mrs. Trumbull. Have her send his things to him.

He turned back toward the ball field and his car. He couldn't spare the time to pick up his stuff. Mrs. Trumbull could keep his TV. She didn't have one.

Heading back, he hurried. He was moving

pretty fast by the time he came to the swale. He wasn't watching where he stepped and he skidded down the slope. He tumbled into the small valley, his feet slipped in a damp spot, and he fell, facedown. He lay still. Didn't try to get up. Gasped for breath. He would lie here forever. Maybe it was all a bad dream.

The dinner party broke up amid compliments on the food and requests for the cook's recipe.

"Delightful young man, sorry he had to leave early," said the buxom blonde to Samantha's father. She kissed him wetly, full on the lips. "I hope whatever he's got isn't catching."

"A fine fellow." Daddy pulled his handkerchief out of his pocket. "He certainly didn't look well."

The last car pulled away and he returned to the dining room. The cook had already cleared away the remains of the meal.

Isabella approached, holding a phone out to him. She wore her dark hair loose, brushed back so it hung partway down her back in soft waves. She'd changed into a loose silk dressing gown, green, printed with bright red hibiscus flowers. "Darling, don't you want to call your daughter to report in?

Here's your phone."

He took it from her, pulled out a dining room chair, punched in Samantha's number. He turned the chair and sat facing one of the windows with his feet up on the sill.

Sammy's ringtone ended and a robotic voice said she wasn't available. He smiled and disconnected.

"No answer, darling?" Isabella put her hand on his shoulder.

"She's off-Island for a few days. Probably having a night out with the girls."

"You mean boys," said Isabella. "Correction, any old males."

He lowered his feet from the windowsill and stood. "Watch yourself. That's my daughter you're talking about."

"A chip off the old block."

"What d'ya mean by that?"

"She's like you, darling." Isabella laughed. "A slut."

"God damn you!" He drew his arm back and slapped her. "Shut your mouth."

Isabella put her hand up to her cheek and backed away from him. "A slut! Slut!"

He took a step toward her. She turned. He snatched at her gown and grabbed a handful of silk. She wrenched herself free. The gown ripped and she ran.

He looked at his watch, reached for his

black suede jacket, and headed for the garage. Chose the green Jaguar, backed out, and headed down his long driveway to North Road.

"That bitch," he muttered. "She'll be sorry."

"Zack couldn't have had a better dinner than ours." Victoria folded her napkin and set it beside her empty plate.

"He probably didn't have much appetite," said Elizabeth. "I guess Samantha's father is enough to terrify anyone."

Victoria glanced out the window. "Junior Norton is here with a copy of the arson report."

The police car stopped and Junior got out.

He came in and took off his hat. "Evening, Elizabeth. Evening, Mrs. Trumbull." He looked at the empty plates still on the table. "Looks like I missed another great Trumbull meal."

"We've got leftovers," offered Elizabeth.

"Thanks, but no thanks. I've got to run. Here's the copy of the report the chief wants you to have. The parsonage fire was deliberately set." He handed a manila envelope to Victoria.

Victoria took it. "Do they know how it started?"

"Not yet. But it's amazing what the arson team can do with nothing but ashes."

Junior had left, and Elizabeth had finished carrying dishes to the sink when a car door slammed and a tall, thick-set man came up the steps. He was about to knock when Elizabeth opened the door.

He might have been nice looking with his close cropped silver hair and tan, but at the moment his jaw was set and he looked, to Elizabeth, as though he was in very tight control of himself. She backed away.

"May I help you?" she asked.

The man stepped up into the kitchen. "Would you mind telling me where he is?"

"I beg your pardon?" said Elizabeth.

"I'm looking for Zack, or whatever his name is."

Victoria stepped up into the kitchen, still holding her napkin. "Good evening. I don't believe we know you, do we?"

"I beg your pardon." He turned. "I'm Bruno Eberhardt. I need to talk to Zack." He glanced at Elizabeth. "Can you tell me where he is?"

"Would you be Samantha's father?" asked Victoria. "If so, I believe he was planning to have dinner at your house this evening."

The man's clenched hands were down by his sides. "That's right."

94

Victoria was at a loss. She set her napkin on the table. "Won't you sit down? Didn't he show up?"

"I beg your pardon. I'm upset." He sat, but immediately stood again. "Do I understand correctly that he lives here?"

"He rents an upstairs room." Victoria sat at the kitchen table. "He was heading for your house a little before seven. That's the last time we saw him."

Eberhardt nodded. "He arrived but left as dinner was served."

"May I ask what this is all about?"

Eberhardt sat again and sighed. "It has to do with mushrooms that he intended for my daughter. She brought them to me."

Victoria sat forward. "Mushrooms?"

"Black trumpets."

"Zack gave them to your daughter? They're quite a delicacy."

"I know, I know," said Eberhardt.

"He and I went on a walk earlier this week, and I pointed them out to him. I told him they were rare and we don't pick them," she said with some asperity. "It seems he went back and did just that."

"When the cook brought in the dish, black trumpets in a cream sauce over wild rice, Zack left in a hurry."

"I know he wasn't feeling well," said Victoria.

Eberhardt sat still for a moment. "Am I doing him an injustice?"

"I don't understand," said Victoria.

"Did he know they were edible?" Eberhardt asked.

"I assume so," said Victoria. "I simply showed him a patch of them I'd found. He'd never seen them before."

"You told him they were black trumpets?"

"Black trumpets, yes," said Victoria. "Black trumpets of death."

"Ah," murmured Eberhardt.

"He told me the only mushrooms he'd ever eaten were the white button kind that come in blue pasteboard boxes in the grocery store."

"You told him they were a delicacy?"

Victoria thought. "I told him they are rare, and I recall telling him they are expensive if you can find them in a specialty store."

Eberhardt shook his head.

"Just what is the trouble?" asked Victoria.

"I'd been led to believe he thought they were poisonous."

"By whom?" asked Victoria. "I didn't indicate any such thing."

"The 'whom' is someone who can be overly dramatic on occasion." Eberhardt turned to her. "Do you know where he might be?"

Elizabeth exchanged glances with Victoria and shrugged.

"I must say, when I came here looking for him, I was upset. Is it possible I am misjudging him?"

"I'm sorry we can't help," said Victoria. "Give me your phone number." She handed him a notepad. "We'll call if he shows up."

Eberhardt scrawled his name and phone number. He stood. "I'm sorry to have bothered you."

They listened to his footsteps on the stone steps. Headlights flashed on. The car door shut with an expensive thunk, and the car headed out of Victoria's drive.

After silence returned, Victoria said, "What do you suppose that was all about?"

"I can't imagine," said Elizabeth. "But I'd never have believed I'd feel sorry for Zack."

CHAPTER 10

Zack, stunned by his fall, wasn't sure at first what had happened. He was cold. He lay still for a few minutes and recalled sliding down the slope, tripping in mud, and falling. He sat up. His head hurt. He ran his hands up and down his legs, felt his arms, gently fingered his head. No obvious injuries. He got to his feet slowly. The night's darkness had closed in and a chill dew had settled. His shirt was muddy.

His flashlight. Must have rolled off to the side of the path when he fell. He had to find it. He bent down to look, holding his throbbing head, and saw a faint glow under a heap of fallen leaves. He had to get that light. Needed it to get back to his car, and fast.

He glanced over at the pile of leaves. The pile seemed large. It was faintly illuminated by the glow from his flashlight. Somebody must have raked it up here. Maybe the wind had piled the leaves up. As he reached his hand toward the leaves he thought of snakes nesting there. Snakes terrified him. Everybody said there were no poisonous snakes on Martha's Vineyard, but the idea of a cold, clammy, slithery body, or worse, a whole nest of snakes . . .

This Island was full of poisons — ivy, jellyfish, and mushrooms.

He had to stop thinking like this. He had to get back to his car. First he had to retrieve his flashlight to see where he was going. He thrust his hand into the leaves and touched something soft, yielding, and cold. He withdrew his hand with a startled yelp.

Snakes!

He had to get outta here, now. He could picture a nest full of aroused snakes coming after him, coiling and sidewinding and hissing.

The light. Snakes or no snakes, he had to get that light.

Despite the chilly night air, he was sweating profusely. He approached the glow under the leaf pile again, kicked the light out from under, and headed back to his car.

He reached it out of breath, stinking of sweat.

Voices. A campfire. Shadows dancing

around it.

What was going on? A gathering of witches. Who were all these people?

A tall lanky guy loomed out of the darkness. "How're you doing?"

Zack gulped.

"That your car?"

"Yeah. Is there some problem?"

"Not for us. The team's about to have a cookout and we saw your lights were on. Turned them off."

"Thanks. Thanks a lot." Zack wiped the sweat off his forehead with his forearm. "Appreciate it."

A small boy ran up to them, backlit by the bonfire so Zack could only see a black silhouette.

The man tousled the boy's hair. "This is Robin, the guy who noticed your lights were on."

Zack put his hand up to his aching head. "Thanks, Robin."

"Don't know how long they were on," said the man. "Hope your battery's still got juice in it."

"Thanks," said Zack, again. "Thanks a lot."

"We're having a pep rally, really, really late," said Robin. "That's how come I saw your car lights."

"Thanks," said Zack.

The boy darted around the car and went back to the fire.

The man stuck around. "You okay?"

"Yeah, yeah, sure. I'm fine."

"If you haven't eaten, we've got the fire going and we'll be putting hot dogs and hamburgers on the grill." The guy's face was hard to see. "Join us if you want. Rally for the softball game tomorrow."

"Thanks. Really nice of you." Zack wiped his forehead with the back of his hand. "Think I might be coming down with something. Don't want to give it to the kids. But thanks again. See you."

"I'll wait. See if you need a jump start."

Zack got into his car, the engine caught after a few feeble coughs, as it normally did, he gave the man a wave, and headed out.

His dashboard clock read nine o'clock. Maybe he could make the last ferry. Nine thirty, he thought. He had to hurry.

He drove as fast as he dared, not wanting to invite the attention of either West Tisbury or Vineyard Haven police, and made it to the Steamship Authority dock as cars were being directed onto the boat. He parked at the end of the standby line and dashed into the waiting room where the ticket counter was. Sweat poured down his forehead, down his back, and down from under his arms. He was covered with mud from his fall. I must stink, he thought.

"Can I get my car on this boat?" He was out of breath.

"Passengers only," said the man behind the glass window. His badge read STEP. "No cars." He peered at Zack over the top of his glasses.

"I have to get my car over," said Zack.

"Best we can do is give you a reservation on the eight a.m. boat tomorrow morning." Step checked something on his computer. "The six and seven o'clock boats are booked."

Zack peered out the window at the cars still driving onto the ferry. "Can I go standby?"

The guy shook his head. "Not a chance. They're lining up standby for tomorrow's boats."

"I've got to get off-Island now."

"You can go as a passenger, but you better hurry." Step leaned over and looked out the window. "Nope. They've closed the doors. Too late."

Zack set both hands on the ticket counter and lowered his head.

"I can sell you a reservation for eight a.m. tomorrow." He glanced at Zack. "You better get a good night's sleep, buddy. Looks like you could use it."

Zack paid for his reservation and put the receipt in his pocket.

"You can try standby tomorrow morning for an earlier boat, six or seven. But you're all set for the eight a.m. for sure."

"Thanks," said Zack. He made his way back to his car. Three vehicles had parked behind him and the drivers had left. Gone someplace for a night's sleep. Maybe he should crash here. He thought about that. No, he'd better park someplace else and sleep in the car. Try for an earlier boat, but definitely get on the eight o'clock.

Where, though? Not Mrs. Trumbull's. Not the ball field. Once he found a place to park he'd think about what to do then.

There was only about two feet of clearance between his car and the one in back and the same for the one in front. He had to inch backward and forward several times before finally getting out of the line.

What now?

The Park and Ride lot. That would be a safe place to spend the night. The lot was at the top of a hill only a short drive from the ticket office.

South Boston was a sanctuary. No one would find him there.

He drove up the hill and turned into the first row, where he found a parking slot midway down the line of parked cars. He backed in to get a quick start in the morning.

He padded the space in the middle of the front seat with a beach towel from the backseat and curled up around the gear shift.

In the early part of the evening cars drove into the lot, slowing as they passed his car. He had an awful feeling they were looking for him. The front seat was not designed for a comfortable night's sleep, but he wanted to be ready to take off at daybreak and he didn't intend to do more than just rest.

He pulled his jacket over his head to block out the light from the lot's illumination. The chill night air and terror kept him awake.

He'd try to make one of the earlier boats. At least he had a confirmed reservation for eight o'clock. Once he was on the boat, he'd be home free. His breath steamed up the windows. A gusty wind arose. Loose duct tape flattered against the convertible top. He must stay awake. He had to get off the Island.

Robin arrived at Victoria's house shortly after eight o'clock on Saturday morning, more than an hour before he was to report to the ball field. He leaned his bicycle against the railing and bounded up the steps. He was wearing a long-sleeved jersey with wide purple and white stripes, his name in large block letters across the back, and he carried a new-looking bat and an equally new-looking glove.

"Good morning, Robin. You're awfully early."

He thumped his bat on the floor. "Yeah. I guess." He shifted from one foot to another.

"Are you nervous about the game?"

"Nah." Thump, thump. His red baseball cap was on backward as usual. His glasses had slipped down his nose and he pushed them back into place with a finger.

Victoria indicated the bat and glove. "It looks as though you have brand-new equipment."

He nodded. "My grandfather got it for me."

"That's sure to bring you good luck."

"I thought, you know, since we're walking we better go early."

"Of course," said Victoria. "We're likely to get there first." She saw his anxious expression. "But it's a nice day for a walk."

"It might take us a long time to walk there."

"Well, I've packed a snack in case we get hungry." She held up a brown paper bag. "Shall we head for the ball field?"

They crossed the road and started off along the bicycle path. The ball field was about a half mile from Victoria's. The morning was clear and crisp, a perfect day for the game. They walked slowly, Victoria swinging her lilac wood stick and Robin swishing his bat at the underbrush. They'd been friends since he was in third grade, a long time ago, and didn't need to talk, at least not much.

A flock of wild turkeys scurried across the path. Farther on, a rabbit hopped out in front of them and then disappeared into the underbrush. The path veered away from the road and dipped into a hollow, where it was sheltered by overhanging trees.

Suddenly, there was a rush of wings, a loud cawing, and several crows took flight from the undergrowth, startling them.

Robin stopped abruptly. "What was that?"

"Crows," said Victoria. "They're feeding on something."

"That was kinda scary."

"Crows are very bright. Let's see what they found to eat."

A heap of leaves had been pushed off to the left side of the path and made a mound about three feet high and almost eight feet long. The crows had uncovered something inside the heap of leaves.

Robin reached it first. He stared, then stumbled backward in a hurry, his hands up to his face.

"What is it, Robin?"

"Something awful." He looked up at Victoria and she saw that his face had paled.

"What do you mean?"

"Like," he paused. "Like, somebody's arm?"

Victoria approached the mound carefully. He was right. The crows had uncovered an arm. She glanced at Robin, who was holding a hand to his mouth. "We've got to call the police. Do you have a cell phone?"

"No." His freckles stood out a greenish hue against his pale face. "I think I'm going to be sick."

"No wonder," Victoria reassured him. "Go back a ways so you don't disturb anything. Then I want you to run ahead to the ball field and get someone to call 911. If no one's there yet, call from the fire house. I'll wait here."

While Victoria waited, she leaned on her lilac wood stick and studied the pile of leaves. She must be careful not to move around anymore than was absolutely necessary. In the distance, she could hear activity at the ball field. Others had come early. Kids shouted, she heard grown-up voices. Laughter.

Who had dumped leaves here and why? It was an odd place for a leaf dump. Had someone raked the bicycle path and this was a convenient spot to dump them? She shook her head. Hardly. The trees sheltering the path were mostly oak, and still had their leaves. The leaves on the pile were a lighter color than oak, most likely maple.

Was that arm still attached to a body? She hated to think of either case, a detached arm or an attached one. Had it, or its body, arrived with the pile of leaves when it had been dumped here? The leaf pile was certainly out of place on the side of the bicycle path.

She had glanced at Robin's discovery and had no more than a fleeting image of an obscenely grayish-green bare arm the crows had uncovered in the leaf pile. Bent at the elbow, a hand, forearm, and upper arm. When she sent Robin to get help, she'd assumed it was attached to a person. But when she thought about it, perhaps not.

She looked at her watch. It would take Robin only a few minutes to get to the ball field. He'd raced off, a terrified rabbit, zigzagging along the path until he was out of sight. Only a minute or two to tell the grown-ups at the ball field what he'd seen. Most of the adults were volunteer firemen, ready for almost any emergency. They'd contact the state police and the police should be here shortly.

Her paper bag of snacks was light, but her arm was beginning to throb from holding it stiffly. She started to set it on the ground, then decided she'd better not disturb the immediate area around the leaves.

She didn't want to think about the arm. It wasn't visible from where she stood. But the sight was burned into her mind. How would Robin deal with the memory of that? A nightmarish arm. First she'd worried about Robin. Then she'd been afraid he might contaminate what was certainly a crime scene.

She heard voices.

A squirrel scampered down the trunk of one of the oak trees, in quick starts and stops headed for the leaves.

"No!" Victoria called out. "Get away!" She looked for something to toss at the squirrel, but it had stopped. It stood on its haunches, took a quick look at Victoria, and scurried back up the tree.

She heard a chickadee call "pee-wee." Voices were louder and pounding footsteps approached. Three men raced toward her.

She called out, "I haven't moved since we discovered . . ."

The men halted abruptly. The leader, Ira Bodman, called out to her. "The state cops are on their way, Mrs. Trumbull. They'll be here momentarily." He paused. "How're you doing?"

"Fine," said Victoria.

"We'll take over from here, unless, I mean, I know you work with the West Tisbury police . . ."

"I'll wait here," said Victoria. "But I'd like to sit down."

Ira beckoned to the other two. "One of you go back quick and get a folding chair."

"I'll go," said the younger of the two and raced off.

He was back within minutes, and Victoria seated herself with a sigh to await the state police. It wasn't long before they arrived.

"Morning, Mrs. Trumbull." Sergeant John Smalley touched his fingers to his hat. Smalley was a big man, a former football player who'd kept in pretty good shape. "We contacted Chief O'Neill. She's on her way." He motioned to his two troopers. "Tim, you and Ben start clearing the leaves away. You know the drill, a few leaves at a time, careful not to disturb anything. Expose enough of the body or whatever we've got so Doc Jeffers can do his work."

It was a relief to sit after standing for such a long time. She was on the opposite side of the path from the body, so she could watch the troopers work, both of whom she'd known since they were children. When they had cleared enough leaves, she could tell the arm was attached to a body, and when a not so faint unpleasant odor drifted her way, she knew the body had been dead for some time. She couldn't tell whether it was male or female, young or not so young.

Smalley and the troopers took photos and measurements, speaking so quietly she couldn't hear what they said, then Smalley left.

Casey arrived in uniform, tan trousers and short-sleeved white shirt, with the town insignia on one arm. Her heavy utility belt with its arsenal of police paraphernalia hung low on her hips. She had parked at the ball field and walked to the site.

"Now what, Victoria?" Casey hoisted the heavy belt into place.

"Robin White and I were walking to the ball field where he's to play a softball match this morning. When we heard crows cawing he investigated." Victoria shifted on the uncomfortable log. "A horrible experience. He was terribly upset."

"I can imagine. How old is he, eleven?"

"Yes."

Casey stood next to Victoria. There was a sheen of perspiration on her forehead. She brushed her hair away from her face.

On the other side of the path, the pile of leaves now formed a nest around the body. The body was distorted by death. It was dressed in ragged jeans and T-shirt. The arm Robin had seen was limp, flopped down on a bloated stomach. The face was grotesque. How could anyone identify this. Victoria looked away.

The two troopers stood some distance from the body.

"We'll keep watch until Doc Jeffers shows up," said Casey.

Chapter 11

Doc Jeffers, the medical examiner this week, arrived on his Harley within a half-hour. He swung one leg over the seat of his bike, stood up, and stretched. He was tall and broad shouldered with thick arm muscles and looked more like a motorcycle mechanic than the number one doctor at the hospital.

"Morning, Mrs. Trumbull." He tugged off his leather motorcycle gauntlets and stuffed them into his pockets. "How are you doing?"

"I'm fine, thank you." She nodded at the exposed body.

Doc Jeffers stepped across the bike path just as Sergeant Smalley returned along with Ira Bodman.

"Any identification, John?" Doc Jeffers asked.

"Didn't check," Smalley replied.

The doc pulled on latex gloves, tugged an

iPhone on a cord out from under his shirt, knelt next to the body, and spoke into the phone. "Victim is in bad shape. Face especially." He checked the head, throat, and chest. Examined lower body and limbs. "Young woman, early twenties, probably in good physical condition. Blow to the back of the head. Dead for three, four days. Crows worked on her. That's about it." He checked her jeans pockets, the only obvious place where she might have had some ID.

"Nothing, I suppose," said Smalley.

"Nope. Even her own mother would have trouble recognizing her." He stood, tucked the iPhone back into his shirt, peeled off his gloves, and turned to the state troopers. "Not likely she did that to herself." He snapped his medical bag shut. "I can pronounce her dead with reasonable assurance."

No one laughed.

"You want to phone Toby or shall I?" Doc Jeffers called out to Smalley, who was on the other side of the leaf pile.

Toby owned the mortuary and his hearse would be used to carry the girl's body off-Island for autopsy.

"We'll take care of it, Doc," said Smalley.

After the medical examiner left, Ira held a hand out to Victoria, and she got up stiffly from her folding chair. She'd been pondering life and death. A young woman. The arm she'd seen had belonged to a girl who'd had a full lifetime ahead of her.

"You okay, Mrs. Trumbull?" asked Ira.

"Not really." Victoria nodded toward the leaf pile and the body resting there. "I'm thinking about her."

"Yeah," said Ira. "Why her, right?"

Victoria ached from sitting still. She tried stretching the way she'd seen runners stretch. It helped slightly. "I suppose we'd better go back to the ball field. Will you go ahead with the game?"

"Yup. Best thing for the kids."

"Are you going to tell them about the body?"

Ira kicked an acorn out of the path. "They already know. Word travels fast. I'm sure Robin told them what he saw, and I'll give them what information we have. They can take it. They're good kids."

Victoria nodded. Robin was likely the center of attention now, his queasy stomach settled by a new sense of celebrity.

At the ball field, Tim Eldredge, one of the state troopers, was questioning Robin, and a group of curious boys and grown-ups stood back some distance, watching.

Tim looked up. "Hello, Mrs. Trumbull. Robin, here, had the presence of mind to write down the plate number of a car parked here last night. Black Volkswagen convertible, lot of duct tape."

Robin hopped from one foot to another. "He was acting really weird." He wrinkled his nose. "And sweating."

Tim, who looked as though he could be Robin's older brother, patted Robin on the back. "Good work." He turned to Victoria. "Ben and Adam are searching for the car now. We alerted the Steamship Authority to be on the lookout. Could be the driver has nothing to do with the body, but we'd like to rule him out."

"A black Volkswagen convertible held together with duct tape," Victoria said. "My tenant, Zack, drives a car like that."

Zack awoke with a start. Where was he? Someone was rapping on his misted window. He sat up, bumping his head on the dashboard. Rubbed his eyes. Wiped drool from his mouth. He ached. The sun was high. The figure at the window was backlit, a dark silhouette.

What time was it? Late. It all came back to him in a rush. He had to get off this Island. He had to be on that morning boat.

Damnation. Six a.m. was long past. He'd also missed his eight o'clock reservation.

Another rap.

A state trooper. Good God!

He lowered his window.

"I'd like to see some ID, buddy." The trooper held out his hand.

"What is it?" asked Zack. "What's the matter?"

The trooper continued to hold out his hand.

Where was his wallet? He'd taken it out of his back pocket while he tried to find some comfortable position in the front seat. Where was it? The glove compartment. He reached toward it.

"Not so fast." The trooper jerked the door open.

"My wallet. My driver's license," mumbled Zack.

"Out of the car, please."

"What?"

The trooper stepped back and Zack saw a second cop and behind the second cop a squad car with flashing blue lights.

He was trapped. They'd reported him.

He swung his legs out, set his feet on the macadam, and eased himself to a standing position.

"Turn around, please, hands on the car."

Zack obeyed.

The trooper patted him down.

Zack twisted his head around. "I didn't mean —"

A second trooper interrupted him. "Sir, we simply want to take you to the county jail to question you."

"Are all of them —"

"I wouldn't say anything at this time, sir, if I were you," said the trooper.

The first trooper went around to the passenger side, opened the glove compartment, and handed Zack his wallet.

The second trooper said, "Come with us, please. You want to lock up your car?"

Zack tucked his wallet into his back pocket and rubbed his beard. "I guess not. The locks don't work."

After the noonday meal on Saturday, Phil Smith, owner of the Beetlebung Café where Zack washed dishes, was in the kitchen clearing up the luncheon mess. He checked his watch. Zack was late. He wasn't fond of the boy, half-stoned half the time. But, he had to admit, Zack was a reliable worker.

Will Osborne, Zack's fellow dishwasher, pushed through the swinging kitchen door with a tray of dirty dishes.

"You hear from Zack?" Smith asked. "Not

like him to be late."

"I'll call the place he's staying. He could be sick. I saw him last night at Eberhardt's dinner, and he looked like hell."

"Yeah, I'd appreciate that." Smith rolled up his sleeves, took off his watch and put it on the windowsill above the sink and then started the tedious process of scraping, rinsing, and stacking dishes in the dishwasher.

He looked up when Will returned. "Well?"

"Mrs. Trumbull hasn't seen Zack since he left for the dinner last night."

"Is his car at her place?"

Will shook his head. "Nope."

"Strange." Smith gestured at the full sink. "Help me with these."

"No problem," said Will, rolling up his own sleeves.

Smith turned on the hot water spray full blast and sloshed it over the dishes. "I hope he's got a damn good excuse. What was he doing at the Eberhardt's?"

"He told me he's engaged to Samantha, Eberhardt's daughter." Will began stacking plates upright in the dishwasher.

"Samantha Eberhardt engaged?" Smith laughed. "I doubt it." He turned back to the dishes. "Piece of work, that girl."

While Will Osborne and Phil Smith were

wondering where Zack was, Bruno Eberhardt was wondering the same thing. Furthermore, he was wondering where his daughter was. She should be home by now.

He'd gotten no response to messages he left on her voicemail. Since she'd said she'd be visiting friends off-Island, he hadn't expected her to call as often as usual.

He had an uneasy feeling that his unpredictable daughter had run off with Zack. That would explain why Zack was missing. It would be like her. Not the first time she'd run off with some guy and he'd had to save her from something stupid, like getting married.

He gave up trying to reach her by phone and drove to the house she was renting. Correction: that he was renting for her. Her car was gone, as he expected. She'd have taken it off-Island, of course.

As always, the place was a mess. Clothes strewn around, towels dropped on the bathroom floor, crumpled tissues on the counter. God, what disaster that girl left. Half-full wine bottle on the kitchen counter. Two wineglasses with a sludge of wine, buzzing with fruit flies. Week-old dirty dishes in and around the sink. He'd told her he'd pay for his cleaning woman to come twice a week. What was wrong with her? She wasn't brought up this way.

He started to clean, but gave up before he made much of a dent. At least he'd washed the dishes, put the wine in the fridge, picked her clothes off the floor and piled them on her unmade bed.

He paused in front of the bed, shrugged, and looked out over Vineyard Sound. White sailboats, white gulls. The Elizabeth Islands seemed close today. Brilliant blue sky.

The only available chair had a stack of magazines and clothing on it. He lifted the stuff off, moved the chair closer to the large window, and sat down with a sigh. He loved that daughter of his, so much like him in so many ways. Wild. By her age, though, she ought to have settled down. He had by then.

He missed her. At least she could have called.

A hawk soared overhead, distracting him. Suddenly, several crows tore after it, scream-ing their raucous "Caw! Caw! Caw!" A murder of crows, that's what they called a flock. Fascinated, he watched as the hawk dove and climbed to get away from his tormenters. Farther and farther away they flew until the caw-cawing of the crows faded, and they were too far away for him to see.

He didn't like the idea of Samantha not

answering her phone.

He'd tried to track down some of her friends, but he didn't know where to start. All he knew were first names of a few of her Island friends. He didn't know any of her off-Island friends.

Well, she certainly had a bunch of pals. He smiled at the thought. A popular girl. What in hell was the matter with Isabella that she didn't like Sammy? Calling his baby girl a slut. Isabella was jealous, that was the problem. Sammy, obviously, didn't like Isabella. That was enough to send her away. He'd take care of that when he got home.

He'd met a couple of guys Sammy dated. Decent enough. Now he'd met Zack. The kid had good manners. Dressed right. He thought about the black trumpets. Was Sammy pulling one of her cute tricks, telling him Zack was trying to poison her?

It would be like her.

Kind of far-fetched to think he planned to kill her with them. Sammy hated mushrooms anyway. She would dramatize things. Fantasize her boyfriend was trying to kill her.

But why did Zack suddenly bolt when the mushroom dish appeared?

He said he felt ill. Actually, he looked ill. Mrs. Trumbull had said he hadn't been feeling well.

Sammy, Sammy. When will you grow up?

Eberhardt had almost convinced himself that his daughter was playing some obscure trick on him and Zack.

Although the way Zack had bolted from the dinner table last evening at the moment the black trumpet dish appeared could be explained by the fact the kid thought those mushrooms were deadly.

Eberhardt stood and then turned back to the chaos of his daughter's place. He'd get his cleaning woman, Maria Lima, to come in and do a thorough job, so when Sammy came home things would look nice.

He punched in her number on his iPhone.

"No problem, Mr. Eberhardt. I'll clean it good so it will look nice when she gets back."

"Today, Maria?"

"Sure, Mr. Eberhardt. I'll be there around five."

"An extra fifty for the quick response."

"You don't need to do that, Mr. Eberhardt, but thank you."

Eberhardt put his phone back in his pocket. Sammy had probably lost track of time. Having fun with the off-Island girlfriend. He sighed. He cared too much for his baby girl. Keeping too tight a rein on her. Had to let go.

Chapter 12

The police assured Zack they were simply taking him in for questioning. They asked him politely to hold his hands behind his back and snapped on plastic handcuffs.

"What's that for?" Zack protested.

"Your personal safety, sir," said the second trooper. "We always do this. Doesn't mean anything."

"I had hoped to make the eight o'clock boat," Zack said to the trooper who had patted him down. "I had a reservation."

"Afraid you missed it, buddy," said the first trooper. "It's about eleven."

"Damn," said Zack. "Have they already seen the guests?"

The troopers exchanged glances. One opened the rear door of the cruiser, and the other politely helped Zack, who was handicapped with his hands cuffed behind him, into the backseat.

The radio was spitting out static. The

trooper on the passenger side turned down the squelch and picked up the mike. After introductory official talk, he said, "We're leaving the Park and Ride lot with a person of interest and are heading to the jail."

Except for the intermittent crackling of the radio, they drove in silence, down the hill from the parking lot, turned right at the foot of the hill, and made their way slowly along State Road. When they reached the Vineyard Haven–Edgartown Road they turned onto it and sped up, still silent.

Zack shifted in the backseat trying to get comfortable. He could only imagine what lay in store for him. He'd never been in trouble before, never even had a traffic ticket. Only a close shave when he had the good luck to leave a party before the cops came and found a lot of stuff and hauled everyone off to who knows where.

Now he was faced with poisoning eight people. How sick would they be? Would someone die? If so, they'd lock him up forever on death row. Except the county jail didn't have a death row. They'd send him off-Island to Walpole or some prison fortress, where he'd be raped by inmates. Would solitary confinement be worse?

He groaned.

The officer glanced at him in the rearview

mirror. "Sorry about the cuffs, sir. Only a few more minutes and we'll be in Edgartown."

Who could he call for help? Zack lowered his head and tried unsuccessfully to wipe his eyes on his shoulders. Mrs. Trumbull, that's who he'd call. Victoria Trumbull.

From Edgartown's Main Street, the jail looked like any one of the other white painted captains' houses that lined the street, but once you were inside, it lost its charm. Victoria had been here before.

Sheriff Grimsey Norton met Victoria at the front entrance. Even though Victoria was close to six feet tall, he towered over her and had to bend slightly to talk to her.

"Sorry to involve you in this, Mrs. Trumbull, but Mr. Zeller was insistent." He led her into his office, which looked vaguely like a onetime downstairs bedroom. The office had a large desk that took up most of the room. Behind the desk and to one side bookcases were stacked with files and Massachusetts law and criminal justice tomes.

The sheriff held the seat for her and Victoria sat.

"What seems to be the trouble?" Victoria asked, once he'd seated himself behind the desk.

He straightened papers on his desk before answering. He sat back and ran his fingers through his hair, which was thick, wavy, and an attractive dark auburn. He sighed. "We're calling him a 'person of interest,' Mrs. Trumbull. Has to do with the death of the unidentified young woman found near the fire station."

"Zack?" Victoria sat forward.

He nodded, hands folded over his flat stomach.

"I don't know what to say. Robin White and I found the body, you know."

"Yes, I know. Must have upset the boy. I've got a ten-year-old son myself."

"Why are you questioning Zack?"

The sheriff turned his swivel chair slightly to face the window. "Last evening, Robin and others saw a car parked at the ball field with its lights on. Nobody was around, so they turned the lights off."

Victoria nodded. "Robin told me."

"Shortly thereafter," the sheriff continued, "the driver showed up, quite upset. Got in the car and left. Robin noted the license plate number. Smart kid." He swiveled back to face Victoria. "This morning, after you and Robin found the body, the state troopers tracked down the car at the Park and Ride lot. Mr. Zeller was asleep in the front seat. He told the officers that he had a reservation on the eight o'clock boat, but it was close to eleven when the state troopers woke him up." He stood. "Mr. Zeller will be in an upstairs room we call the conference room. Can you handle the stairs, okay, Mrs. Trumbull?"

"Yes, of course I can," said Victoria, lifting herself out of the chair.

The conference room was a bleak place with a barred window and a long, scarred wooden table that looked as though it dated back to when the house was built on Main Street, Edgartown, in the mid-1800s.

Zack, pale and untidy with his unshaven chin and rumpled clothing, was sitting with his back to the window. He stood when Victoria entered with the sheriff.

"You came!"

"Of course I came," said Victoria.

"There'll be a deputy sitting just outside the room with the door open, in case you need him," the sheriff said.

Victoria turned to him. "I'll be fine, Sheriff, thank you." She sat at the head of the table, but before she could speak, Zack poured out his misery.

"I'm guilty, Mrs. Trumbull. I didn't mean to make those eight people sick. I only meant the mushrooms for Samantha."

"Stop, Zack!" Victoria held up her hand. "What are you talking about?"

"Sammy. I changed my mind, though, and couldn't get them back in time."

"You're not telling me you planned to poison Samantha?"

He nodded and lowered his head. "Just make her sick."

"Good heavens, Zack. Why?"

"She told me she was pregnant. I figured if she was, the poisonous mushrooms would end the pregnancy."

Victoria pushed her chair away from the table. "Zack!"

The deputy, standing by the railing around the stairway, strode into the room. "You okay, Mrs. Trumbull?"

"Yes, yes," said Victoria. "I'm fine."

The deputy, a slender boy with sandy cropped hair and acne, looked barely out of his teens. "I'm not supposed to be, like, where I can hear what you're saying, you know." He ran a hand over his hair. "You need me, Mrs. Trumbull, I'm here. Just call out." He patted his thin chest.

"Thank you," said Victoria. "Zack and I are good friends. We're fine."

When the deputy left, Victoria leaned forward, her elbows on the table. "What on earth were you thinking?"

"Guess I wasn't thinking too clearly, Mrs. T. I don't even think she's pregnant. I figured if she got sick enough it would teach her a lesson." Zack scratched his beard. "I didn't want her old man making me marry her."

"That's not the way things work these days," said Victoria. It wasn't often that she was stumped. Elizabeth thought he was on some kind of drugs. That was about the only explanation. Victoria looked away. She had been captivated by his good manners.

He leaned forward. "Did any of the guests die, Mrs. Trumbull?"

It ran through Victoria's mind that she would not tell him all eight of the dinner people were alive and well. She stood. He was entitled to rot in this nice jail.

He stood too, always polite. "Mrs. Trumbull?" He looked at her with those deep brown moist eyes of his.

She saw the pain. She sat again.

So did he.

"The dinner guests are all fine."

Zack stared at her. "What?"

"They enjoyed the mushrooms and they're all fine. Black trumpets are a great delicacy."

"Trumpets of death?"

"As I told you, old-timers imagined the

131

dead buried in the ground were playing on trumpets. The mushrooms look like tiny black trumpets. That's how they got that name."

He ran his fingers through his hair. Scratched his beard. Shifted in his seat. Leaned forward again. "Then what am I doing here?"

"The body of a young woman was found on the bicycle path." Victoria took a deep breath. It was difficult to believe she was the one who'd found the girl. "They are holding you, Zack, because they need to question you. You parked at the ball field near where the body was found." Victoria looked away from him. "When you returned to your car, the softball players thought you acted suspicious and one of them noted your license number."

Zack slumped back in his chair. "So I didn't kill anyone, but they think I killed someone I didn't kill."

"No," said Victoria, getting a bit testy, "they simply want to ask you a few questions, and it would be a good idea if you told them the truth."

CHAPTER 13

After Victoria left, Zack was returned to the cell, waiting to be questioned. He perched on his cot, staring mindlessly at the bright pink walls that closed in on him. He had never wanted to get high so badly. He ran his fingers through his hair. Why had they painted the walls that ugly color? He must be imagining things. Were all the cells painted pink? Was he suffering from some weird withdrawal symptom that made those walls shimmer? His stomach vibrated too. But out of sync with the walls. Nauseating. He was inside the belly of a beast. The walls breathed in and out. He was spinning. He closed his eyes. Worse. His mouth watered. Was he going to be sick? He'd have to call that baby-faced deputy.

That awful thing he'd touched under the bed of leaves. He'd actually touched a dead body. Cold. What a horrible thought. Worse than a snake. Would his fingerprints show up on the corpse?

Footsteps. Jangling keys. The cell door —
cell door! — opened. Zack turned toward
it. Was he free? From this nightmare? Dear
God, he swore he would never, ever plan
anything that would put him in a place like
this. One afternoon was enough.

"Mr. Zeller, we'll be asking you a few
questions, sir." A tall man with a soft voice,
in uniform. "I'm Sheriff Grimsey Norton.
Sorry you had to wait. And sorry it had to
be in one of the cells."

Zack took a deep breath. Mrs. Trumbull's
advice was good. Tell them everything. Then
they'd understand why he'd acted suspi-
ciously. "Can I ask you a question?"

"Depends," said the sheriff.

"Are all the walls in this jail pink?"

The sheriff tossed his bunch of keys from
one hand to the other. "Well, we redecorated
one time when we incarcerated a female."

Zack laughed. The world righted itself. A
touch of humanity, even in this place.
"Okay, Sheriff, your turn to ask."

The sheriff stood by the open cell door.
"We'll be upstairs in the conference room."

"Where Mrs. Trumbull came to see me,
right?"

"Right," said the sheriff. "But this time
we'll have a couple of attorneys present, and

a court stenographer. Come with me." He stood aside, and once Zack passed through the barred door, someone slammed it shut. Zack glanced behind him. That baby-faced deputy. The kid had an empty holster dangling from his belt.

The sheriff looked straight ahead. "We'll also have a videographer. That way there'll be a record of everything that transpires. For your protection, sir." He glanced at Zack.

"Understood," said Zack, feeling better all the time. He hadn't killed anyone after all. And he certainly hadn't killed whoever it was under those leaves. He shuddered at the thought of that coldness he'd touched that wasn't a nest of snakes.

Upstairs in the conference room where he'd met with Mrs. Trumbull, a video camera was set up on a tripod at the end of the room. He could see a couple of people sitting at the table.

"You're entitled to legal representation any time you feel you need it," the sheriff said as he held a chair for Zack. "Want you to meet two good people, Harrington Peabody and Miranda Smith, both lawyers. Ms. Smith is a public defender, in case you need one."

The woman was sleek, like something he'd

seen slithering into the Mill Pond. She was slender and pale-faced, about the same age as Elizabeth, Mrs. Trumbull's granddaughter, who was in her early thirties. She had long black hair that she kept running her hands over and was wearing some kind of shiny black one-piece outfit, like a leather jumpsuit.

Both extended their hands across the table to Zack, and he shook one after the other. The woman's hand was cold, damp, and limp. The man's hand was puffy and warm.

He only got the man's last name, which sounded like Pee-Biddy. The man was probably close to seventy. White hair, big belly, red face, rimless glasses, little screwed-up mouth, wearing a long-sleeved white shirt with a black-and-white polka-dotted bow tie.

"Mr. Zeller, we're making a video of this interview with you as we do with everyone we question," said the sheriff, and repeated, "For your protection, of course."

Zack nodded. "Thank you."

"I've asked Miranda to sit in to make sure your rights are protected. She's a public defender. As I said, you're entitled to a lawyer of your own any time you say."

Miranda nodded and her shiny hair slid across her shoulders from her back to her front, as if it were oiled.

Zack was feeling pretty much okay, almost confident. "Sounds good to me, Sheriff. Don't think I need a lawyer, though."

Once he'd learned from Mrs. Trumbull that the guests were alive and well, the world had turned right-side up again. He wished he didn't feel so scruffy in his slept-in clothes, unwashed face, and un-brushed teeth. Didn't smell great, either. Touching that thing under the pile of leaves had given him a good scare, and he still reeked of leftover fear.

The sheriff told the video camera the date and time. "We are questioning Zack Zeller in connection with the as-yet-unidentified body of a young woman found on the bicycle path near the firehouse in West Tisbury."

Zack, at the sheriff's request, gave his name, date of birth, and his address at Victoria Trumbull's.

"You parked your car at the ball field near the West Tisbury fire house, is that correct?" asked the sheriff.

"That's right," said Zack.

"Would you please tell us why you parked there."

Zack shifted in his chair. "It's a long story."

"We have time," said the chubby Mr. Peabody, with a smile.

"Well," said Zack, "My girlfriend and I, you see, we weren't getting along, and she was pregnant, or said she was, so I said to myself, I'm going to make her so sick she'll —"

"Stop!" Miranda stood and held up her hand. She turned to the court stenographer. "Delete that."

"But I didn't kill her," Zack protested. "You won't understand why I parked there unless I tell you the whole story."

"Just say why you parked there and not somewhere else," said Miranda. She sat again, flicked her hair over her shoulder, and studied Zack.

"Well, I usually park at Mrs. Trumbull's, but I saw the police car there —"

"Stop!" said Miranda. "Delete that." She turned to Zack. "You usually park at Mrs. Trumbull's and instead you decided to park at the ball field."

"That's right," said Zack.

"Miranda," said Mr. Peabody with a sigh. "Don't put words in his mouth."

"Keep it simple, Mr. Zeller," she said, ignoring Peabody. "Kiss, kiss. 'Keep It Simple.' " She didn't add "Stupid."

Zack smiled. "I parked at the ball field

and started to walk back to Mrs. Trumbull's, but then I remembered —"

"Watch it," said Miranda.

"Well, I turned back —"

"Simple!" ordered Miranda.

"I turned back to my car, got in, and drove to the Park and Ride, where I spent the night, okay?"

"Did you notice anything along the bicycle path?" asked the sheriff.

"Yeah, I did. I slipped in the mud or something and fell, and my flashlight rolled under a pile of leaves." He looked over at Miranda, who nodded. "When I reached for my flashlight I thought I'd touched a snake and it startled the hell out of me and I went back to my car in a hurry."

"You thought you'd touched a snake?" asked the sheriff.

"Something cold and slimy feeling. I'm a city boy. I hate snakes."

"I think we do need to know Mr. Zeller's reason for parking at the ball field, Miranda," said the sheriff. "It's pertinent. This isn't a trial, you know. We need all the information we can get."

"O-kay," said Miranda. "Go ahead, Mr. Zeller. Why did you park at the ball field instead of at Mrs. Trumbull's?"

"I was coming back from dinner at my

girlfriend's father's, and I thought I better get off the Island in a hurry."

"May I ask why?" said the sheriff.

"I thought the dinner guests had all gotten sick because of me."

Miranda pushed her chair back and stood. "Mr. Zeller!" She glanced at the sheriff. "He didn't say that."

"But they didn't get sick," protested Zack. "Mrs. Trumbull said I should tell you everything."

Silence around the table. All stared at Zack.

Miranda plopped back down into her chair.

Zack glanced from one to the other. "I thought the mushrooms I gave my girlfriend would make her sick. But she didn't eat them. She gave them to her father and he served them to his guests. I still thought they were poisonous."

Miranda sighed and leaned back in her chair.

"You can see why I wanted to leave the Island. I thought they'd all gotten sick and possibly someone died. I went to Mrs. Trumbull's, but there was a cop car there, and I thought they were after me, so I parked at the ball field and was going to walk back and get my belongings, and then

I thought I'd better not waste time, since the cops were probably waiting for me."

"Mr. Zeller . . ." said Miranda.

"But when Mrs. Trumbull came to see me this morning, afternoon, I guess, she said the mushrooms were perfectly good to eat, and all the dinner guests were just fine. No one died." Zack held up his hands, palms up, and leaned back in his chair. "So there you have it."

Silence.

Mr. Peabody doodled on the pad in front of him. Miranda continued to stare at Zack. The sheriff pushed his chair back and folded his arms over his chest. The videographer kept the camera focused on Zack.

"You know, I haven't eaten since yesterday noon." Zack peered at the faces around the table, all avoiding his eyes. "Any chance I can get something to eat?"

CHAPTER 14

The identification of the deceased young woman came through quickly on Saturday afternoon. At least three of the Island's six police departments had some record of her various exploits, as did the state police.

Sergeant John Smalley, who had been at the scene when the body was uncovered, had not recognized her then, but on closer inspection at the funeral parlor, which served as the Island's morgue, identified her as Samantha Eberhardt.

It was his job, as head of the state police barracks, to notify her next of kin. This was the only part of his job Smalley hated. Moped accidents. Car crashes. Boating accidents. Calling on a parent or husband or wife, knock on the door, they answer, smile fades when they see his uniform. First reaction always is, What have I done? Then they see his somber face and the second reaction is, Oh, my God! He says, "May I come in?" They nod, not able to speak. He says, "I'm afraid I have bad news. You might want to sit." Their hands go up to their faces. "Is my daughter all right?" "My son?" "My husband?"

This was even worse, if possible. Telling a guy his daughter, his only child, has been murdered. It was going to be particularly odious breaking the news to Bruno Eberhardt. "Mr. Eberhardt, we believe a young woman found dead on the bicycle path, is your daughter. Would you please come with me, sir. We need you to identify her . . ." Just stop there. Don't say "body" or "corpse" or "remains." To her father, she's still alive and will be until he sees what she has become.

Bruno Eberhardt slumped out of the funeral parlor onto the loading ramp at the rear, stopped, and leaned against the wall.

"Sammy," he mumbled. "My baby girl. She can't be dead."

Smalley kept enough distance between them to give Eberhardt privacy, but he was ready to catch him if he collapsed. You could never tell with these tough-as-steel guys. They were often more shaken up than their fragile-looking spouses.

"That bastard," muttered Eberhardt,

standing up straight. "That goddamned bastard. I'll get him, believe you me, I'll get him. The law can't compensate me for what that bastard did." Eberhardt turned and suddenly punched the wall with his fist. Then he held it up and stared at the blood oozing from his knuckles. "You heard me, Smalley. I'll make that bastard pay and pay and pay for this." He punched the wall again.

Smalley winced. He refrained from saying what he should say now, that Zack had not yet been convicted and was deemed innocent until he was proven guilty. This was not the time for that. Nor was it the time to record the threats Eberhardt was making. He, Smalley, would probably voice the exact same threats under the same circumstances.

"I'll take you home, Mr. Eberhardt," Smalley said. Apologies were too feeble. Less said the better. He'd never liked the guy, arrogant prick. But he was a human being in distress, and Smalley hurt for him.

Zack had finished eating a combination of supper, breakfast, and lunch, a meal that was better than most upscale restaurants served, when he heard footsteps coming down the hall outside his cell. At last, he would be free of this nightmarish place with its hot pink walls. But at least he'd had one of the best meals he could remember. He'd have something to tell his buddies at the restaurant about his cell, redecorated for a female incarcerent, according to the sheriff.

He stood and went to the cell door, held on to the bars, and peered out. Funny, that was exactly what he'd seen prisoners do on TV shows. Hold on to the bars of their cell doors.

The sheriff and two others. He was about to be free, at last!

He called out, "Excellent meal, Sheriff. Thanks!"

"You're welcome," said the sheriff. He looked awfully serious.

Then Zack recognized Miranda, the sleek lawyer lady. A uniformed state cop accompanied them. They, too, looked serious. What was this all about? Trailing along behind the three was the baby-faced deputy with the large empty holster bumping against his leg.

The sheriff stopped at the cell door and without looking at Zack, beckoned to the state trooper, who stepped forward.

"Mr. Zeller," said the sheriff. "I'm arresting you on suspicion of the murder of Samantha Eberhardt."

"What are you talking about?" Zack shook

the bars of his cell door. "Samantha's not dead. Mrs. Trumbull said I didn't kill anyone!"

The sheriff turned to his deputy. "Read Mr. Zeller his Miranda rights."

"Miranda?" Zack interrupted the deputy who had taken a card out of his pocket and was reading something. "She's my lawyer."

"Mr. Zeller," said Miranda, the lawyer, "you're not listening. You have a right to a lawyer of your own choosing. In the meantime, I will act as your attorney. Like the man says, I urge you to remain silent. Anything you say they can hold against you."

"But I only *thought* about making Sammy sick, I —"

"Mr. Zeller!" warned Miranda.

"But she didn't eat them." Zack's knuckles were white from holding the bars so tightly.

The deputy unlocked the cell door.

"Please turn around, Mr. Zeller," said the sheriff. "Hands behind your back." To the deputy, "Handcuff him."

"I didn't know she was dead!" cried Zack. "Ouch! That hurts."

"Follow me," said the sheriff.

After her visit to the jail, Victoria changed out of her good suit into her gray corduroy pants and turtleneck shirt, and she and Elizabeth went out to the garden and harvested a large crop of tomatoes.

They worked at the kitchen table, preparing them for the freezer by trimming the stem ends. Back copies of the *Island Enquirer,* wetly pink from tomato juice, protected the table. The kitchen smelled of autumn harvest and the ritual of preparing for winter, changed only because the fruit was headed for the freezer, not glass jars.

The phone rang. Victoria wiped her hands, got up, and answered. The conversation was short. She returned to her seat, somber. "That was Zack." She picked up her paring knife and set to work.

"What does he want now?" Elizabeth scooped up a pile of the discarded stems and dropped them into the compost bucket. "I didn't think inmates were allowed to make calls from jail."

"Apparently the sheriff is liberal about phone calls. By the way," Victoria continued, "I owe you an apology. You were right about him." She set down her knife.

Elizabeth plucked a tomato from the basket and dug her knife into it. "I think he's on some kind of mind-altering substance." She removed a neat cone of stem. "So, what was the call about?"

Victoria laid both gnarled hands, stained with juice, on the table. "He's been charged with murder."

The tomato she'd just cored slipped out of Elizabeth's hand. It rolled off the table and fell to the floor with a splat. Neither she nor Victoria moved to clean it up. "What? What did you say?"

"Murder. He's been charged with the murder of that girl Robin and I found on the bicycle path."

"I don't believe it. Why on earth would Zack . . ." Elizabeth paused. "Have they identified the girl yet?"

"Yes," said Victoria.

"Who?"

"His girlfriend."

Elizabeth set down her knife. "Samantha?"

Victoria nodded.

"I don't believe it. Samantha." Elizabeth picked up her knife and set it down again. "He told us he was trying to get rid of her. I didn't dream he meant permanently. Do you think he actually did it?"

"No." Victoria shook her head. "No. I don't. Not for a minute."

"But you said he planned to feed her poisonous mushrooms."

"Poison is an abstraction. He hoped to

induce an abortion with the mushrooms, not kill her." Victoria picked up her own knife again and reached for another tomato. "Samantha was killed by a blow to her head. I don't think Zack has the courage to smack anyone over the head with a weapon of any kind."

"What are you going to do about it?" Elizabeth looked down at the tomato splayed out on the floor. "Good grief, look what I've done."

"It won't be wasted. Put it on the compost heap," said Victoria. "I'm going to find out who killed her." She went back to work.

Elizabeth got up, reached for a spatula, and cleaned up the mess on the floor. "You know, Gram, he doesn't deserve the time and effort you're going to have to spend to clear him."

"Yes, he does." Victoria's jaw was set. She looked very much like the stony-faced ancestor whose portrait graced the front hall.

Elizabeth sat down again and stared at the half-full basket of tomatoes. "A stay in prison might clear his mind."

"He didn't kill her," said Victoria. "He doesn't belong in prison for that. Besides, the real killer is loose, and we have to find him."

"Or her." Elizabeth got up again, went behind her seated grandmother, and put her arms around her. "Good for you, Gram. I hope when I grow up I can be like you."

Victoria patted her granddaughter's hands.

"Zack's a jerk," said Elizabeth. "He doesn't deserve a minute of your time." She hugged her grandmother more tightly. "Tell me how I can help."

Victoria folded up the wet newspapers and put them out on the brick floor of the entry. The papers would be added to the compost heap tomorrow along with the tomato trimmings.

All of the prepared tomatoes were in plastic bags, ready to go into the freezer where they would become hard as billiard balls. Next winter, with the coming of soup and stew weather, Victoria would dip a few of the rock-hard tomatoes into hot water, slip off the peels, and drop them into the pot.

Elizabeth stowed the last full bag into the freezer. "All done, Gram. What next?"

"Supper," said Victoria. "I'm hungry."

CHAPTER 15

Late on Saturday, Sergeant Smalley called Joel Killdeer, head of the forensics lab off-Island.

"Need your help, Joel."

"Again?" asked Killdeer. "Seems like we were there not too long ago. Thought you wrapped things up."

"This is a different case," said Smalley. "The body of a girl was found by the bicycle path. We don't know where she was killed. Figured we'd better start with her house."

"It's Saturday, you know."

"Yeah. I know." Smalley was back in his office at the state police barracks, his tie loosened, his usually immaculate shirt rumpled, his boots in need of a buffing. A coffee mug with an inch of cold coffee was perched on his desk.

"Kind of late on a Saturday."

"Damnation, Joel, don't you think I know?" Smalley took a sip of the coffee and put his mug down with a grunt.

"What was that?"

"Never mind. We'll put your guys up overnight and feed them, okay?"

"Has anyone been in the house since she was found?"

"Not that I know of," said Smalley. "Not us."

"I'll think about it."

"I owe you a beer."

"Make it two. I'll need to bring my fishing gear. Got a longstanding date with Janet Messineo."

"Right." Smalley looked down at his dusty boots, leaned over and wiped them with his hand, smearing them. He grunted again.

"You sound bad," said Joel. A drawer squeaked open. Paper rustled. "Okay, I'm looking at the boat schedule. We can make the eight-thirty. Gets in at nine fifteen. If we miss that, I'll let you know. There's a late boat."

"I'll be at the ferry dock to lead you to the place," said Smalley. "It's up-Island. We circled it with crime scene tape. One of my guys is there now and will stay until you're done."

"See you in a couple hours," said Killdeer and disconnected.

■ ■ ■ ■

The forensics mobile lab arrived on schedule, nine fifteen. Smalley had parked his police vehicle near the dock and was on foot to meet them as they drove off the ferry.

Joel Killdeer was driving. He was chewing gum. His skin, the color of black coffee, made his face hard to see in the dim light. He wore a Red Sox baseball hat that covered what Smalley knew was a shiny, shaved head.

"Thanks, Joel. I'm parked over there." Smalley pointed.

"No problem. Two beers. Wow." Killdeer smiled, showing great white teeth.

"Follow me," said Smalley.

This time of year, this time of night, traffic was light. They made the trip up-Island to Chilmark in a half hour and turned off the paved road onto a dirt road, up a slight incline and onto the drive that led to Samantha's rental house. Smalley led the way and parked outside the circle of yellow tape draped around bushes and stakes driven into the ground.

Killdeer parked next to him and got out of the van. Two others joined him, a young woman with spiky green hair, and an equally young man with a large mustache. It was too dark to make out much about them.

Killdeer introduced them.

"We've met before," said Smalley, shaking hands with the woman and nodding at the man.

"Nobody's been inside, right?" asked Killdeer.

"Not since we identified the girl's body this afternoon."

Killdeer nodded to his crew. "Okay, you guys, suit up and we'll get to work."

It was fully dark now and a chilly dew had settled on the grass. The Milky Way was a gauzy band of light stretched across the sky. The three forensic specialists stepped over the crime scene tape and donned white suits, covered their shoes with white shoe covers, slipped white hoods over their heads. Three white ghosts in the dark night.

"I'll be in my vehicle," said Smalley.

Actually, he was standing outside leaning against his car gazing up at the stars, hoping to see a meteor on this clear, crisp night, when the team reappeared fifteen minutes later. Smalley had expected them to take hours, even with such a small house.

They tugged off their white apparel, blending into the dark night once again.

"What's up?" asked Smalley, surprised to

see them.

"Nothing," said Killdeer. "Nothing at all. Someone cleaned the place like an operating room."

"Nothing?" asked Smalley.

"We'll come back tomorrow and give it a thorough go-through in daylight, but I have to tell you, I'd like to hire the cleaner who did this place. Do my house."

Bruno Eberhardt couldn't sleep. He got out of bed and paced. He thought about his dead daughter, her entire beautiful being transformed into that grotesque thing he'd had to identify.

Zack Zeller. A hateful name. The law will never mete out to that beast, that worm, the justice he deserves. Eberhardt lost no time in planning *his* strategy. He would deal with Zack Zeller in his own way. At some point, Zeller would be transferred from the local jail to a secure facility off-Island.

How much time did he have before that took place?

He went downstairs and sat at the head of the table in his dining room, at the very same place he had sat when Zeller fled from that ludicrous botched attempt at killing Samantha. With mushrooms. Black trumpets. Well, the edible, delectable, prized trumpets of death didn't work, did they. So you tried again and succeeded.

He set his elbows on the table and laid his head on his hands. His daughter. His only child. Zeller didn't deserve to be in a prison where he'd be cossetted the rest of his life. Where else on this planet would prisoners dine on meals prepared by a French chef, incarcerated for drug possession? On the other hand, he didn't deserve the easy way out by death. Had Samantha died quickly? Had she suffered?

Eberhardt glanced at the window, seeing nothing but his reflection, the dark night mirroring him.

Thoughts tangled in his mind. Imprisonment. For life. What about constructing a high-security facility of his own in which to confine Zeller, a facility in which Zack would spend every second of the rest of his life regretting that he'd ever met Samantha.

He'd get him out somehow.

Once Zeller was out of jail and off-Island, he, Eberhardt, would hold him in a secure place until he could fashion a prison that no one would know about, no one could find, and no one could escape from. Zack would vanish.

He smiled. He had a plan he could deal

with unfolding before him. Now to find how much time he had before Zack was moved.

CHAPTER 16

Early on Sunday morning the phone rang. Victoria, dressed in her Sunday churchgoing clothes, had just started breakfast. She turned off the burner and, holding a spatula, went into the cookroom to answer.

"Casey here, Victoria. Calling about the parsonage fire investigation."

"Any news?"

"They found a piece of jewelry in the ashes. A wampum necklace."

Victoria set the spatula down on the table. "How did it survive such a devastating fire?"

"Fires are freaky," said Casey. "They skip over stuff you'd think would burn and burn stuff you'd think wouldn't. They found the necklace under a pile of newspapers. The wampum pieces are twined in copper wire and attached to a leather lace. Definitely a one-of-a-kind piece of jewelry."

"The newspapers didn't burn?" Victoria was still standing. She moved her chair closer and leaned on it.

"The top layers were scorched, but no, the papers didn't burn."

"Do you know who the necklace belonged to?"

"This is why I called you."

Victoria could hear papers rustling on Casey's desk.

"Do you have any thoughts, Victoria, about who might have owned a wampum necklace like that? Asking you is a long shot because everybody's into wampum jewelry these days."

"The jewelry is expensive, which narrows the field a bit." Victoria fished an envelope out of the wastepaper basket and selected a pen from the jar on the table. "I'll see what I can find out."

They disconnected.

Victoria sat down and turned to face the view of the village. The view always calmed her. From the window, she could see the church steeple rising above the trees on the distant hillside. Sunlight glinted on the weathervane on top of the steeple, and she could almost make out the hands of the clock. The church had been the town center when she was a child. It held pleasant memories of music and the special smell of the worn hymnals, of the vases of flowers in season or bare branches in winter that flanked the altar. Of the long sermons she hadn't understood, her grandmother holding her small hand and patting it in sympathy. The warm homemade cookies and punch in the parish hall afterward.

She looked at her watch. The bell would ring in about an hour, summoning her to church.

This peaceful village shouldn't be the setting for the deaths of two young people and the destruction of a treasured building.

She returned to her notes.

She had a feeling that Sebastian's death and Samantha's death were connected. After church, she would write down all the questions she could think of. Answers might then come.

At Beetlebung Café, where Zack worked, Phil Smith, the owner, and Will Osborne, Zack's fellow dishwasher, were in the kitchen clearing up the Sunday luncheon mess and getting ready for supper.

"I found out why we haven't seen Zack," said Will. "He's in jail." Will was scraping plates and stacking them in the dishwasher.

"Yeah?" said Phil. "Drugs?"

"Nope," said Will. "You'll never guess."

Phil sighed. "I'm sick of guessing."

"Murder."

"Murder? Who'd he kill?"

"Samantha."

Phil said nothing. He was sorting through recipe cards.

"I wouldn't have thought he had it in him," said Will, continuing to load the dishwasher. "Samantha worked here at one time, didn't she?"

Phil was sitting at the prep table. "Yeah." He scowled and continued to sort through recipes.

Will glanced over at his boss. "What's your problem? I asked a simple question." He turned back to the dirty dishes.

Phil shoved the recipes aside. He stood up, hands on his hips. "Yeah. I knew Samantha. Answer your question?"

"Okay, okay." Will continued to load the machine. "Zack introduced me to her when he started going with her. Not a bad looker. Her old man's loaded." He scraped leftovers off a plate and rinsed it with the spray. "I tended bar at his dinner party, you know. He introduced Zack to everyone as Samantha's fiancé."

Phil continued to sort recipes, setting some aside.

"The cook brought out some gourmet dish," said Will, "and Zack practically shit

161

his pants getting out of there. Said he was sick. Looked it."

"Just shut up, will you?"

Will turned off the spray. "I don't think Zack killed her, is all. He said he was breaking up with her, I said good for you, and then they must have made up, since her old man introduces him as Samantha's fiancé."

Phil slapped a card on the table.

"What's with you, anyhow?" asked Will.

"What's with me," said Phil, turning away, "is I don't want to hear any more about her."

Will shifted back to the sink. "All I was saying is I don't see Zack killing her. Killing anyone, for that matter."

"Everyone can kill, given the right circumstances," said Phil. "Change the subject, will you?" He gathered up the stack of recipe cards. "Bluefish special tonight. Fries, coleslaw, pureed carrots."

"I'll take care of the coleslaw. Want onions in it this time?"

"Leave them out. Too many diners don't like raw onions."

Will grinned. "Hot date after dinner, that's why." He finished loading the dishwasher and turned it on. Over the sound of rushing water, he said, "How come you don't want to talk about Samantha?"

"For God's sake, can't you leave it alone?" Phil headed toward the door, but stopped before he opened it and turned to Will. "Samantha Eberhardt is dead. Dead, understand? She got what was coming to her. I, for one, am not going to mourn her loss."

Will glanced at him. "Did you kill her?"

"Did I kill her?" Phil laughed. "I had every reason to. Get back to work, will you?"

The forensics team went back to work at Samantha's cottage on Sunday morning. They examined every centimeter of floor, walls, and ceiling, probed into every crack and cranny, collected every particle of dust and dirt no matter how minute. For the most part, the results were discouraging. The house had been cleaned, and cleaned thoroughly. However, they did collect fingerprints from items in the refrigerator, including an almost empty wine bottle.

"It's something," said Killdeer, holding the bottle with padded forceps high up on the neck where no fingerprints had been detected. "Probably the cleaning woman's fingerprints. But who knows."

Samantha's Mini Cooper was found parked at the Park and Ride lot where Zack had spent Friday night. The forensics team went over her car in great detail.

"Anything?" asked Smalley.

Killdeer snapped his chewing gum and thrust his hands into his pockets. "Nope."

"Fingerprints?"

"The steering wheel was wiped clean. Rearview mirror, clean. Anything the perp might have touched, clean. All other prints belong to the girl."

On Sunday morning Bruno Eberhardt drove into Edgartown to check out the jail. Officially it was the County of Dukes County House of Corrections. He'd passed the building dozens of times, thinking it was one of the captains' houses that lined Main Street, never realizing what it was.

He parked near the tall white Whaling Church and walked back to the jail. Several people he didn't recognize offered condolences. He bowed his head and kept walking. How could they have learned about his baby girl so soon?

He turned down a side street to check out the back of the building. Hardly high security, but then it usually housed local transgressors, not murderers. Once Zack was indicted, he'd be transferred to a high-security facility. Eberhardt decided he would have enough time to carry out his plans.

At the mortuary he'd shouted at Sergeant Smalley, told him he would kill Zack if he got his hands on him. If Smalley had passed on his threat to the sheriff, he, Eberhardt, would be in trouble. But Smalley was an Island cop, likely to understand and ignore a father's rage at the murder of his child, dismiss his angry threats.

Eberhardt walked back to his Jaguar and got in. He'd intended to drive home, but instead decided to return to Samantha's place. At some point he would have to go through her belongings, sort them out, feel them, smell them, grieve over them, and curse the man who'd cut her life short.

He drove back along the Edgartown Road, past the West Tisbury firehouse and the low spot near the bike path where they'd found her. He didn't want to see that. Her final resting place. They hadn't given him any details of her death beyond the fact that she'd been hit with some blunt object and didn't suffer. How did they know? He supposed they had to say that. Was it comforting to think your baby girl didn't suffer while some monster killed her?

He drove on, past Mrs. Trumbull's house, where the monster had lived. Through the village, with its church, library, and art gallery. To the hills and stone walls of Chilmark.

He turned onto the dirt road that led to her drive. He would spend a quiet time with her possessions. He lowered his window to take in the smell of sun-warmed pine and the sound of chewinks scratching in the oak leaves. The drive to her place had always been calming. He heard a bell buoy in the distance. A last turn up her rutted road and he would see her house.

But as he made the turn, a parked police vehicle blocked the road. He jammed on the brake.

A sturdy-looking cop got out and strode over to him. "May I see some identification, sir."

Eberhardt blurted out, "What are you talking about? This is my daughter's house."

"Sorry, sir. No unauthorized persons are permitted access. The area is a crime scene, sir."

"This is my daughter's house. I'm her father —"

"Yes, sir."

Eberhardt smacked his steering wheel. "I intend to spend some quiet time there —"

"I'm sorry, sir. You can't enter until the police are through with their work."

Eberhardt felt blood rush to his head. "That creep murdered her. We know who killed her. Why in hell are you doing this to me?"

"This is a crime scene, sir," repeated the cop.

"What are you doing? Think it will bring her back to me, pawing through her things? That what you think?"

The cop shook his head. "We can understand how you feel, sir."

"The hell you can." Eberhardt took a deep breath. "You hope to find evidence to clear him, that it?" He shook his head. "Make sure his rights are protected. What about me?" He pounded his chest. "What about my rights? Me, her father. What about that, hey?"

"Yes, sir." The cop took a step back. "I understand, sir."

"You don't understand one goddamned thing." Eberhardt felt a throbbing in his head.

"Sergeant Smalley will notify you when you can return, sir." The cop looked up. "Sir, an official vehicle needs to get past you."

Eberhardt, defeated, backed his car into a wide space in the dirt road and turned away. The vehicle passed him. There was an official seal on the door. Once it passed, he headed away from Samantha's house and toward his own place.

Before he could return, every item she owned, had touched, had looked at, would be pawed over, examined, dusted for fingerprints, photographed. Every essence of her would be destroyed by these officials coldly seeking, what? Truth?

Truth. What was truth?

He'd lost her a second time. They would wipe out every last remaining vestige of his daughter.

He had a second, horrible thought. He'd been through her house himself and it must have been after she was . . . He couldn't bring himself to think the word. He'd touched things of hers, held them, moved them. Cleaned up her dishes. Left his own fingerprints. Had he obliterated the fingerprints of Zack, her killer?

Oh, God! He'd forgotten. He'd asked Maria to clean the house. He told her he'd give her extra to clean real well. She cleaned the operating rooms at the hospital. She'd have done a thorough job.

He lowered his head until it touched the steering wheel and moaned.

That bastard will pay.

CHAPTER 17

It wasn't until mid-afternoon that Victoria could get back to work. After an hour of pondering, all she had on the back of her envelope were questions. No answers.

In a way, Casey was right. She mustn't meddle in the business of trained investigators. She could too easily damage whatever case they were hoping to build.

But she, Victoria, was in the unusual position of being semi-official, and that by courtesy. She wasn't obliged to answer to anyone. Furthermore, she knew more about the Island and the ways of its inhabitants than any official she could think of.

So it behooved her to investigate in her own way, taking a different path from that of the others.

She went back to her notes.

How did the wampum necklace figure in this, if at all?

It was ridiculous to think that Zack had

killed Samantha, yet Zack had admitted to every official who'd listen to him that he'd planned to poison her. Sicken her. Abort the pregnancy, if there was one, teach her a lesson if there wasn't. She knew him well enough to know there was no way he could possibly have pulled off her killing.

Where had Samantha been killed? In her house? The forensics team would determine that. She made a note to ask Casey what evidence the forensics people had found.

Then there was the leaf pile in which Samantha's body had been concealed. The pile was on the left side of the bicycle path, as one headed toward Edgartown, in a slight hollow, created by glacial water runoff. When, during the past four days, had her body, along with the leaves, gotten to the bike path? And how? Certainly not by car. The leaf pile was large. Had the vehicle, a dump truck or pickup, backed up onto the bike path and unloaded the leaves?

Unloading a pickup would mean shoveling everything out of the back. A tedious job. A dump truck would have been less trouble, but probably more noticeable. Although there were a lot of landscaping and construction dump trucks on Island roads these days.

Something else about the leaf pile puzzled

her. This was early September and autumn leaves had not yet begun to fall. It would be unusual to see a landscaper transporting fallen leaves now.

The leaves she had seen in the pile seemed to be mostly maple, a lighter color, broader shape, and flimsier than oak, and quite different from beech. The maples still held their late-summer green leaves. The leaves in the pile were a golden tan, and so must have been from the previous fall. She knew, from adding maple leaves to her compost heaps, that they disintegrated more readily than other leaves.

Therefore, the leaves in Samantha's burial pile had to have been protected by something, sheltered from wind and rain. The source of the leaf pile would have to be found. She made a note.

The mechanics of depositing that load, right there, also puzzled her. Why there? At this time of year, early September, someone surely would have seen a dump truck backing onto the bicycle path. The load would have been covered by a tarp, of course. That was the law. So it wouldn't have been obvious to passing cars that the truck was carrying not only leaves, but a body.

She left the question of leaves, and moved on to the question of Samantha's car. It had been found at the Park and Ride lot. That meant she probably had not been killed in her house. She might have followed someone she trusted to a place where he then killed her, placed her body in the load of leaves, and dumped the load by the bicycle path.

Victoria kept coming back to the question, Why there? Why dump a body in that particular spot? She could think of a dozen places on the Island where a killer might leave a body and it would never be found. Did he have to get rid of the load quickly for some reason?

Or was it a deliberate message of some kind. But what? And to whom? And why?

Her immediate concern was to clear Zack by finding Samantha's killer. She would put aside investigating Sebastian's death and the parsonage fire until she knew more.

She would start by talking to the parents whose teenagers had been caught up in Samantha's net, but she didn't know who they might be. She decided to ask the Alley's porch regulars, who usually convened after work, and who knew more about Island intrigues than anyone else she was acquainted with.

■ ■ ■ ■

Monday afternoon, Victoria and Elizabeth went to Alley's to pick up their mail. They went later than usual to be sure the porch sitters were there.

Sarah Germaine was already sitting on her bench next to a sign that read CANNED PEAS. She had come from tribal headquarters, where she worked, and she was wearing a white T-shirt with TWO BRAVE HAULERS printed in bright red above a drawing of some kind.

Victoria stopped to examine the drawing.

"Hey, Mrs. Trumbull." Sarah pulled out her shirt so Victoria could see the picture better. It depicted a Wampanoag brave carrying a piano on one shoulder while a second Wampanoag rode on the other shoulder playing the piano.

Victoria laughed.

"Have a seat." Sarah smoothed her shirt back into place and moved over to make room for her. "They're actually wicked strong, you know. Bucky and his older brother Leo. And they're pretty careful."

Victoria seated herself beside Sarah. "Aren't they grandsons of Charity Minnowfish? She was one of my best friends in school."

"I think they're great-grandsons."

Joe shifted slightly against the porch support, where he was standing.

"Good afternoon, Joe." Victoria fanned herself with a letter she had been about to mail. "A warm day for September."

"Can I get you a Coke?" Sarah stood.

"Thank you. That would hit the spot."

"Be right back," said Sarah, stepping up into the store. The screen door slammed behind her.

Joe reached into his shirt pocket, brought out a package of Red Man, and carved off a chunk with his pocket knife. "I hear your tenant is in jail for killing his girlfriend." He tossed the chunk of chewing tobacco into his mouth.

This was exactly what Victoria wanted to talk about.

"I'm afraid so," she said.

Joe lifted his cap and scratched his forehead. "Think he did?"

"I don't see how he could have," said Victoria.

"Me neither." Joe shifted his wad of tobacco into the other cheek. "He doesn't have the balls."

"I agree," said Victoria.

At that point, Sarah returned with three

Diet Cokes. Victoria reached into her pocket for money.

"It's okay, Mrs. Trumbull. It's on Joe." Sarah handed him two of the cans. He popped the lid off one and gave it to Victoria.

"Thank you." Victoria held up the icy can.

"No problem," said Joe. He examined the label. "You trying to tell me something, Sarah? Diet?" He took a swig and made a face.

Victoria wondered in passing if he was swallowing tobacco juice along with the soft drink.

"Right off the bat I could name ten people who wanted to kill that girl," said Joe, wiping his mouth with the back of his hand.

"Woman," said Sarah. "You talking about Samantha?"

"Who else?" Joe took another swig.

"I thought Samantha was a nice young woman," said Victoria, settling in for a chat.

"Samantha?" Joe laughed. "You thought she was nice?"

"I didn't really know her," said Victoria.

"That's for sure."

Victoria wiped the condensation from her own can with a napkin she'd saved from the senior center. "What was her problem, Joe?"

"She is — or was — a rich, spoiled, nymphomaniac."

"Watch your tongue, Joe," said Sarah. "Mrs. Trumbull doesn't need to hear that."

"Actually, I'm interested," said Victoria.

"It's the truth," said Joe. "She had the hots for everything that moved. Probably for things that didn't move, too." Joe glanced over at Victoria and grinned. "You can put that in your column."

"Thank you," said Victoria. "I'd like to exonerate Zack by finding out who did kill her. She lived in Chilmark. Was there anyone up-Island whom she might have antagonized?"

Joe chortled. "Up-Island, down-Island, mid-Island. Men, girls, boys, sheep, for all I know."

"Stop it, Joe." Sarah looked off to the right, where an ancient truck was turning into the parking area. "Here's Lincoln. I was afraid he was going to sink into a depression after Sebastian . . ." she stopped. "I wouldn't blame him."

"He could tell Mrs. T a thing or two about her."

"Don't mention her name to him, Joe. He hurts too much."

At that point, Elizabeth, who'd been in the store for longer than it took to simply pick up the mail, came out with a handful of catalogs and a brown paper bag of groceries. She glanced at her grandmother who gave her a thumbs-up sign. Elizabeth nodded. "If you don't mind, I'll stop in at the library for a few minutes, Gram."

"No hurry," said Victoria.

Lincoln parked his truck and shambled over to the porch. He looked haggard. His sandy hair was dull, his face was gray. He'd aged in the past couple of days. He stepped up onto the porch and took his usual spot by the door.

"Good afternoon, Lincoln," said Victoria. "My condolences. I'm sorry about Sebastian, so terribly sorry."

Lincoln nodded.

"We're discussing the untimely death of Ms. Eberhardt," said Joe.

"Joe . . ." warned Sarah.

"Surprised it took so long," said Lincoln.

"Mrs. T, here, thought she was nice. You want to add anything?"

"Joe, cut it out!"

"It's what he needs right now," said Joe. "To cuss her out."

Lincoln settled himself against the doorframe.

Victoria sat quietly.

"Whether she had anything to do with that fire or not, she killed my boy," said Lincoln. "She did a nice job on him."

"Sebastian?" asked Victoria. "He was only thirteen or fourteen, wasn't he?"

"Sixteen," said Sarah.

"Yeah, sixteen," repeated Lincoln, looking away.

"I'll tell you about Samantha," said Sarah. "She is, or was, like, in her mid-twenties, too grown up, you know, mixed up something terrible. She starts telling Lincoln's kid how manly he is, and, like, a lot of other stuff. The kid fell for it."

Lincoln looked down and kicked a loose pebble that had found its way onto the porch. The pebble flew into the road, narrowly missing a car.

Sarah continued. "Sebastian had been saving up for college ever since he started earning money. He bought her a wampum necklace that must have cost him."

Victoria sat up straight. "A wampum necklace?"

"Three hundred bucks," said Lincoln.

Victoria whistled. This was not the time to mention the necklace found in the ashes of the parsonage fire.

"Yeah." Joe spit off to the side of the porch again. "I'd put good ole Lincoln down as number one suspect."

"I wish," said Lincoln.

"Were there others she toyed with?" asked Victoria.

"She had a girls' club," said Sarah.

Joe laughed. "Women."

Victoria set her can down on the bench.

"Girls," Sarah repeated. "High school girls. And you know what that was all about, don't you?"

"I'm afraid to ask," said Victoria.

"Dope," said Joe.

"Pot," said Sarah. "Grass. Marijuana. Heroin. Opiates. Prescription drugs. She paid for the stuff, the girls got it for her."

Victoria wanted to take notes, but was afraid that might stop the flow of information. She needed to tell Casey about the necklace Sebastian had bought. But right now she had to follow up on the conversation about Samantha.

She asked, "Who were the girls?"

"You know a couple of them, don't you, Joe? I know one was the daughter of that Oak Bluffs selectperson."

"Selectman," said Joe. "Board of Selectmen. Legal name."

Victoria picked up her drink can.

Joe wiped his mouth with the back of his hand again. "Dana Putnam's girl."

"How many members were in the girls' club?" asked Victoria.

"It wasn't anything formal, you know," Sarah said. "Maybe four girls? Three or four."

"Then there was that teacher's kid," said Joe. "Teacher at the Charter School. Single mom, raising a teenager alone, Samantha comes along, and teacher thinks, 'She seems like a nice friendly person her kid might have fun with.' "

Lincoln rubbed his back against the doorframe.

"Give us a day or two, Mrs. T," said Joe. "I could give you a list of a dozen names."

Victoria saw Elizabeth walking away from the library toward them and set the empty Coke can down. "I've got to leave. But if you're serious about giving me a list, I would appreciate it."

"I can add another half dozen names," said Sarah.

Joe chortled. "Keep Mrs. T out of trouble following up on all of them." He turned to Lincoln. "Take it easy, Linc."

Lincoln thrust his hands deep into his pockets. "Don't get involved, Mrs. Trumbull."

"Lighten up, Linc," said Joe. "You're giving Mrs. T a challenge she can't resist."

Lincoln turned his back on the group.

"I'll be fine, Lincoln. It's you we're concerned about." Victoria got to her feet. "Let me know if there's anything Elizabeth and I can do to help you get through this awful time." She turned to the others. "I'll see you tomorrow, then."

As soon as she got home from Alley's, Victoria called the police station. "Casey, I know who owned the wampum necklace."

"That was quick. Who?"

"Lincoln's son, Sebastian, bought a piece of wampum jewelry for Samantha. Do you want me to talk to him about it?"

"No, I'd better. That's a promising lead. Thanks, Victoria. I'll check it out with Lincoln and get back to you."

CHAPTER 18

Casey tracked down Lincoln, who was planting bulbs at the home of a Chilmark client whose grounds he was landscaping. She had considered asking him to come to the station to question him about the necklace, but decided informal would be better. Lincoln was too shattered, she was sure, to deal with his personal tragedy in an official setting.

The weathered, gray-shingled house where he was working was at the top of a slight hill and overlooked Menemsha Pond. Lincoln was kneeling by a newly dug-up bed that bordered the drive. The bed was at least twenty feet long and about three feet wide.

Casey parked the police vehicle at the foot of the hill and walked up to where he was digging. He had scattered bulbs on top of the dirt and was so intent on planting them he didn't notice her until she spoke.

"Lincoln?"

He dropped the bulbs he was holding and got to his feet. "Morning, Chief." He slapped dirt off his hands and wiped them on his jeans. "To what do I owe this honor?"

"It's too nice a day to stay indoors, and I wanted to ask you something. Do you mind if I interrupt?" She glanced away from him to the pond below them. His thin face was so marked by grief she found it difficult to look at him.

A sailboat was anchored in the pond, its sails neatly flaked along the boom. A light wind rippled a cat's paw across the pond's surface. Several gulls wheeled and settled near the boat. "What a beautiful spot," Casey said. "Peaceful."

"A good place to be right now," said Lincoln. "What have you got on your mind, Casey? The bulbs can wait a few minutes."

"What are you planting?"

"Daffodils." He bent down and picked up a chunky double bulb and showed it to her. "They're about the only spring bulb that deer and rabbits won't eat. No sense in planting tulips here."

Casey was not usually uncomfortable with asking questions, but somehow this business of the necklace seemed intrusive. Neither of them spoke. A sudden gust of wind tossed one of the paper packets that had protected the bulbs across the border. Lincoln went after it, his long legs straddling the bed. He dropped the empty packet into the bushel basket that still held a half dozen packets of bulbs to be planted.

"Well?" he asked.

"Did you ever see the necklace Sebastian bought?" She couldn't bring herself to say "for Samantha."

Lincoln tossed the bulb he'd been holding into the basket. "Yeah, Casey. I did. Never saw anything quite like it. Beautiful. Expensive for a kid. Three hundred bucks. Sebastian had been saving up his money for college." He kicked at a dirt clod and it flew across the border. "Why do you ask?"

"The arson investigators found a wampum necklace at the scene."

Lincoln said nothing.

"The necklace was made up of separate pieces of wampum shell, the way you pick it up on the beach, not cut or anything, wound with copper wire and strung on a leather cord."

He bent down and picked up his digging tool. He flipped it from one hand to the other.

Casey waited.

Lincoln took a deep breath. "Yeah. It was like that." He looked away. "So it survived the fire."

"It was protected by a pile of newspapers." Casey shrugged. "How it got there, I guess we'll never know. Had Sebastian already given the necklace to Samantha?"

"He was planning to. That was the last time I saw him. He'd wrapped it up real pretty in blue tissue paper. Tied it with a pink ribbon." He slapped the palm of his hand with the tool. "I suppose you want me to take a look at it."

"Yes, Lincoln. I'm afraid so."

"At the police station."

"Yes." Casey nodded. "I'll ask them to bring the necklace to me there." They stood, Casey with her hands in her jacket pockets, Lincoln with his down by his sides, one hand still holding the digger.

"Let me know when. You have my cell number?"

Casey nodded. "I don't know how to tell you how sorry I am, Lincoln."

"Thanks."

Casey walked back down the hill to her vehicle, feeling depressed. Lincoln was too decent to have these things happen to him.

After school on Monday, Robin dropped by Victoria's to show her his new T-shirt and the trophy he'd won for batting in the most runs.

Robin's school had won Saturday's game with the Charter School after it had been delayed more than an hour because of the body in the leaf pile.

The bright red T-shirt had CHAMPION! in bold black and white letters splashed across the front. Below was a picture of a fire truck and below that, crowded into four lines that sprawled across his slight chest was WEST TISBURY/VOLUNTEER FIRE DEPARTMENT/ ANNUAL 6TH GRADE/SOFTBALL CHAMPI-ONSHIP.

Victoria had worried about him. Finding the body must have been traumatic, a scene that would haunt him for the rest of his life. Talking about a horrible experience, she knew, would be therapeutic. She approached the subject cautiously.

"I hope you didn't have a problem sleep-ing Saturday night," she began.

"Who, me?" Robin looked surprised.

"That was a terrible experience," Victoria said.

"It was them that had the terrible experi-ence." Robin held up his trophy to empha-size the point. "We creamed 'em. Eleven to two."

"That's beautiful," Victoria said, taking

the trophy from him and examining the lettering. "Your parents must be proud of you."

"My dad is building a shelf to put it on."

Finding the body didn't seem to have bothered him as much as Victoria feared. In fact, Robin looked taller and broader and had a self-confident look that Victoria hadn't seen before.

She handed the small silver-colored trophy back to him. "Weren't you upset by finding the body?"

"Oh, *that.*" He stood still taller. "The kids wanted to know all about it. Both teams. About how I saw this creepy arm sticking out of the leaf pile, and how I ran to get help, and how the cops came. And how I got that license plate the night before."

"That was smart of you."

"He left his lights on, and when he came out of the woods he said thank you about a million times. He looked awful. I figured he must've done something. And my teacher told us how we should be on the alert for weirdos and always get license numbers."

Victoria nodded. So much for a therapeutic chat. "Do you have time for some lemonade?"

He shook his head. "I gotta get home. I just wanted you to see my trophy." He went out the door, stowed his trophy in his bicycle basket, swung his leg over the seat, and took off.

At Alley's Store still later that afternoon, Joe handed Victoria a scrawled list of names and phone numbers. "I'll give you more tomorrow."

"Five is enough to start with," said Victoria. "Thank you, Joe."

"No problem." Joe touched his baseball cap with a finger.

Once home, she looked over the names. The five included four parents of girls in Samantha's so-called club — a Charter School teacher, a builder, a garage owner, and a landscaper. The fifth name was familiar to Victoria, Abilene Butler, the granddaughter of a girlhood friend, Mattie.

Joe had noted, "Lover" next to the name. Victoria hesitated, not sure how to approach her. She knew Abilene, who looked so much like her grandmother had when she was in her early twenties, that Victoria had called her Mattie more than once. She was a slight young woman with light brown hair usually worn in a ponytail.

Victoria dialed and a soft voice answered, "Lily Pond Yoga."

"I hope I'm not intruding on you at an awkward time," said Victoria after introducing herself, "but I want to talk to you about Samantha . . ." She didn't get any further.

"Sammy!" The soft voice had gone sharp. "I can tell you a lot about Sammy. I'll stop by tonight, if you want."

"I don't want to inconvenience you," said Victoria.

"No inconvenience," said Abilene. "Someone needs to set the record straight. About seven?"

"I look forward to . . ." Victoria had started to say, but realized that was not exactly the right thing to say. But Abilene had already hung up.

She called the second name on the list, Connie Burrowes, the teacher.

"Sure, I'll talk to you about Samantha, Mrs. Trumbull. I'll stop by your house after school tomorrow, if that's convenient."

Victoria put a check mark next to her name, then looked at her watch. It was after five, and she hadn't yet made plans for supper. Elizabeth wouldn't be home from work until after eleven. This was a late night at the harbor, with boats coming in for a last cruise before they were put away for the winter. Scrambled eggs would do. She decided to call one more name, Anderson Jones, a man she didn't know.

"Andy's Moped Rentals at your service,"

a deep voice answered.

"This is Victoria Trumbull," she said.

"Right. Connie just called and said you might be contacting me. Sure, I'd love to talk to you about Samantha Eberhardt." He laughed. "Word travels fast on the Island, right?"

"Yes, it does," said Victoria. "Where shall I meet you, and when?"

He paused. "I can come to your place after work tomorrow, if that's okay."

"Connie will be here then."

"Probably good to hear both of us. Different takes on the same story."

"Thank you," said Victoria, and hung up.

CHAPTER 19

Victoria was washing her supper dishes when there was a gentle knock on the side of the open kitchen door.

"Mrs. Trumbull?" A soft voice.

She looked up and, as had happened before, was transported back more than three-quarters of a century when she saw Mattie's granddaughter. She forgot for a moment where she was.

"May I come in?"

Victoria recovered quickly. "Of course. I was seeing the image of your grandmother and forgot myself for a moment."

Abilene stepped into the kitchen. "I remember hearing her say how you and she were close friends."

"We used to bird-watch together. You're like her, you know."

Abilene nodded. "I was only a child when I knew her. She seemed terribly old to me, although she was only in her seventies."

"Let's sit where we can talk." Victoria led the way into the cookroom. They sat at the table.

"I understand you knew Samantha well," Victoria said. "I didn't know her at all and I'm hoping to learn something about her."

Abilene folded her hands in her lap and looked down at them. "I guess I don't know where to begin."

Victoria stood up. "Would you like a cup of tea?"

"Do you have herbal tea?"

"I do. Do you like honey and lemon in it?"

"Yes, indeed." Abilene stood. "I'll help."

Together they went through the tea-making ritual, discussing tea and the location of spoons.

Seated at the table, Abilene said, "I might as well begin. Sammy and I were really close."

"I know," said Victoria. "I understand you were lovers."

Abilene looked down into her tea. "Not everyone understands."

"Were you still close at the time of her death?"

Abilene looked up again, and Victoria could see pain in her eyes. "Everybody saw Sammy as a spoiled rich girl who had everything." She stopped.

"But you saw her differently?"

"She was all that." Abilene paused. "Sammy's mother divorced her father when Sammy was just a little girl. She was tossed back and forth in one court case after another, her parents fighting for custody. You can imagine what that does to a kid."

Victoria nodded.

"He won. He had the money and the lawyers. Her mother lost. So he brought her up, if you can call it that." Abilene sipped her tea and set the cup down. "Anything that money could buy. His idea of love is shoving money at his kid."

Victoria was quiet.

"I'm no psychologist," Abilene continued, "but it was so obvious. Sammy seeks love, and Daddy hands her more money. Sammy tries to attract his attention with crazy stuff, he never stops her, just throws more money at her. She wanted to see just how wild she could get before he did stop her."

"And he never did," said Victoria. "Did she end up hurting you?"

"Yes, she did. I loved her and she responded like a drooping plant when you water it. She was starved for love and I gave it to her."

"From the little I know about Samantha,

193

she had an Island-wide reputation for wildness," said Victoria.

Abilene nodded. "She was what she was. I guess I was a small haven for her when she was desperate. I knew all about her drugs and drinking and boyfriends. I thought I could handle it. I understood where she was coming from. I never expected her to change."

"Do you have any thoughts on who might have killed her?"

"She hurt a lot of people. Especially a small group of high school girls who got all caught up in the 'wicked' stuff they were doing." Abilene made quote marks in the air. "Fun and grown up messing around with drugs and sex."

"You were close to Samantha despite how difficult she must have been," said Victoria. "Right up to the end, weren't you?"

Abilene shrugged. "Sounds stupid, doesn't it."

"Love can take us to strange places." Victoria thought for a moment. "Tell me about your yoga practice. Do you have a studio?"

Abilene smiled. "I share a really nice space I rent along with three other people."

"That sounds like a good arrangement," said Victoria. "How often do you hold your yoga classes?"

"Every weekday morning, from seven until noon."

"No wonder you're in such wonderful shape," said Victoria.

Abilene smiled again. "Yoga is good exercise. Come over to my place sometime and I'll show you around."

"Thank you." Victoria wrote herself a note and checked her watch. "I've taken up a lot of your time, Abilene. You've been most helpful. Losing such a close friend is difficult enough without having to talk about it."

"You're going to hear a lot of Sammy-bashing," said Abilene.

A car pulled up. Abilene looked out the window. "I'd better leave. I don't want to face anyone right now."

Victoria pointed to the back door that led out of the cookroom, and before her next visitor knocked on the door, Abilene had disappeared.

Victoria anticipated the knock and opened the door. It took her a moment to recognize her caller.

"Mr. Eberhardt. Good evening. This is a surprise."

Eberhardt looked gray and weary.

"Please, sit down," said Victoria. "What

195

can I do for you?"

"I needed to talk to someone, Mrs. Trumbull."

Victoria glanced at him. He was a parent who'd lost a child in the most chilling way possible and he was in anguish.

"I think you need a stiff drink," she said.

He nodded.

"Sit down." Victoria pointed to a chair.

He looked behind him and sat on the nearest seat. Set his elbows on his knees and lowered his head into his hands.

"I can only imagine how you must be feeling," she said.

He shook his head as though in denial.

"What can I do to help you?" Victoria stood watching him for a moment. "I seem to recall that you prefer bourbon. Will Jim Beam do?"

He looked up. "Yes. Thank you."

Victoria fetched the bottle from the cabinet under the coffeemaker and set it on the table in front of him along with two glasses. He didn't move.

"We'll be more comfortable in the cookroom. If you'll take the glasses and bottle to the table in there, I'll bring ice."

He stood, but didn't move.

She looked at him with concern. "When did you last eat?"

He shook his head. "I don't remember."

"Not for a while, I imagine." She turned to the refrigerator and opened the freezer. "Here's the ice. You pour yourself a drink, while I make an omelet."

"I can't eat. I don't want anything."

"Pour me a very light one, just a finger's worth." She held up her forefinger. "With water."

He moved. Dutifully dropped ice into their glasses, refilled the ice cube tray with water, made her a light drink and himself a heavy one, and went to the cookroom. He pulled out a chair. She heard the chair squeak as he sat. She heard him take a deep breath.

She busied herself with the omelet. A hearty one with bacon and onion. She toasted two slices of bread. Buttered them and slathered them with strawberry jam.

She glanced over to the cookroom. Eberhardt hadn't touched his drink. His arms were folded on the table and he was staring out the window into the dark night.

She carried a plate with his supper into the cookroom and sat in her usual chair. He looked at the omelet.

"I can't eat."

"Try a bit, otherwise you'll hurt my feelings."

He lifted the fork. Cut into the omelet with its bacon and translucent onion. Took the smallest of mouthfuls. Chewed and swallowed. Looked up at Victoria again, this time with a faint smile and dug in.

They said nothing until he'd scraped his plate clean, eaten every crumb of toast, and reached for his drink.

"The world looks better once you've eaten." Victoria reached for her own drink and took a small sip.

He nodded.

"You said you needed to talk. I'm a good listener."

"I'm not accustomed to asking anyone for anything, Mrs. Trumbull." He folded his napkin and tossed it onto the table next to his clean plate. "Yet here I am, seeking you out."

"Losing a daughter like that would drive any parent to distraction."

Victoria waited.

Eberhardt stared at his empty plate. "I don't know where to start."

"We have plenty of time," said Victoria.

He took a deep breath. "Sammy was popular. She had a lot of friends." He glanced at her.

Victoria was not about to let him know

what she had learned about Sammy's friends.

"I didn't know most of them. Zack. She didn't say much about him. Had no idea they were so involved."

Victoria took another small sip of her drink.

"She was sure he intended to poison her," said Eberhardt.

Victoria looked down at her hands and said nothing. What could she say?

He glanced at her. "I spoke with you after dinner that night and become convinced she was wrong. That he had good intentions."

Victoria looked up at the baskets hanging from the beams. She looked at the bookcases under the window that held her gardening books. She couldn't meet his eyes.

"I thought Sammy was probably overreacting," he continued. "Which she's inclined to do." He studied his empty plate. "But Sammy was right. He intended to kill her. And this time he succeeded."

Victoria said nothing.

"I identified her body at the mortuary. My baby girl." His voice broke. "You can't imagine what it was like. I wouldn't have recognized that rotting flesh as my beautiful baby girl."

Victoria had seen the body.

He began to speak again. "She had tattoos. I recognized them. The police officer was polite. Sensitive." He took a small sip of his drink. "I swore I'd get even with that bastard. I swore I'd kill him. Swore that, right in front of the cop."

Victoria said nothing.

"If that cop took me seriously . . ." His voice trailed off.

"He understood," said Victoria.

"No one understands," said Eberhardt. "I told myself killing was too good for him. I want to see him locked away in a prison where no one will ever find him. Every day I will curse him and the day he laid eyes on my Sammy." He took a small swallow of his drink and set the glass down. "That stupid boy will not destroy me, too."

They sat quietly. Eberhardt stared at the window. The window reflected his image back to him. Victoria toyed with her drink, turning her glass around and around on the red-checked tablecloth.

She broke the silence. "You're right about his being stupid. He is a stupid boy. You're wrong, though, about his killing your daughter. Someone else did."

"He intended to kill her." Eberhardt

picked up his glass and slammed it down on the table. "He killed her."

"He didn't succeed," said Victoria. "She was assaulted. He doesn't have the nerve to assault anyone." She set her own glass down. "We have to find who did kill her."

"I've found him, Mrs. Trumbull. And I'll make sure he pays. He'll regret the day he was born."

"He'll be punished. He's likely to be locked up for attempted poisoning, but he's not the one who killed your daughter." She took another small sip of her drink. "Surely, you don't want the killer to go free."

"I know who the killer is, Mrs. Trumbull."

"I don't think so, Mr. Eberhardt. Zack might poison, yes. Blunt instrument, no."

Eberhardt shook his head.

"With your help, we'll find the killer," said Victoria.

"No."

"Assume for a moment that Zack could not possibly have killed Samantha. That means we don't know who the killer is. We need to track down the killer and see that he's punished."

"Are you backing me into a corner, making me say I don't want her killer punished?" Eberhardt wiped his forehead with his napkin. "Mrs. Trumbull, Zack wanted my

Sammy dead. That's enough for me."

How was she going to get through to this thick-headed man? Zack had no intention of killing Samantha with the trumpets of death. She would try a new approach.

"You're a risk taker, Mr. Eberhardt, aren't you?"

"That's how I got where I am."

"I'm a gambler, myself. Shall we make a bet?" Victoria occasionally bought a lottery ticket.

"What are we betting?"

"Give me the support I need for the next ten days and I will find the real killer."

"Financial?" He raised his eyebrows.

"Financial, and your time."

"And if you find the real killer is the one I've already identified?"

"I'll apologize."

He laughed. "Some bargain."

"It will take your mind off your suffering for the next ten days. At least, partly."

"And suppose you identify no one?"

"We'll find the killer, whether it's a him or a her."

He held out a hand and she shook it. "I suppose you'll want a signed affidavit to the effect of this agreement?"

"The handshake will do," said Victoria.

CHAPTER 20

When Mrs. Trumball pointed to the back-door so she could avoid her visitor, Abilene slipped out of the cookroom into the former woodshed, where Mrs. Trumbull now kept her plants. From the woodshed a back door led to the outside, and Abilene could escape unseen.

But Abilene wanted to know who was visiting Mrs. Trumbull. When she closed the cookroom door, she found she was on a flight of three steps leading down into a room. She sat on the top step. A half-moon shone through skylights, the only illumination. By moonlight she could make out the shapes of plants on the floor and hanging from the ceiling.

She heard the kitchen door shut. She heard Victoria exclaim and a man answer, but couldn't make out words. She pressed her ear against the door.

Footsteps into the cookroom, a chair

scraped, a chair creaked as someone sat heavily on it.

More footsteps, lighter, clearly Mrs. Trumbull.

"I can't eat," she heard the man say.

Abilene recoiled. She heard him clearly. That familiar voice. Sammy's father. That rotten excuse of a father. That arrogant, egotistical prick of a man. What was he doing here?

They were speaking clearly enough so she stopped leaning against the door. She felt her face flush with anger.

He's playing a new role, grieving parent. The faker. How can Mrs. Trumbull possibly believe him? Grief? Love? His only thought during Sammy's entire life was to keep her away from her mother. He'd buy her anything. Anything. He had no idea she was into drugs. Didn't even know the names of her friends.

She'd heard enough. She had to get out of here before he returned to his car and noticed hers. He'd recognize it.

She stood and winced as the step creaked, a sound everyone in the vicinity surely heard. She eased down the steps and tiptoed past the potted plants and gardening tools, hoping she wouldn't knock over something she couldn't see in the darkness.

Once outside, she could smell the faint odor of skunk. That's all I need tonight, a run-in with a skunk, she thought. The night air was chilly and she shivered. She brushed against the shrubbery growing near the woodshed door, and the right side of her jeans got soaked with cold dew. Despite the bright moon, she could make out stars, millions and billions and more of stars. Phoenicians had navigated by those same stars. Now the Hubble Space Telescope was out there exploring the universe and its tens of thousands of galaxies. Hundreds of millions of galaxies. Too many to conceive of.

And here she was, nothing. Not even a dust mote in the universe. Not even a recognizable entity on Earth. Even on this Island. Mrs. Trumbull called her by her grandmother's name. Sammy really, truly, hadn't given a damn about her. She'd thought she understood Sammy. But who was she to Sammy? Was there any purpose to her life? Abilene, hot tears of self-pity dripping down her face, reached her car without encountering the skunk. She slipped behind the wheel, started up the engine, and stole out of Mrs. Trumball's drive without turning on the headlights.

She would pay another visit to Mrs. Trumbull. Maybe Mrs. Trumbull would recognize her as Abilene Butler, a person in her own right, not the grandmother she hardly knew. As she'd listened to Samantha's father and Mrs. Trumbull talking, she felt sick at the way Daddy had maneuvered Mrs. Trumbull into feeling sympathy for him so easily. That cold-blooded bastard.

At the end of the drive she flipped on the headlights and waited for her eyesight to adjust before she turned onto the paved road.

After Eberhardt left, Victoria was thinking about their conversation when Elizabeth came home from work. Victoria had just taken her typewriter out of its case and was about to work on her column.

Even after a day's work, Elizabeth looked trim in her white uniform shirt and creased tan trousers. "I'm exhausted," she said, flopping down in the chair Eberhardt had vacated. "How was your day, Gram?"

Victoria told her about her visitors.

"Lucky those two didn't meet," said Elizabeth. "I'd hate to see the bloodbath."

Victoria pushed her typewriter aside.

"What did Samantha's father have to say for himself?"

"He fell to pieces after he had to identify his daughter."

"That I can understand. Awful for anyone. Even Bruno Eberhardt."

"Mr. Eberhardt was planning to take matters into his own hands," said Victoria.

"He told you that?"

"Pretty much so. He told Sergeant Smalley at the mortuary that he was going to kill Zack."

"What on earth was he doing here?" asked Elizabeth.

"He had no one to talk to."

Elizabeth stood. "Why you? I mean, I'd go to you when I needed someone to talk to, but that power-hungry excuse for a father?" She started toward the kitchen.

"He was broken," said Victoria.

Elizabeth turned. "Don't believe anything he says."

Victoria heard the refrigerator door open and shut.

"I feel sorry for him," Victoria said.

"Yeah, right."

"Are you finding something to eat?"

"I'm making a sandwich. What did you say to him?"

"I told him Zack couldn't possibly be the killer and I asked him to help me find the real killer."

"You asked him *what*?" Elizabeth carried her sandwich into the cookroom and sat down. "You're not serious about asking for his help to clear Zack? And he agreed?"

"Not to clear Zack, to find the killer."

Elizabeth shook her head.

Victoria said, "Bruno Eberhardt has money and connections."

Elizabeth wiped her mouth. "What did Abilene have to say?"

"She's devastated by Samantha's death. She says she was one of the few people who understood Samantha."

"Don't trust Abilene, either. She's steel inside that sweet exterior. She hated Samantha."

"Abilene reminds me so much of her grandmother."

"Abilene isn't her grandmother," said Elizabeth.

"I hope you're wrong, Elizabeth, about both Bruno and Abilene."

"We'll see, Gram." Elizabeth took her plate into the kitchen and rinsed it. "Look who was right about Zack."

"Point taken," admitted Victoria.

CHAPTER 21

When Bruno Eberhardt drove away from Victoria Trumbull's he wondered what there was about the old lady that had induced him to open up to her? She was about the same age as his dead mother, but she bore no resemblance to his mother, who'd been a remote and feeble presence in his life. Surely he hadn't gone to Victoria Trumbull in his time of desperate need looking for a mother substitute.

Why on God's green earth had he called on her? And how had she conned him into agreeing to help her with her sleuthing? He wasn't quite sure what had happened back there.

He scarcely noticed his surroundings. The warm day had given way to a chilly night and dew formed a gray mist on his windshield. He turned on the wipers.

He shook his head to clear it. He'd lost control of himself there at Mrs. Trumbull's.

He couldn't recall ever before needing anyone, let alone a listener. She'd listened to him. But he didn't much like what she had to say. She was wrong about Zack Zeller.

A skunk sauntered into the road from the grassy edge. Eberhardt was deep in his misery and swerved automatically, without being aware that he had. The skunk hurried off. An owl flew low in front of him, almost touching the car. He drove on.

Sammy. He slapped the steering wheel. Dead. She was gone. That boy, that kid, had intended to kill her. And now she was dead.

Why in hell would Mrs. Trumbull defend him? And somehow, she'd twisted things around so he'd agreed to work with her. To find the killer. Well, Mrs. Trumbull, I know who the killer is. I'll work with you, Mrs. Trumbull, for the reason you gave. It's a distraction from the anger that's eating me up. I'm a street fighter. You might be a local heavyweight, but I know how to turn my opponent's weight to my advantage. I'll get that kid if it's the last thing I do.

The straight road of West Tisbury gave way to the hills and curves of Chilmark and he reached his turnoff. No cars had passed him. The sprinklers were on in the center of his rutted road, and the spray of water shushed against the underside of his car.

The last turn and there was his house, looking like an ad for the architect who'd designed it. Every light in every window was on, blasting out lumens in an attempt to look welcoming. Well, it didn't look welcoming. He'd told Isabella to stop lighting up the house like that. It looked like a cheap hotel. Indian from Gay Head. She loved to play that card calling herself Native American from Aquinnah.

She was probably in bed with a half-empty box of chocolates next to her. With all the lights on to greet him. On purpose. At one time he'd thought she was so exotic, slender, with that long, sexy, black hair and those green, slanted eyes. Now, all he could envision was her lying down on the rumpled bed with a box of chocolates. She'd put on weight, and it didn't look good on her. He was tired of her. Sammy hated her. A good excuse to evict her. Sammy was always telling him that Isabella was using him. He knew she was, and he was fed up with her. She'd have to go.

The garage doors opened automatically at his approach and he drove in, left the key in the ignition after turning it off, and went out of the garage through the side door.

As he went up the steps onto the porch he

had a jarring feeling that something was wrong. He approached the front door cautiously, pressed down the thumb-latch, stood back, and shoved the door open with his foot.

The door swung inward.

He glanced around. Nothing was out of place that he could see. It would be like Isabella to turn on all the lights to aggravate him. Before going upstairs to her bedroom, he checked the great room, the dining room where they'd had that memorable dinner of black trumpets. The kitchen. The breakfast room. The study. The library.

Everything was brightly illuminated. Everything was still.

That was why he felt uneasy. The TV was usually blaring, tuned in to a soap or a shopping channel.

He headed up the stairs and went into her bedroom. Not there.

"Isabella?" he called out.

No answer.

"Isabella!" he shouted.

Nothing.

He checked the other bedrooms, the bathrooms. Her bathroom was its usual mess. No sign of her. He went back downstairs and through all the rooms. No note. She hadn't taken one of the cars, he'd have noticed that, even in his misery.

He went into the dining room again and sat down. Had she gone off with some girlfriend unexpectedly? Some emergency? Had she taken anything with her?

He went upstairs again and checked her closet. Empty. The floor of the closet was littered with discarded coat hangers. Her suitcases. Gone. He went into her bathroom again. Wet towels on the floor. An empty lotion bottle dropped in the basin. A clutter of tissues tossed toward the wastebasket. A sprinkling of powder. He opened the cabinet over the sink. Her toiletries were gone.

So. She'd walked out on him. Ironic. He laughed. Just when he was going to throw her out. She'd thumbed her nose at him, lighting up the house in defiance.

She hadn't taken a car. They were all there in the garage. Someone had picked her up.

During the two years they'd been together, he'd always given her whatever she asked for, paid her credit card bills. Never gave her money. She had no money of her own.

He stood. Search for the money.

He kept an emergency supply of cash in his study, fifty thousand dollars, in a safe that was a discouragement against a casual burglary, not a high-tech deterrent.

He opened the door to his study and

stopped. The Doug Kent painting, a ruse that any self-respecting burglar would look behind, was facedown on the floor. The combination lock was hanging by a couple of red and black wires from the open door of the safe. The door itself was a torn and blackened piece of metal hanging from one hinge with a fluff of insulation leaking out of it.

And, of course, the cash was gone. So was some damned expensive jewelry he'd given her during their two years together.

He laughed. The goddamned bitch had gone to all that trouble. He'd have given her fifty thousand to pack up and leave.

Who the hell was her accomplice? Some guy with a car and a knowledge of burglary.

Call the cops?

No.

He'd seen enough of cops to last a lifetime. He'd deal with this on his own.

Victoria slept late Tuesday, the morning following her talks with Abilene Butler and Bruno Eberhardt. She awoke to the smell of coffee brewing and bacon cooking. Such good aromas. All was well, and she would solve the murder of Bruno's daughter, and he would help her. If Samantha's murder was tied in with Sebastian's death, and she was sure it was, she would unravel the snarled facts.

Her granddaughter hadn't been so sanguine about Bruno's cooperation. But Victoria believed she understood people, and she would bring him around.

She dressed hurriedly in her corduroy slacks and a rose-colored turtleneck shirt, selected a necklace of polished beach stones in shades of rose that matched her shirt, and headed for the stairs.

By the time she got downstairs, Elizabeth had set the table and was sliding a pan of blueberry muffins out of the oven.

"Morning, Gram."

"Almost afternoon." Victoria glanced at her watch.

"It's only nine thirty. You had a full day yesterday. Are you meeting with more of Samantha's fans today?"

Victoria seated herself in her armchair, where she could watch the bird feeder. "Connie Burrowes and Anderson Jones this afternoon, probably after five o'clock. I know both by sight, but that's all." She spread her napkin on her lap. "Do you know either of them?"

"I know Connie and her daughter, Brooke, slightly." Elizabeth passed the warm muffins to her grandmother. "Connie teaches fifth grade at the Charter School. Last spring I gave a talk to her class about working in the harbor. She wanted me to let the girls in her class know they can work at any kind of job they want."

"Does Brooke attend the Charter School?"

Elizabeth shook her head. "She's at the Regional High, either a sophomore or a junior."

"What do you know about Brooke?"

"You mean, how did Samantha screw her up?"

Victoria nodded. "Were you aware of anything amiss?"

"Sort of. Mostly hearsay. Apparently Samantha conned a small group of girls into a relationship with a local drug dealer."

"What sort of relationship?"

"I don't think it was sex, Gram." Elizabeth picked up a piece of bacon. "Samantha could be persuasive. She introduced the girls to this exciting and forbidden drug scene and the characters who buy and sell drugs. The girls changed, all of them, from normal, nice kids to these fake sophisticates. Some of them started smoking, thinking it was cool, and who knows what else." She paused. "Maybe sex." She bit off a piece of the bacon. "Possibly sex. *Probably* sex."

"What about Anderson Jones?" Victoria took a sip of her coffee.

"I don't know much about Mr. Jones. He's African American, lives in Oak Bluffs, and runs a moped rental place in the summer. I have no idea what he does in the winter."

"And his son?" asked Victoria. "What about him?"

"I didn't even know he had a son." Elizabeth checked her watch. "Gotta run." She dropped her napkin onto the table and stood. "See you this afternoon." She carried her dishes into the kitchen. A moment later the screen door slammed and Victoria heard the car start up.

She finished breakfast slowly, savoring the muffin, the coffee, the eggs, and thought about her meeting later this afternoon. Between now and then, she had work to do, planning how best to use Bruno Eberhardt.

While Victoria was planning her day, Isabella Minnowfish, Bruno Eberhardt's erstwhile live-in girlfriend, was unpacking one of her suitcases in her friend, Tank's, apartment in the tribal housing complex in Aquinnah.

Tank watched from the bed they'd shared the previous night, feet crossed, hands behind his head, as she hung up one dress after another in his closet, shoving his scanty wardrobe of work pants and shirts to one side. She lined up five pairs of high-heeled shoes on the floor next to his scuffed work boots, and then turned to look at his bureau.

"You can have the second and third drawers. I cleaned them out for you," he said. "Where you gonna wear those clothes around here? You'll get laughed out of town."

Isabella pouted. "I like pretty things."

"Me too, Izzy." Tank made a kissy sound. "That's you. You're a lot prettier now you put some meat around your bones."

She turned to him. "God, you romantic hunk, you."

He waved a massive hand at the closet. "Didn't that guy buy you any real clothes? You got nowhere to wear that stuff."

"I haven't finished unpacking."

"Yeah, sure. I forgot the dozen suitcases."

"Only four, stupid."

Tank got up off the bed and went toward her. "Time to get serious, babe. He's not gonna be real happy when he sees his safe."

"He's not going to call the cops. Trust me."

"Maybe not, but he's likely to show up here with some of his buddies."

218

"He won't come here."

"Yeah. Maybe just send the buddies."

Isabella closed the suitcase she'd unpacked with a snap and gestured to the second suitcase in line. "Pass me that, will you?"

He handed it to her. "He knows where you lived before you took up with him."

"You know my brothers." She glanced at him with a broad smile.

"Yeah. There's that. 'Two Brave Haulers.' "

"And, honeybunch, there's you to protect me."

"Ugh. Me big brave. Braver than Bucky and Leo." He thumped his chest.

"I mean it. He wouldn't dare set foot on tribal land, even with all his 'connections.' " She made quote marks in the air with her fingers. "I'm starved. What's to eat?"

Tank thumped his chest. "You squaw. Me brave. Me defend squaw against mean white man." He made a grab for her. "You cook. Me eat."

She slipped out of his grasp. "Me squaw. Brave cooks." She slapped him gently. "New order around here."

CHAPTER 22

Bruno Eberhardt went back to his library and stared at the blasted safe. He set a chair in front of it, turned the chair around, and straddled it, resting his arms on the back.

When he'd first seen the safe, his reaction had been to do nothing. No police report, no retaliation. But the more he thought of the bitch getting away with fifty thousand, the more his blood boiled. Action was needed.

Action. He had to take his mind off his daughter.

Obviously, Isabella would go back to Aquinnah, to tribal housing where she had lived before she moved in with him. She'd never lived anyplace else. She didn't know any other life. She'd figure she was safe there, guarded by the tribe and those two big brothers of hers, great brutes who ran that trucking business.

He stood up and moved the chair back

against the wall. He'd call the security firm off-Island first thing in the morning to replace the safe.

Then he would get even. More than get even. He made a fist and pounded his left palm.

The money. Yes. Get it back, by all means, with interest.

Jewelry. Yes. He'd given her some mighty expensive stuff. Get that back.

Clothes. She'd bought clothes. Probably fifty thousand dollars' worth. What could he do with women's clothes? Not take them back. Yes, he would take them back. What in hell could he do with them? He'd think of something.

But first, access to tribal housing. An outsider would never get in. It would have to be an inside job. He thought about that.

Ahh!

The chief of tribal police, Josephus Van-Dyke, owed him big time. He'd taken care of a serious gambling debt the chief had incurred, and not only that: the characters involved would never bother the chief again.

He'd explain to Chief VanDyke that his property had been stolen by a tribal member and he wanted his stolen property back. Quietly. He'd say he didn't want Isabella to get in trouble over the theft. He simply wanted to get back the money, the jewelry, and, if it wasn't too much trouble, the clothing. No fuss, no bother. No Island or state cops interfering with the sovereign nation's business.

There'd be a recovery fee payable, of course. Wink, wink.

Eberhardt left the library and walked from room to room of his vacant house, feeling marginally better. From the library, through a hall lined with landscape paintings, to the great room that overlooked the sound. His head ached. His eyes felt scratchy. His stomach hurt. He didn't miss Isabella, but he missed the hysterical background noise of that TV channel she watched.

Most of all, he missed those daily calls from Sammy. For all those years, he'd considered her calls a nuisance, had cut her off most of the time. Right now he'd trade anything to have the phone vibrate and hear her voice again.

Yes, he'd work with Mrs. Trumbull. He'd graciously accept her apology when he proved to her, without a doubt, that Zack Zeller killed his daughter.

That afternoon Victoria was clearing away her notes for her column when her first visitor arrived.

She greeted the young woman with short blond hair.

"I'm Connie Burrowes," she said. "Thanks for asking me. We really need to talk to you."

"Anderson Jones is coming, too. He should be here shortly."

"I know he'll have a lot to say."

"Elizabeth, my granddaughter, set out snacks in the parlor. We can talk in there." Victoria led the way.

Victoria sat in her usual seat in the wing chair and Connie sat on the uncomfortable sofa. Once they were seated Connie said, "Elizabeth spoke to my class last spring about people working in nontraditional jobs. Both women and men. She's very inspiring."

"Vineyard women have always been strong," Victoria said. "Their menfolk would go to sea for years at a time, so the women worked in every job there was. They ran farms and mills and grocery stores, and thought nothing of it."

A knock on the door. "Hallo!"

"Come in. We're in here, Mr. Jones," Victoria called out.

Anderson Jones was a large man, so tall his head barely cleared the top of the doorframe and the rest of his body seemed to fill it. His skin was dark, his hair was short and gray, and when he walked into the parlor and Victoria could see his eyes were a clear, light hazel.

He bowed slightly to Victoria. "Mrs. Trumbull." Then nodded at Connie. "Nice to see you." Back to Victoria. "Ms. Burrowes and I have a lot to say."

Victoria indicated the big armchair. "Please have a seat, Mr. Jones. There's wine, if either of you would like a glass."

"Call me Anderson." He poured wine before sitting and passed a glass to Victoria, one to Connie, and took one himself. He set his wineglass on the small table next to his chair and sat, large hands on his knees. "Where would you like to start, Mrs. Trumbull?"

"I've heard about Samantha Eberhardt's treatment of Sebastian Sibert, Lincoln's son, and about her girls' club."

"She didn't actually call it a club, Mrs. Trumbull," said Connie. "She called it a fellowship, a nice, warm, friendly sounding name."

"Warm and friendly, that was our Samantha," said Anderson.

Victoria turned to him. "Tell me about your son."

"Benjy, yes. He was just a kid when he met her. Thirteen, bright, straight-A student, freshman at the high school." He leaned forward. "He's sixteen now. Dropped out of school. I finally got him in a drug treatment center. Off-Island."

"I'm so sorry." Victoria could think of nothing else to say.

"Let me tell you about Samantha, Mrs. Trumbull," said Connie. "First of all, we live on the Island because it's a safe place to raise our children. We didn't reckon on drugs. Samantha was clean-cut looking, sort of outdoorsy. She was charming. She spoke well, had good manners — when she wanted to." Connie shifted on the hard sofa. "We parents thought, what a nice influence on our children. We hadn't the least notion of what was coming. The kids loved her. She talked about all the adventures she'd had and got them — and us parents — under her spell." She leaned back.

Victoria looked from her to Anderson.

"Drugs, Mrs. Trumbull. Drugs."

"How did she obtain them?" asked Victoria.

"There are a number of dealers on this Island," said Anderson. "Unfortunately. And when you're dealing in drugs, morals and ethics go out the window." He held up his right hand and rubbed his thumb and third finger together. "Money, money, money. All about money. The kids ran errands for her, buying and selling stuff. They didn't have a clue."

Connie picked up. "When we were kids we hid behind the barn and smoked corn silk wrapped in toilet paper. We thought we were wicked."

Victoria nodded. The three wineglasses were untouched.

Connie continued, "She had the kids smoking, but not corn silk. One thing led to another. Harder and harder drugs. The kids got hooked."

"Who paid for the drugs?" asked Victoria.

"To start with, she got the kids to 'invest' their allowances or savings or whatever, promising she'd make a lot of money for them. Then she bought drugs from her dealer friends and her kids sold small quantities around the school. She'd give her investors enough to keep them happy and she'd take a big profit."

"Is this what happened to your daughter?" Victoria asked Connie.

"My Brooke attempted suicide."

Victoria was silent.

"She's in counseling that I can't afford to pay for. But I can't afford not to pay for it."

"Will she be all right?" Victoria asked.

Connie shrugged. "She'll never be the

same. A sweet, gentle girl with a lot of wonderful dreams. Now it's nightmares."

"Benjy." Anderson said his son's name and no more.

Victoria picked up her wineglass and took a sip. "Do you both live near the high school?"

Connie looked at Anderson, who shook his head.

"Neither of us does," said Connie. "I live just this side of the Edgartown Triangle. A quiet, woodsy area, but within walking distance of the town."

"I know the area," said Victoria.

"It's a nice place for kids," said Connie. "My late husband built a treehouse for Brooke. She'd play up in the branches for hours when she was little."

"I loved scuffing through fallen leaves when I was a child," said Victoria.

"Brooke did, too. I used to let the leaves lie all over the grass so she could run through them. Now I rake them into a pile behind the house so they don't smother the grass."

"I didn't realize your husband had died," said Victoria. "I'm sorry."

"Thanks. It's tough without him. Maybe if he'd been around Samantha wouldn't have snared Brooke."

"Stop!" Anderson held up his hand. "Don't think that way, Connie. Drive you crazy if you do."

"And you, Anderson? Where do you live?"

"I'm one of the few year-round Camp Ground residents."

"Do you live in one of the lovely old gingerbread houses?"

"Yes, ma'am."

"It must be lonely in winter."

"Well, there are about two dozen of us year-rounders out of about three-hundred-fifty cottages. We're a close community off-season. Potluck suppers and bridge. When summer comes, it's too busy."

"No tree house for Benjy?"

"As a matter of fact, yes. I built a tree house for Benjy in a big old maple behind my cottage, but he never took to it. Didn't like heights." He lifted a hand from the chair's arm and dropped it again. "I've got a small garden, really small, and I pile up the leaves for compost. Can't have a real compost heap with kitchen scraps because of rodents."

Victoria smiled. "I know all about rodents and compost heaps. Fortunately, my compost is far enough away from the house that I don't mind having the rats turn it for me."

"We've gone from Samantha to rats," said

Connie. "That's appropriate."

"Don't bad-mouth rats," said Anderson. "They're pretty nice animals, actually."

Silence.

Anderson broke the silence. "A dozen parents, and probably every one of us feels relieved that Samantha is gone."

Connie nodded.

Anderson said, "I'm afraid you're not going to find much cooperation from us parents in hunting down the killer. More likely you'll find us protecting the killer, whoever it is."

CHAPTER 23

Abilene Butler lived on Tisbury Great Pond in what Islanders called a camp. It was really no more than an unheated shack with no running water, no electricity, and an outdoor privy. Her great-grandfather had built it as a hunting lodge more than a hundred years before she was born, on land her family had owned for a hundred years before that.

In spring, summer, and fall, she hiked along the shore to a brook at the head of the pond where she bathed. In winter she carried buckets of water from the pump behind the camp and heated it on a small kerosene stove for her bath. A couple of years earlier, Lincoln Sibert's son, Sebastian, who was only thirteen or fourteen at the time, helped her build a stone chimney and fireplace on the north side of the shack. The fireplace gave out enough heat in winter to keep her quite cozy.

Until recently, Abilene hadn't worried about supporting herself. Her grandmother, Victoria Trumbull's girlhood friend, had left her a small legacy that, along with writing and teaching yoga, was enough.

The recent development looming before her was her neighbors. On either side, wealthy newcomers had bought pond-view property and built large summer houses. Property values soared and now Abilene's small holdings were taxed beyond anything she could hope to pay.

Her new neighbors were not sympathetic. To them, the ancient, ramshackle camp was an excrescence that marred their summertime view of the water. Its eccentric inhabitant was not someone they cared to have crossing in front of their houses, nor someone they wanted their children to associate with, let alone associate with her themselves. They wanted her out.

Abilene felt like an autumn leaf blown before the storm of lawyers who suggested, then recommended, urged, and insisted that she sell her acre of pond view and were now threatening to sue. She would never be able to fight a lawsuit.

Abilene was alone and desperate when she met Samantha.

Samantha had shown up at Lily Pond

Yoga, Abilene's yoga studio, for a regular Friday night Free-for-All. Every level of competence came for the no-cost evening of yoga. Abilene had not known who the young woman with long dark hair was at first. She was obviously new to yoga and Abilene paid special attention to her.

Samantha soon let Abilene know whose daughter she was, the connections Daddy had, and the money she, Samantha, had access to.

Abilene decided to court her.

She'd heard of Samantha's background, motherless with a father who equated money with love. Abilene knew enough about psychology to recognize a troubled young woman seeking acceptance, and she coolly took on the risk of friendship with this unstable, rich land mine.

But then she fell in love. And became dependent upon Samantha. The love alternated with hatred.

Sammy had been Abilene's one and only lover. When they first got together, Sammy had promised to make Abilene's small holdings safe forever from the predatory neighbors. For a while, Sammy had lived up to her promises. She had paid Abilene's taxes. She had started legal action against the neighbors and paid the legal fees until recently, when things changed.

Suddenly, Sammy had no more money, or so she claimed.

Sammy had gone wild with her promises of help. More lawyers, more legal fees. The debts that Sammy had incurred were mounting, and Sammy was no longer paying them. Abilene was stuck with them.

Abilene knew that Sammy was hooked on drugs. Lately she had burned up every cent she could get her hands on buying drugs. Eating them up, smoking them up, shooting them up.

Sammy's death was both desolation and relief.

Abilene knew beyond any doubt that it had never occurred to Sammy that she might die someday. And she was equally sure Sammy had left no will. Even if she had, there'd be no mention of Abilene in it.

Abilene was left with bills she'd never dreamed of before Sammy came into her life. Bills she would never be able to pay, and the imminent loss of her camp on the Great Pond.

The morning after Victoria spoke with Connie Burrowes and Anderson Jones, she walked to the police station to report to Casey.

It was a crisp, cool, day. The air smelled of late harvests and the first of the falling leaves, and was what Victoria called "a typical Vineyard day," although this kind of day was rare. The Island's fall colors were subtle, not like the brilliant reds and oranges of the Vermont mountains. But the beetlebung trees beside the brook displayed their wine-red leaves, the Norway maples had turned a muted gold, and the oaks' tan and red-brown leaves would hold far into the winter. In some areas a streak of vivid red or orange punctuated the scene, where poison ivy twined up a tree trunk or fence post.

Doane's hayfield had been mown for the last time this year, and Victoria inhaled the sweet scent as she walked past, briskly swinging her lilac wood stick.

When she reached the grounds of the police station, she shook out the stale bread she'd brought with her, and the noisy flock of waterfowl assembled.

"All gone." She stowed the empty bag next to her police deputy hat, which she always carried with her.

Casey greeted her at the top of the steps. "Morning, Victoria. Come on in."

Victoria seated herself in the armchair she considered her own. Casey went behind her desk and sat.

"What's up, Victoria?"

"I'm here to report on my investigations into Samantha Eberhardt's death."

Casey shoved papers to one side and set her elbows on the desk. "It's not our jurisdiction, you know."

"Yes, I know," said Victoria.

"The state police are handling the case and they have the suspect in custody." She lifted up the beach stone paperweight from the top of the papers and tossed it from hand to hand.

"Zack didn't kill that girl," said Victoria.

"Let it go," warned Casey.

"The police have in custody a slow-witted boy who doesn't know when to keep his mouth shut." Victoria leaned forward. "And furthermore, the police want to appease the girl's suffering father by nabbing someone, anyone, as quickly as possible."

"Not our problem, Victoria," Casey warned.

Victoria rose. "I'll be working with Bruno Eberhardt."

"What?" Casey, too, stood.

"Mr. Eberhardt is going to help me find the killer."

"You can't be serious."

"I'll report back," said Victoria, and

turned to leave.

"Okay, okay," said Casey. "Keep me informed. I'll give you a ride home, and you can tell me all about what you've been up to."

Isabella finished unpacking her suitcases at Tank's condo, and the two set about counting the money released from Bruno Eberhardt's safe.

Tank stared at the stacks of hundred-dollar bills laid out on the bed. "You did okay, Izzy. Fifty thousand."

"I worked my ass off for that money."

"Pretty soft job." Tank kicked off his untied boots and stretched out on the bed beside the piles of bills.

"Soft? Bruno Eberhardt?" She turned her head and spat.

"Hey, watch it! I just cleaned this place." He put his hands behind his head.

She paced the small room, back and forth. "He's a control freak. An egomaniac." She kicked at one of her empty suitcases. "Narcissist. Bastard. Steals his daughter away from her mother," she stopped pacing. "Money, lawyers, more money. Until the ex is broke. Then he fucks his daughter up good just to get back at mama. 'Anything you want, sweetums.' His daughter was as sick as he is. Jealous bitch. He's neurotic, psychotic, and rigid as a stovepipe except where it counts, if you get my meaning."

"Now, now." Tank chortled. "Spitcat. What I'm calling you from now on. You know he's coming after you for this money, don't you?" He waved at the green stuff on the bed.

"He wouldn't dare."

"Doesn't sound to me like he's the kind of guy to forget his fifty thousand bucks."

She started to say something.

He held up a hand. "I know, you're about to say fifty thousand is peanuts to him. The way you talk about him, it's the principle of you getting away with something. Something of his."

"My brothers won't let him get near me."

"He's got money, and money talks."

"He wouldn't dare touch me."

"I wouldn't bet on it."

She'd started pacing again, kicking everything that was within kicking distance. "And that bitch, Samantha . . . !"

"You calling that pretty little white girl nasty names?"

She pursed her mouth as though to spit again.

He pointed a finger at her. "Don't you do that, or you'll mop the floor with the seat of your panties."

"You'd better not mention that bitch to me."

"You heard she's dead, didn't you? You have anything to do with that?"

She turned away.

"What'd she do to you?"

"Don't ask."

He held out his arms to her. "C'mere, Spitcat. Let's roll around on all this green stuff and the world will seem a better place."

While Tank and Isabella were counting their money, Victoria got a phone call from Casey.

"I have a favor to ask you." Casey sounded hesitant.

"Of course. Whatever I can do for you." Victoria held the phone to her ear, moved her chair closer to the window, and sat.

"Well, it's like this," Casey began, and paused.

Victoria watched a chickadee dart to the feeder, snatch a seed, and dart off again.

"You know Lincoln Sibert's situation," said Casey.

"It's sad. He's not over his wife's death yet, and now this."

"Well," Casey said again, "I was thinking of inviting him to my place for supper.

238

But . . ."

"Wonderful!"

"Wait, Victoria. I'm the town's police chief. I can't do that."

"This isn't New York or Boston," said Victoria. "Invite him."

"No, no. The reason I called is, I was wondering if you would mind extending an invitation to him."

"Oh. Of course. I wish I'd thought of it myself." Victoria smiled. "Would it be all right if I included you and Patrick?"

She heard a sigh of relief.

"That would be great. Patrick's old enough to behave."

"He's nine now, isn't he?" asked Victoria.

"Almost ten."

They set a date and Casey gave Victoria Lincoln's unlisted number.

"Thanks so much, Victoria."

"You're the one I should thank," said Victoria.

After she disconnected, she called Lincoln Sibert's number. It rang six times before a sleepy voice answered."

"Lincoln? It's Victoria Trumbull."

"Yes, ma'am."

"Did I wake you up?"

"I was dozing in my chair. Should have been up and about."

"If you're not otherwise engaged, Elizabeth and I would like to invite you to supper on Saturday night."

"Well . . ."

"Baked beans," said Victoria. "Cooked in a proper bean pot all day Saturday."

"Ummm . . ." said Lincoln.

"With salt pork and molasses."

"Well," said Lincoln. "I can almost smell it, Mrs. Trumbull. What time's supper?"

"Seven," said Victoria, and hung up, satisfied. She then called Casey.

"What can I bring?" asked Casey.

"Dessert," said Victoria, and that took care of Saturday night's supper plans.

Bruno Eberhardt went into his study, the one room never tainted by Isabella or anyone else. He put his feet up on his desk and made a call to Josephus VanDyke, the tribal police chief. He felt his blood pressure rising along with his impatience after tapping in too many of those damned numbers in the automated system.

"If you'd like to reach the Shellfish Constable, tap One. If you'd like to reach the Fence Viewer, tap Two. For the Tree Warden, tap Three. For the Trench Inspector, tap Four. For the . . ." Just as he was about to toss the phone across the room, Chief Van-

Dyke himself answered.

"Always good to hear from you, Mr. Eberhardt. What can I do for you?"

"How does anyone reach you in an emergency?" demanded Eberhardt.

"I beg your pardon?"

Eberhardt leaned back in his swivel chair and took a deep breath. "Your goddamned high-tech phone system. What do you have, a staff of thirty that someone who wants to reach you has to go through?"

The chief said nothing.

"Well, Josephus, I'm about to do *you* another small favor," said Eberhardt, emphasizing the word *you.*

"I already owe you for the many favors you have done for me, Mr. Eberhardt," the chief said quietly. "And you say you are about to put me in further debt?"

"I'll collect one of these days, Josephus." Eberhardt took another deep breath. Mustn't let inanimate stuff like phones get to him like this. "But here's the situation now. You knew, of course, that Isabella Minnowfish was living with me for the last two years."

"A lovely young woman," said the chief.

"I was fortunate to have had her companionship for that time." Eberhardt paused, and the chief said nothing. "But all good things come to an end."

"True," said the chief.

"Isabella has decided to return to her roots. Back to the tribe."

"Ah," said the chief.

"I assume you heard as much." Eberhardt swiveled his chair slightly, his feet still up on the desk.

"I hear many things," said the chief.

"When she left, she and a friend borrowed some items of mine that I would like to have returned with the least amount of bother to everyone concerned."

Silence from the chief.

"She or the friend accessed my safe. Violently, I'm afraid, in order to borrow the items."

The chief paused before he said, "And the items are?"

"Fifty thousand dollars in hundred-dollar bills. And jewelry worth somewhat more than that." Eberhardt leaned his chair back. The springs squealed.

"Ah," said the chief. "I'm sure you have evidence of your ownership of these borrowed items."

"I do. I have a list of the five hundred numbers on the hundred-dollar bills they borrowed. I also have receipts for my purchase of the jewelry that was borrowed. I

242

also have photographs of the jewelry."

"You are a thorough man," said the chief. "And you are calling me because you would like me to get your items back as a favor to you?"

"Not at all," said Eberhardt, with a touch of indignation. "Certainly not as a favor to me. As a service to the tribe."

"A service to the tribe, Mr. Eberhardt?"

"You'll agree, I believe, that it is in the best interest of the tribe as well as Ms. Minnowfish to have these borrowed items returned quietly rather than to involve the non-tribal authorities."

Silence.

"There is a finder's fee for the return of the items," said Eberhardt.

"How soon do you need these borrowed items back?"

"Immediately." Eberhardt paused again. "There are a number of other borrowed items I would like to have returned as well." He leaned forward, opened a desk drawer, and drew out a notebook. He riffled through pages.

"And those are, Mr. Eberhardt?"

"Women's clothing I loaned to Ms. Minnowfish. You will want a copy of the list of clothing, receipts, and photographs as well."

"What sort of clothing, Mr. Eberhardt?"

Eberhardt paged through the notebook. "Shoes, cocktail dresses, suits, sportswear, coats, jackets, furs, ski attire, riding boots, riding habits —"

"Yes, yes," said the chief.

"Not intimate apparel. Lingerie she may keep. Silk underwear, nightgowns, and robes, that sort of thing. A gift from me."

"You have always been generous, Mr. Eberhardt."

"I hope to continue to be generous, Josephus."

"And you believe this recovery of items will be a service to the tribe, avoiding the unpleasantness of Island and state police claiming the items were stolen. And certainly an even greater service to Isabella and her friend, not having to face accusations of theft. Although you know, of course, Mr. Eberhardt, that she is a member of a sovereign nation, not subject to your laws."

"I realize that, Josephus. Nevertheless, the publicity and the legal complications would not help the tribe or Isabella."

"I see. I need to think about this."

"By all means. Think about it. However, my offer of a finder's fee will be withdrawn tomorrow. The day after that, I will —"

"I understand, Mr. Eberhardt. May I be so crass as to ask what the finder's fee might

244

be? We are talking about well over one hundred thousand dollars' worth of items."

"Not crass at all, Josephus. You're a prudent man. When you've had time to think about it, I'll give you a written agreement for 7.5 percent of the total value of my recovered property worth, at a rough estimate, 150,000 dollars which, I believe, would bring the finder's fee up to something like 11,250 dollars. Cash," he added.

"I will call you back in an hour, Mr. Eberhardt."

Eberhardt disconnected with a feeling of satisfaction, the first positive feeling he'd had since he'd identified his dead daughter.

CHAPTER 24

Zack, meanwhile, was adjusting to life in jail. He expected to be released as soon as they realized they had the wrong person, that he had nothing to do with Sammy's death. Mrs. Trumbull would get him out.

He was out of his cell in the jail's rec room, working on a jigsaw puzzle, while waiting for supper to be served. The smell of frying onions made his mouth water. About six other guys were sitting around, talking, and watching TV. One guy he'd gotten to know, named Jeff, was sitting at a table, writing.

He was still confined for most of the day in that same cell with hot pink walls. He had trouble sleeping because the walls seemed to close in on him and shimmer in the dim light that was on all night. The sheriff had promised to move him to a more austere cell when one became available. But he didn't expect to be here more than another day. Two at the most.

Fortunately, the sheriff had relaxed the rules about phone calls, so he was able to make a call a day to whoever he wanted. But the only person he wanted to talk to was Mrs. Trumbull.

The puzzle was about half done when he started work on it. It was a partly completed picture of a mill with a big wheel and a stream, most of which was blank. Hard to find pieces for the stream.

Jeff looked up from his writing. "How're you doing, pal?"

"Not bad, considering," said Zack. "I have trouble sleeping in that pink cell."

"Yeah, tell me about it. They put me in there, too, the first night. Guess it's to soften you up."

"You never told me what you're in for," said Zack, looking down at the puzzle. "Hey, found it."

"Found what?" asked Jeff.

"Part of the mill stream."

"That's a miracle," said Jeff. "Most of the time the pieces you need are missing. A real bitch."

"So what are you in for?"

"DUI," said Jeff. "I been here before and should've known better. Had one too many and that friendly state cop, Tim, nabbed me

247

again." He pushed his writing pad back and capped his pen.

"What are you writing, a letter?" asked Zack.

"A book. A memoir. My life story."

"Wish I could write," said Zack. "Who's Tim?"

"State trooper. Has it in for me. Knows where I hang out and parks outta sight. I shoulda known," he said again.

"What are the rest of the guys in here for?" asked Zack.

"DUIs or drugs. Or domestic abuse. You're a celebrity, you know. We never had a murderer before."

In truth, Zack was being treated by his fellow inmates with a respect he'd never known.

"I just meant to make her sick, didn't mean to kill her, in fact, I didn't," said Zack.

"Yeah, sure," said Jeff. "But she ended up dead, right? Lucky you."

"Really weird," said Zack.

"Yeah," said Jeff. "I guess."

"I was afraid I'd killed some of the eight. Maybe all of them."

"Yeah?" Jeff's face went rigid. "Eight people?"

"When the police found me, I was trying to get off the Island, but I missed the ferry."

"You thought you killed eight people?"

"But luckily I didn't."

"Yeah. Lucky you." Jeff pushed back his chair and got up. "Call of nature. Be seein' you around."

Zack found another stream piece and snapped it into place. Jeff was right. He was lucky. He hadn't killed Sammy and he hadn't killed her father's guests. Looking back, he'd been pretty stupid to think he could terminate Sammy's pregnancy with mushrooms. Someone must have hated her an awful lot to kill her.

He looked around for a piece at the edge of the stream that had a head and two angel wings. Looked over all the pieces. Didn't find that one, but did find two pieces of the stream that fit together. Where did the block of two fit? No place he could see, yet. Must be in the center of the stream.

What were they going to do to him? Would he be sentenced to some prison term just because he'd thought about making her sick? Well, the lawyer, Miranda, was supposed to defend him, and Mrs. Trumbull would find a way to get him out of here.

Two guys sauntered over to him. "How're you doin'?" the shorter of the two asked. "I'm Rocky and this here's Butch." He pointed a thumb at the tall, broad guy behind him. "Understand you're here on a murder rap."

Zack had decided he had bragging rights. "Yeah," he said. "What about you?"

"Drugs for me, domestic for him." He jerked his head at Butch.

"Stupid bitch," said Butch. "You hit your G.F.?"

"She's not my girlfriend anymore," said Zack. "She's dead."

"That would do it," said Butch. "You got balls, all right."

A gong sounded.

"Lunch," said Rocky.

Now, in addition to smelling onions Zack could hear the sizzle of frying hamburger.

"Can't complain about the food," said Zack, reveling in the idea that he was respected by the likes of Butch and Rocky.

"Chef's in here for dealing," said Rocky. He cooks stuff we grow out back, like beans and squash."

"I never much cared for vegetables before," said Zack. "These taste pretty good."

"He's teaching cooking," said Rocky. "Couple guys been in here for more than a year and are pretty good cooks now. Probably get good work when they got out."

The gong sounded again.

The guys lined up to go into what they

called the dining hall.

This really wasn't too bad for a couple of days, thought Zack.

Isabella, wearing only her thong, was on her hands and knees looking for hundred-dollar bills under the bed. Tank, in jeans only, was counting them and putting them back in some kind of order. The bills had scattered over and into the bed during their celebration of the heist and had spilled onto the floor.

"Here's another one." She held up a bill and tittered. "A couple more I can't quite reach yet." She wriggled under the bed. "Three more." Her voice was muffled by bedclothes and dust. "Four. Five. How are we doing?"

"Fifteen hundred to go."

She squirmed back from under the bed and sneezed. "Don't you ever clean this place?"

"Waiting for you." He was putting rubber bands around stacks of bills.

"To clean your dump?"

"No, babe. Mess it up like this here."

She stood, brushed off the cobwebs, and held out her arms. "Well, let's see what you mean by that."

At which point, there was a knock on the door.

"Shit," said Tank.

"Don't answer," said Isabella.

There was a harder knock and a loud voice calling out something that sounded like "Police!"

Isabella put her hands up to her mouth. "No!"

"It's okay, babe, they can't touch us. Help me throw the blanket over this stuff."

"Tribal police. We're coming in."

"Josephus VanDyke, that's who it is," said Tank, relieved. "He's one of us. Hurry up, though. Straighten the blanket so it doesn't look like we're hiding something."

The door that led directly from the outside into the living area opened, and from the bedroom they could see Chief VanDyke stride in. He was in full uniform.

Tank patted down his hair and left the bedroom. "Good evening, Chief. What's up?"

Chief VanDyke was in his early fifties, just under six feet tall with a broad, weather-beaten face, a wide, thick chest, and a large belly that overhung his uniform belt. A private guy, even his fellow tribe members didn't know much about his personal life. Married, no kids. That was about it. He stood, booted feet apart, thumbs hooked into his belt.

"Hope I didn't disturb you." He removed his police hat and ran a hand over light brown hair, cut short. He glanced around with those hazel eyes of his.

"Me and Isabella was just celebrating her return," said Tank, running his own hand over his own hair, the same color as the chief's, but worn in a sort of Afro. He was barefoot and shirtless. "You here for anything special? Business or social call?"

"Both," said Josephus. "Got three of my men outside. Mind if they come in?"

"If it's social, can I offer you a beer? Got a six pack on ice."

"Thanks, but no. It's a little more business than social." Josephus turned to the half-open door and called out, "Corbit, tell Monto and Sonny to come on in. All three of you." He turned back to Tank. "Ms. Minnowfish available?"

"I'll ask." Tank stepped into the bedroom, which opened directly into the living area. Isabella was tugging a sweater over her head. "Izzy, they want to talk to you."

She heaved a deep sigh. "I'm in no mood to talk to them."

"You better come on out, anyway. Don't say a word, if you don't want to."

She sucked in her breath to fasten the top button of her jeans and ran her fingers through her hair. "I must look a mess."

"Never," Tank said, gallantly.

The chief and his three men, all in uniform, were standing just inside the door, when Tank and Isabella came out of the bedroom.

The chief was studying the narrow, barely furnished room. It was dominated by a worn couch that might have been green at one time. A large television set faced the couch. At the end of the room near a small kitchen two folding chairs were pulled up to a card table that still had the remains of a nuked frozen dinner in a black plastic serving container, two used paper plates, plastic forks and spoons, crumpled paper napkins.

"Like your decorator," said the chief.

"Yeah," said Tank. Isabella stood behind him, arms crossed over her chest.

No rugs, no pictures, no curtains on the two small windows at either end of the room, or on the large picture window next to the door. The picture window looked out at other houses identical to Tank's.

"Needs a woman's touch," said the chief. "Looks like you might have hope yet." He nodded toward Isabella.

Tank hooked his own fingers in the waist

of his jeans. "What do you want, Josephus?"

"Well," Josephus drawled out, "we're dealing with a tribal matter that I'd like to settle before it gets blown out of proportion."

"C'mon, Josephus. Get to it."

"It's a small matter of some borrowed items that need to be returned to their owner before, as I said, things get blown out of proportion."

"Borrowed items," Tank repeated.

The chief nodded. "Fifty thousand dollars in cash. Five hundred bills with the image of one of America's founding fathers, Benjamin Franklin. I like that. America's founding father."

Tank continued to stand, his thumbs still hooked in his jeans.

"And there's a small matter of borrowed jewelry the owner would like to have returned. With no fuss, you understand."

Isabella snapped, "It's my jewelry. He gave it to me."

"Shut up, Izzy." Tank didn't move.

"We've come to collect the money, the jewelry and," the chief took out a printed list from an inside pocket of his blouse, "I almost forgot. The furs, shoes, dresses, and —"

"Stop!" screamed Isabella. "That bastard, that lousy, fucking bastard! Those are my

255

clothes. My things. My jewelry. My money! I earned it, all of it. It's mine."

"Izzy! Shut. Up."

Josephus handed the list to Tank. "You can have this copy."

Tank didn't move to take it.

Josephus turned to his three men. "Okay, collect the stuff."

"A warrant! You have to have a warrant to touch my things!" shouted Isabella.

Josephus turned back to her. "You forget," he said quietly. "We are a sovereign nation. We do not go by rules that govern others."

"Then why can't she keep her property? He can't come after her here," said Tank. "He gave it to her. The money. She earned that money."

Josephus smiled. His face was leathery from being out on the water, fishing. The deep lines that radiated across his face and ran from his nose to his chin crinkled in amusement. "You can take that up with him." He turned to the three men who'd stood silently since they'd entered. "Corbit, go through the house, you, Monto, and Sonny. Pack up everything on the list. Make sure you don't take anything else. Suitcases are on the list. Use them. Cardboard boxes in the cruiser for the overflow."

"No, no, no!" screamed Isabella. She

broke away from Tank, darted at Josephus, and slashed out at him with her polished red talons.

Tank grabbed the back of her sweater and dragged her back.

The three uniformed tribal cops followed the chief as he headed toward the bedroom.

He paused. "You can help us if you want, Tank. Watch us if you want. Get out of our way if you want. Don't go far, because we are here to pick up every single bill and every single diamond earring and every single glove that's on this list." He held it up and shook it.

Isabella flung herself at Tank. "They can't do this!"

He held her. "Yes, they can."

"I'll get even. I'll get even with that bastard, if it's the last thing I do. I'll kill him. Dead, like that bitch daughter of his."

"I didn't hear you say that," said Josephus.

It took several trips to collect all of the items Isabella and Tank had "borrowed" from Bruno Eberhardt's house, but eventually Chief Josephus VanDyke and his three officers were ready to leave.

"Don't see how you managed to get all that stuff in one car," the chief said.

Tank jerked a thumb at Isabella. "Her

257

brothers."

"Of course. Two Brave Haulers. How can I forget?" He held out a sheaf of papers. "You might want to sign this release saying we've taken away the borrowed items noted. That way you're protected."

"Protected, you asshole!" shouted Isabella, who mourned every item that got packed away in a cardboard box and carted out of Tank's house. "Robbers! Thieves! Burglars!"

"Isabella, will you shut up," said Tank, holding her arms.

"Shit!" said Isabella, when they finally shut the door behind them and drove away. "I'm gonna get him."

"Don't do it."

"My brothers . . ."

"Oh, my god," said Tank.

CHAPTER 25

Saturday-night Boston baked beans are a New England tradition. Victoria's grandmother had served baked beans every Saturday night that she could remember, and Victoria carried on the tradition. Saturday night beans was a company occasion.

On Friday night, she poured two cups of dried beans, the yellow-eyes she'd grown, harvested, and shelled, into the large stew pot and added enough water to cover them and then some. The beans would soak up much of the water overnight.

Elizabeth was stacking dishes in the dishwasher. "Need help, Gram?"

"No, thank you. I'm finished for now. That's it until tomorrow morning. I'm off to bed."

The phone rang and Elizabeth answered. "Hello?" A pause. "Please call back tomorrow." Pause. "She's about to go to bed." Pause. "It's late, Zack. Call tomorrow."

259

Victoria turned back. "I'll talk to him."

Elizabeth, making a wry face, handed her the phone.

Victoria took it and sat down. "Zack, are you all right?"

"I'm fine. I just wanted to talk to you."

She listened while he told her about the food, about the pink cell, about his new friend Jeff, who was writing a book, and his two new friends, Rocky and Butch.

"Has the lawyer visited you since we last talked?" asked Victoria.

"No, but guess who did come to visit me."

"I can't imagine."

"Samantha's father. Mr. Eberhardt."

"What?!"

"He said you and him teamed up. That you're working on my case."

Victoria didn't know what to say.

"You still there, Mrs. Trumbull?"

"Yes, yes."

"He said he planned a way to get me out of jail."

"Legally?"

"I don't know anything about that legal stuff. After hearing the lawyers talk, if we go with the legal stuff it means I'll rot here forever in this crazy pink cell."

"What exactly did Mr. Eberhardt say to you, Zack?"

"He said you said I didn't kill Sammy, and I should be let out of jail. I didn't tell him I was just trying to make her sick."

"That was wise."

"He said he had a plan and he would get back to me."

Victoria was beginning to have an uneasy feeling about this.

"Actually, Mrs. Trumbull, he didn't want me to say anything to you."

"Really! Did he say why?"

"He said it was your idea I was innocent and he wanted to surprise you. Don't tell him I said anything."

"Of course not. How does he intend to free you?"

"He didn't say."

"Do you have any idea when this is to come about?"

"Pretty soon, I guess. Tomorrow or the day after. He said we needed to hurry. You know, Mrs. Trumbull, he's not such a bad guy after all."

Victoria hung up the phone with a very uneasy feeling about the call. She continued to sit, staring at the bare spots on the pine floorboards where the varnish had been scuffed off, without really seeing them. What was Bruno Eberhardt intending to do? Certainly not to free Zack and send him on his way. That would be a legal nightmare for Zack and for him. She thought about calling Eberhardt. Demand to know what he thought he was doing. Remind him that, as partners, they had to communicate.

And then she thought she'd better not call him. Definitely not a good idea. Not only that, but Zack had been warned not to tell her. She would need to approach this a different way.

Warn the sheriff?

The sheriff already knew Zack talked too much and didn't make a great deal of sense. He also knew Bruno Eberhardt was wealthy, successful, and reliable, a father suffering from the death of his child, who believed his child died at the hands of Zack.

If she told the sheriff that Zack said Mr. Eberhardt was planning to free him, the sheriff would laugh politely. She would too, under the circumstances. And if Zack should, by some miracle, be freed by Eberhardt, the sheriff would think Zack had laid out a fantasy involving Eberhardt to cover his tracks.

No, warning the sheriff would never do.

"Gram?" Elizabeth came back into the cookroom, where Victoria was sitting, contemplating. "What is he up to now?"

"He claims Bruno Eberhardt has a plan

to free him from jail."

Elizabeth laughed. "You're kidding."

"Zack was quite serious."

"Why in heaven's name would Bruno Eberhardt want to free Zack?"

"I have an uncomfortable feeling I know the answer," said Victoria.

Elizabeth pulled up a chair next to her grandmother's. "Well?"

"This sounds ridiculous. But when I talked with Mr. Eberhardt the other night, he told me he had a plan for dealing with Zack."

"Like, what kind of plan?"

"I don't know, but it involved taking matters into his own hands."

"Ouch," said Elizabeth.

"I thought I had talked him into at least a shadow of doubt that Zack could be the killer. I got him to agree that we would work together to identify the killer."

"Bet he said he already knows who the killer is. Zack Zeller."

Victoria nodded. "I told him I would apologize if it should turn out that he was right. He laughed. I thought we parted on good terms."

"He's stubborn. He calls that determined. A positive attribute. Set a goal, aim for it, fire away, and reach it. Don't look left or right. That's his road to success. So, what are you thinking of doing?"

"I honestly don't know," said Victoria.

"Talk to Casey?"

Victoria shook her head. "Casey already believes I'm meddling into affairs that rightfully are in the purview of the state police, the sheriff, and the legal system."

"She's right, you know."

"Yes, of course I know." Victoria continued. "Zack said Mr. Eberhardt was going to help free him in the next day or so." She glanced at Elizabeth. "We don't have much time."

" 'We'?" Elizabeth put both hands on her chest. "What's this 'we' about?"

"We won't have any help from Casey, of course. Nor the sheriff."

"I want to go to bed."

"You don't have to work tomorrow, do you?"

"No, but . . . I have other plans."

"I have an idea. This is something I can't do, but —"

Elizabeth interrupted. "Not me, Gram. Count me out, whatever it is."

"I've been thinking. I don't know that anyone has written an in-depth article about our jail."

"No, Gram. I'm not the one to be involved."

"We can work together." Victoria sat forward, a light in her eyes. "This is the way we'll do it. I'll tell the sheriff I'm writing a feature article about our jail for the *Island Enquirer.* Clearly, he won't want to incarcerate me, but I'm sure he would be willing to incarcerate you."

"Me!?"

"You can spend the night in jail and observe what's going on. No one will suspect a thing. You can report to me what it's like and I will actually write the article, but we'll be able to forestall the jailbreak."

Elizabeth shook her head. "No."

"This is going to be a wonderful article," said Victoria. "Even if nothing happens. It will be a great experience for you. I'll visit you. I don't know if they have visiting hours, but I'll check."

"Gram . . ."

Victoria looked over at her granddaughter. "I should have asked. Did you have other plans?"

"I was hoping to do my laundry and wash my hair and file my nails."

"That can wait," said Victoria. "In fact, if you look a bit scruffy, it will help the deception."

"Can we go to bed now?" asked Elizabeth.

■ ■ ■ ■

Early the next morning, Victoria put the beans on to boil, and while they were cooking, got out the ancient bean pot her grandmother had used. The bean pot was at least a hundred years old. Each time she used it she thought of that. And how many years more will it be used by grandchildren and great-grandchildren? She leaned down and took an onion out of the box next to the stove. Too big. She selected a smaller one. Brown sugar. Molasses. The yellow container of dry mustard. Salt pork from the freezer. She laid everything out and started by cutting a square chunk from the salt pork, about two inches on a side. She scored the onion so it would release its flavor into the cooking beans. She mixed brown sugar, molasses, dry mustard, and salt in a cup and added water from the boiling beans.

She lifted a few beans out with a slotted spoon and blew on them. They were ready. The skins cracked and wrinkled back. Just right. She spooned the beans into the bean pot, tucked the square of salt pork into them, and poured the molasses mixture over everything, adding water until it reached the top.

Elizabeth appeared, rubbing sleep out of her eyes. "Ready to go?"

"Just about." Victoria turned the oven on low, put a cover on the bean pot, set the pot on a pie pan, and slid it into the oven.

"Now, I'm ready," said Victoria.

"You know, Gram, if I end up in jail tonight, I'll miss out on the beans."

"I'll save some for you."

"Seeing that starved look on Lincoln Sibert's face lately, there won't be any left."

"I'll make a special pot for you."

"On a weekday?"

Victoria laughed.

After the beans were in the oven, Elizabeth and Victoria drove to the jail, eight miles from their house. Where the Edgartown Road ended, the jail faced them.

Elizabeth had given in, with not much grace. She would offer herself to the jail as the sacrificial goat.

"If this ruse works, which I hope it doesn't, how will you get home, Gram? I'll be leaving my car in the parking lot behind the Whaling Church."

"The bus stops right by the Whaling Church and will let me off right in front of our house."

"And if you plan to visit me, or catch

Bruno Eberhardt in the act of busting Zack out of stir, will Casey give you a ride?"

"She won't see this as stepping on anyone's toes."

"And if she's not available, you'll hitchhike."

"It's perfectly safe," said Victoria.

They parked behind the Whaling Church and walked to the jail.

Sheriff Grimsey Norton unlocked the door. "Morning, Mrs. Trumbull. Elizabeth. You're here mighty early. Mr. Zeller isn't up yet." He beckoned them in and shut the door and locked it with a key selected from an enormous ring of keys chained to his belt.

"We're not here to see Zack," said Victoria. "We're here on quite another matter."

"Come into my office, then. Let's hear what you have to say."

This wasn't the first time Victoria had been in the sheriff's office, but each time she wondered how such a large man could fit into such a small space and manage all the myriad details that go into running a jail without knocking over files with his elbows.

He held the only visitor's chair for Victoria, and she sat.

"I'll bring in another chair," he said to

Elizabeth, who moved to one side so he could get by.

Once he was back with the chair and Elizabeth was seated, he squeezed between his desk and overflowing bookcases and sat behind the desk.

"You're looking well, Mrs. Trumbull," he said. "You know, I can remember stealing green apples off that tree near Brandy Brow, and you driving by. You stopped and scolded me. Told me those apples belonged to poor little old Miss Davis and she'd go hungry if I ate her apples."

Victoria laughed. "I remember that well."

"You set me on the straight and narrow. So here I am. What can I do for you?"

Victoria leaned forward. "No one has ever written about the jail."

"We call it the House of Correction, Mrs. Trumbull."

"Jail is easier to say."

"True." He laughed. "We're proud of it, the way we run it, the way we try to get people to change their bad ways, so they won't steal apples from little old ladies. We have a pretty low rate of recidivism." He leaned back in his chair. "Course most of our inmates are neighbors who drove drunk or got caught with drugs. Not likely to be back."

"I'm writing an article for the *Island Enquirer* about the jail —"

He interrupted. "Is that right? Good! Let me know how I can help."

Victoria glanced quickly at Elizabeth, who sat stony faced and rigid, looking straight ahead at the sheriff.

"We want to be accurate, want the reader to know how it is to be inside."

"Wouldn't have it any other way, Mrs. Trumbull."

"We want to know what a prisoner experiences. What it's like to sleep here at night, what the meals are like, what the prisoners do for recreation, everything."

"We'll trot out a few of our inmates you can talk to."

"Better than that, I had been thinking I'd like to spend a night in jail, but —"

"No, no, Mrs. Trumbull!" His voice had a touch of horror.

"— but," Victoria held up a hand and continued, "we decided Elizabeth would be just the right person. She volunteered to spend a night, or even two, in jail. We'd like you to go through the process you go through with everyone who's sentenced, so I can make the article accurate." Victoria had convinced herself, after the first few minutes, that this article, this series of

270

articles, would win the New England Newspaper Award for Excellence. And by the
time she was through with her presentation,
the sheriff was convinced, and Elizabeth
looked like a convicted felon, sentenced,
and headed for incarceration.

The sheriff stood. "When do you want to
start, Mrs. Trumbull?"

"Now, of course. We'd like to start now.
Just the way Elizabeth would come from
the courthouse, not expecting to be sentenced to some term of imprisonment. I assume she'd be handcuffed?"

Elizabeth, fully in her role as convict by
now, groaned.

"I really don't think we need to go that
far," said the sheriff. "Well, Elizabeth.
Around here I insist on respect for the
inmates and for me, so I'll be calling you
Ms. Trumbull from now on." He helped Victoria rise from her chair. "You can go on
home without a worry, now, Mrs. Trumbull.
I'll take it from here. Elizabeth won't be ar-
riving in the front door. I'll introduce her to
the guys as," he turned to Elizabeth, "want
to be in here on DUI, drugs, assault, theft?"

"Driving under the influence," said Elizabeth. "Probably that's what I'm in for."

"Would you like a ride home, Mrs. Trumbull? Jared, that young deputy of mine, is

available, loves to drive the official sheriff's car."

"Thank you," said Victoria. "That would be lovely."

The sheriff made a quick call, and the baby-faced deputy came skipping down the stairs, accepted keys to the official car, and offered his arm to Victoria. She glanced over at her granddaughter as the sheriff led her away. Elizabeth's face was drawn and pale. Her expression was a combination of misery, worry, and fear.

She was playing her role well, thought her grandmother.

CHAPTER 26

Casey and Patrick, her nine-year-old son, were the first to arrive. Patrick's hair, the same coppery red as his mother's, was slicked down and still damp from a vigorous combing. He was wearing jeans and a blue V-necked sweater over a white collared shirt.

Victoria couldn't recall the last time she'd seen Casey out of uniform. She had on pale blue slacks and a soft flowered blouse in shades of blue and green that complimented her hair.

Casey bent down to Patrick, who was standing stiffly beside her, hands behind his back. "What do you say, Patrick?"

He looked up at Victoria. "Thank you for inviting me to supper."

"You're welcome, Patrick. You look quite grown up tonight."

He grinned. "I had to put on a clean shirt."

"Yes, of course," said Victoria. "It looks nice."

"Here, Mrs. Trumbull." He brought his hands out from behind his back and presented her with a bouquet of goldenrod and Queen Anne's lace. "I picked these for you."

"Thank you," said Victoria. "They're lovely. I'll put them on the table. I have just the right vase."

She brought the vase down from the high cupboard, filled it with water, and Patrick arranged the flowers in it.

"You can put that in the center of the table," said Victoria. "Let's go into the parlor. We can have drinks before dinner."

"Where's Elizabeth?" asked Casey, as they headed for the parlor. "Will she be joining us?"

"She's in jail for tonight. And maybe tomorrow," Victoria answered.

Casey stopped abruptly. "What?! What did she do?"

"Well," said Victoria, "it was my suggestion that I stay in the jail overnight, but she is a more logical felon."

"Victoria, what are you up to now?"

Victoria looked out the window. "Lincoln just drove up and is parking. I'll take drink orders. Patrick, ginger ale or cranberry juice?"

Patrick glanced at his mother, who nodded. "Ginger ale, please."

"Ginger ale it is. And Casey, Elizabeth and
I usually have cranberry juice and rum. Or
wine. Or what Patrick is having."

"Let me help," said Casey. "I'll take white
wine."

They returned to the kitchen.

Lincoln parked next to Elizabeth's convertible, got out of his truck slowly, and
shambled toward the stone steps. He
paused, then climbed the three steps slowly.
He had aged over the past week.

Victoria opened the kitchen door for him.

"Evening, Miz Trumbull. Thanks for inviting me."

"You need to get out. I've invited Casey
and Patrick to join us."

He nodded. "Evening, Chief. Patrick." He
held out his hand to Patrick, and Patrick
shook it.

"I'm taking drink orders," said Victoria.

Lincoln took a deep breath. "You know,
bourbon sounds good to me. With a splash
of water." As Victoria headed for the place
she kept liquor bottles, he said, "I'll make
it."

They took their drinks into the parlor, and
Lincoln waited until Victoria was seated
before he sat in the large throne chair. Vic-

toria held up her drink. "We're glad you could come, Lincoln."

He held up his drink, too. "Thanks. And thank-you to you, Chief, for breaking the news to me as softly as it could be done. I'm grateful."

Casey looked down.

Patrick said, "I like your truck."

"Mr. Sibert, Patrick," said Casey.

Patrick was sitting on the bench under the window. He looked over at Lincoln. "Mr. Sibert."

"It's a good truck. You can call me Linc, Patrick. Everyone else does."

"I like trucks. My mom gave me a model just like yours."

"I'll give you a ride someday."

Patrick looked over at his mother, who smiled.

"Can I ride in the back?"

"We'll see."

They talked about weather and local politics. National politics. Casey told Victoria about finding Lincoln at the beautiful place where he was planting bulbs.

"I know that house," said Victoria. "When I was a child, the grocer, Mr. Pease, drove his horse and truck-wagon up-Island to Chilmark once a week to deliver groceries." She picked up her drink. "One time he let me ride with him. We stopped at that very house and had lunch." She took a small sip of her drink and set it down again. "I remember that lunch well. The husband and wife were silent. They never spoke. Instead they waved their hands, and Mr. Pease did too. Waved his hands."

Patrick was wriggling in his seat. "Why did they do that?"

"They were both deaf," said Victoria. "Many Chilmarkers were deaf then, and they communicated with sign language. Most everyone on the Island knew how to sign." She held up a hand and waved her fingers. "All the fishermen could talk to each other that way. That was before radios, and they could see hand signals when they couldn't hear someone shouting."

They avoided talk of the fires that were burning huge areas out west. Talk of fire was too close for comfort. And they avoided any mention of death.

Casey said, "I've been itching for an explanation of why Elizabeth is in jail tonight."

"Elizabeth in jail? What for?" asked Lincoln.

"I'm writing a feature article about our jail for the *Island Enquirer,* and Elizabeth agreed to spend a night or two there to find out what it's like. She seemed a more logical choice than me, so the sheriff has booked her on a fictitious drunk driver charge."

Casey shook her head.

"Years ago when I was a teenager, I spent a night in jail." Linc took a large swallow of his bourbon. "Taught me a lesson I'll never forget. The nicest jail in the world is still lost freedom."

They discussed Elizabeth's nerve, Victoria's article, and then it was time for supper. Lincoln and Casey carried in the bean pot, the salad Victoria had made, the broiled hot dogs and warmed brown bread.

Victoria sat at the head of the table, Casey to her right, Lincoln to her left, Patrick next to his mother.

The conversation was comfortable. Old times on the Vineyard that Casey wanted to hear about. Lincoln's childhood. Victoria's childhood.

At one point, Patrick, who'd been politely quiet, said, "Do you really mean it about letting me ride in your truck, Mr. Sibert?"

"I do."

Patrick wriggled in his seat. "When can I?"

"Patrick!" warned his mother.

"It's okay, Casey. I meant it and I'd like

his company."

On the spot, they set a day and time after school.

Casey brought out the dessert, a blueberry pie she'd baked.

"My favorite," said Lincoln.

The evening was ending well.

The phone rang.

Victoria answered.

"Gram, it's me."

"Are you all right?"

"I'm okay. However, Bruno Eberhardt is meeting with the sheriff, right now, this minute, and I'm not where I can hear what they're saying. I thought I should let you know."

"I'll be there in twenty minutes." Victoria disconnected and went into the dining room, where Casey and Lincoln were talking together.

"Casey, I need a ride to the jail. That was Elizabeth."

"I have to take Patrick home first and call my sitter."

"I want to go," said Patrick. "I can stay up late tonight."

"Why don't I give Patrick a ride home in my truck," volunteered Lincoln. "I'll stay with him until you get back."

"That's too much of an imposition . . ."

murmured Casey.

"No, ma'am," said Linc. "Not in the least. Better than staring at blank walls at my place."

"Hooray!" said Patrick

"Hurry!" said Victoria, as Casey turned onto the Edgartown Road.

"I will," said Casey. "Only you haven't told me what's the matter with Elizabeth and why we have to go this minute. I think Sheriff Norton probably has things under control."

"She didn't say exactly." Victoria avoided a direct answer.

"O-kay!" said Casey, stepping on the accelerator.

They arrived at the jail fifteen minutes later. Casey let Victoria out in front and parked. Victoria hurried up the steps and rang the bell.

Jared, the deputy, unlocked the door. "Hi, Mrs. Trumbull. Here to see your jailbird?"

"I'd like to see the sheriff first, Jared."

"He's got someone in there with him now, Mrs. Trumbull."

"Mr. Eberhardt?"

"Yes, ma'am."

"I believe I'm supposed to be joining them," said Victoria.

"Okay, ma'am. I'll take you to the sheriff's office, then."

The door was shut. Deputy Jared knocked.

"I'm with someone," the sheriff said through the closed door.

"It's Mrs. Trumbull. She's supposed to be meeting with you and Mr. Eberhardt."

The sound of a chair being pushed back, and Victoria could imagine the sheriff squeezing himself between his desk and the bookcase to come to the door. He opened it partway.

"Mrs. Trumbull. I didn't expect you. Mr. Eberhardt didn't mention that you'd be joining us . . ."

Bruno Eberhardt's voice came through the half-opened door. "Of course Mrs. Trumbull is welcome to join us. An oversight on my part. I should have invited her."

Victoria felt the blood rush to her face.

"Jared, a chair for Mrs. Trumbull, please."

"Yes, sir."

Eberhardt rose from his chair when she entered and offered it to her. She sat.

"Did your granddaughter drive you here?" he asked.

"Chief O'Neill brought me." She did not care to let him know Elizabeth had alerted her. "Didn't you mention to the sheriff that we both planned to meet with him tonight?"

The sheriff had seated himself again, and the deputy brought in the second visitor's chair.

Eberhardt sat. "I must not be thinking clearly, Mrs. Trumbull."

"Understandable," said Victoria. "I'm surprised you're able to function as well as you are. You've had a horrid shock, something no parent should face. I can only extend to you again my condolences."

Eberhardt nodded his thanks. His expression was inscrutable.

The sheriff set both of his large hands flat on his desktop, leaned back in his chair, and watched first one then the other.

Victoria leaned toward Eberhardt. "After we discussed my belief in the likelihood of Zack's innocence," she said, "and agreed to be partners in finding the real killer, I am delighted to know you came here hoping to have Sheriff Norton release Zack."

Eberhardt said nothing.

The sheriff leaned his chair further back.

"I'm proud of you," said Victoria, "for being willing to let go of your strongly held belief in his guilt."

"Mr. Zeller can't be released under any circumstances until he's been cleared legally," the sheriff said. "Mr. Eberhardt hadn't suggested a release."

"Oh," said Victoria, turning to Eberhardt. "I understood from," she paused, not wanting to incriminate Zack, "from you that you planned to get Zack out of jail tonight or tomorrow. Am I mistaken?"

The bell rang at the front door, Jared, the deputy, answered, and a moment later he knocked on the sheriff's door.

"Chief O'Neill is here, sir."

"Can you find another chair?"

"Yes, sir."

The sheriff stood as Casey entered. "Are you involved in this matter?" he asked her.

"What matter?" Casey looked at Victoria. Victoria looked away. Then she looked at Eberhardt, who stared coldly back at her. Then at the sheriff. "No, I'm here unofficially to give Victoria a ride home."

"I believe that's the signal it's time to leave," said Eberhardt. "I'll talk to you another time, Sheriff."

The sheriff was still standing. It seemed as though he was taking up most of the small room, yet three others had been squeezed in.

"If it concerns Zack, of course you'll let me know," said Victoria to the sheriff. "Mr. Eberhardt is under considerable strain and may neglect to tell me."

Casey said nothing until they were outside, stepping down onto the sidewalk. Then she said, "I don't suppose you want to check on your granddaughter?"

"I can explain everything," Victoria said.

"Yeah, yeah."

CHAPTER 27

The next morning, Sunday, Elizabeth phoned Victoria from the jail. "I think I've got enough material for your article. Including quotes from Zack and the pals he's made here. Any chance you can get me released? Nice as it is in some ways, it's still jail. If you get me out in time, I'll drive you to church."

Victoria phoned the sheriff. "Thank you so much for allowing us to get the firsthand material for my article."

"Not at all, Mrs. Trumbull. We'll release Elizabeth right away."

"I'll be sure to show you the article before I send it to the editor."

"I'd appreciate that. By the way, I was interested in that meeting with Bruno Eberhardt last night. Care to shed any light on it for me?"

"Only what I said last night. Mr. Eberhardt is under a terrible strain and I wouldn't blame him for forgetting a meeting."

"By coincidence the night your granddaughter is here to help with the article."

"Yes, indeed," said Victoria.

"Here's my take on things, Mrs. Trumbull. Eberhardt is a powerful man who can pull strings right and left to get his way. I don't trust him one inch. He hinted, not so subtly, that he wants Mr. Zeller released to his custody."

"Is that possible?"

"Anything is possible if you have enough money and connections."

"Mr. Eberhardt wants to take matters into his own hands," said Victoria. "Zack didn't kill that girl."

"I'm inclined to believe you, Mrs. Trumbull, but he's not helping his case by all his talk."

"I suppose planning to poison someone, even though the supposed poison is innocuous, comes with a penalty?"

"Depends. I don't want to speculate on what the legal system is likely to do," said the sheriff. "Me, I'd put him in jail for a couple of weeks to teach him a lesson. Who knows, though. They may send him away for months or they may let him go with a slap on the wrist."

Victoria had just hung up the phone when Casey stopped by.

"That was a really nice supper last night. Many thanks."

"Lincoln and Patrick seemed to hit it off," said Victoria. "Elizabeth is due back any minute. Do you have time for coffee?"

Casey looked at her watch. "I guess there's time before church."

They took their coffee into the cookroom and settled in their usual seats.

"How did Patrick enjoy the ride in Lincoln's truck?" asked Victoria.

"Couldn't have been nicer." Casey stirred two spoonsful of sugar into her coffee, tasted it, and added a third. "Linc tucked him into bed and read him a bedtime story from *The Wind in the Willows.*"

"Mr. Toad's wild ride?"

"You guessed it."

"I was Patrick's age when *The Wind in the Willows* was first published. Every few years I reread it." Victoria drank some coffee. "About the necklace. Are there any new developments?"

"Before we get into that," said Casey, pushing her coffee mug away from her, "What is going on between you and Eberhardt? How about you explaining that mad dash to the jail last night."

"I wanted to see Elizabeth and it happened that a meeting was going on between Mr. Eberhardt and the sheriff. So I joined them." She glanced at Casey, who had pulled her mug back and was stirring her coffee vigorously. "I don't believe my joining them was any sort of interference with the authorities' investigation."

Casey sighed. "I wanted to let you know the state cops are working on another case that's come up that takes precedence over the parsonage fire. They've set it aside for now."

Victoria, surprised, said, "Even though the parsonage fire involves arson and a death?"

Casey shrugged. "They're shorthanded. Budget cuts. We're all shorthanded." She took a sip of her coffee. "Smalley told me to give you free rein to see what you can come up with. You stir up ideas and new ways of thinking about a problem, he said. I already knew that." She set her mug down. "I don't know what I'd do without your help, Victoria." She stood, leaving her mug on the table. "See you in church in a little while."

Isabella topped the silk undies that she had been allowed to keep with one of Tank's T-shirts and the jeans she'd worn the previous day. She started to say something, but

Tank held up a hand. They were in their bedroom.

"I've heard it all, Izzy. Enough, already."

"I wasn't going to say another word about Bruno the Ape stealing my clothes. And my money. And my jewelry, the bastard."

"Izzy!" Tank leaned against the doorframe and folded his arms across his chest.

She bent over and straightened out the rumpled sheets and blanket. "All I was about to say is I'm going over to see my brothers."

"Don't do anything stupid, will you?"

She looked up. "They don't know about Bruno the Thief."

"Keep those two hotheaded bozos out of it, will you?"

"I want my clothes back." She gave the blanket a final smoothing and then fluffed up the pillows. "And don't you call my brothers bozos."

"You can't wear that stuff anywhere on this Island."

"It's the principal of the whole thing."

"Oh for Christ's sake," said Tank, turning away.

Isabella made the short walk from Tank's to the garage that housed Two Brave Haulers in less than five minutes. A moving van was parked outside the garage. A cartoon on the side showed one man carrying a piano, another sitting on his shoulder, playing the piano. The logo TWO BRAVE HAULERS was scrawled across the side of the van in scarlet letters sixteen inches high. The haulers' office was a two-car garage that housed a pickup on one side, and on the other side a desk with a computer on it and a card table where Isabella's brothers, Bucky and Leo, sat playing cards.

"Hey, Sis, what's up?" asked Leo, the older of the two. He laid his cards facedown on the table and stretched his arms over his head. "Thought you'd be wearing that pretty stuff we released for you."

"You haven't heard?" said Isabella.

"Heard what?" Leo brought his arms down and crossed them over his chest. His arm muscles bulged. He wore his mane of light brown hair in a loose, single braid that hung down his back. Like other members of the tribe, he had hazel eyes.

Bucky, the middle child of the three siblings, turned to examine her. "You look like hell, Izzy. You and Tank at it already?"

She gave him a light slap on his arm. "Tank and I are good. Wait until you hear what happened."

Bucky and Leo traded glances. Leo said,

"Now what, baby sister?"

Bucky and Leo were enough alike to be mistaken for twins, except for Bucky's hair, which he wore in a Mohawk, shaved on both sides. He called it a scalp lock and claimed it was a courtesy to his enemies, who would have something to hold on to when they scalped him.

"Aren't you going to invite me to sit down?" asked Isabella.

"Fetch a chair, Bucky," said Leo.

It was a mild day, and the garage doors were open. A breeze wafted in from the Atlantic, the view hidden by a house like Tank's that blocked it.

Bucky shoved his chair back and ambled over to the far side of the garage where two folding chairs leaned against the wall, and returned with one. In the meantime, Isabella had taken his seat. She picked up the hand of cards he'd set facedown on the table and looked at them. "Whooee!" she said.

"Put it down, will you? Me and Leo don't need some fucking girl screwing up our game."

"Now, now!" Isabella plucked one card out of the hand and laid it face up on the table. "A king. Your turn, Leo."

"You stupid broad," snapped Bucky.

"Okay, I won't tell you what I was going to."

"Grow up, Izzy," said Leo. "Stop baiting him, will you?"

Bucky snatched the cards out of her hand, picked up the king, stuck the cards in his jeans pocket, unfolded the folding chair, turned it around so the back faced his brother and sister, and straddled it, arms crossed on the back.

"Okay, what?" he said.

"Welll," she drawled out, "last night, guess who came to see us?"

Bucky sighed. "Oh, for God's sake, Leo, tell her to go back to Eberhardt, will you? We had some peace those two years."

"Come on, Izzy. We got work to do and can't wait all day for you to spin out some story."

"Work?" Izzy eyed the cards on the table. "I see." She moved her chair back and got up. "Well, I won't bother you then."

"Stop playing your games," said Leo. "Either tell us what's on your mind or get outta here, will you?"

She stopped and looked at them. "Bruno got Chief VanDyke to take all my stuff away."

They stared at her.

Outside, a kid went by on a bicycle and

waved at the three inside. They didn't notice.

"Everything?" asked Leo.

"Everything. My fifty thousand cash." She sat down again. "My jewelry, worth another fifty thousand easy. My clothes."

"Another fifty thousand right there," said Leo, and laughed.

"It's not funny," said Isabella. "You better not lean back on that chair like that, or it'll fold up on you."

"Chief VanDyke?" asked Bucky, leaning over his crossed arms. "Took all that stuff we hauled for you? How come? He's one of us."

"VanDyke owes Eberhardt a mega-favor, that's why," said Leo. "Settled a gambling debt. Guess it's payback time." He started to lean back in his chair, but stopped. "So, what do you want your two big brothers to do about it, as though we didn't know."

"I want it back. All of it. Money, jewelry, clothes."

Bucky sat up straight. "You mean, like, taken out?"

"Don't look so eager, Bucky," said Leo. "She doesn't mean permanent, she means teach a lesson. Right, Sis?"

"Actually, permanent has a nice sound to

it. The end of one crappy father-daughter pair."

"Daughter being Samantha," said Leo. "What did she do to you? And did you have anything to do with the latest involving her?"

"When you're not too busy," a nod at the cards, "I'll tell you."

In front of the garage the leaves of a large maple tree were beginning to turn. Sunlight shifted slightly, and the leaves, flickering in the slight breeze, cast a trembling bright gold light into the area where they were sitting.

"Back to particulars," said Leo. "If we steal the stuff again, Eberhardt and his toady VanDyke will know exactly who stole it."

"It's not stealing," Isabella slapped the table. "It's getting my rightful property back."

"Yeah, sure," said Bucky. "Busting into some dude's safe ain't stealing, right?"

"He can't touch us," said Isabella, turning to him.

"Permanent is the best solution," said Bucky. "As Izzy says, they can't touch us. Eberhardt gone, VanDyke won't owe nobody nothing."

"No way." Leo scooped up his cards. "The tribe won't go for it."

"Sure they will. VanDyke will buy us a case of champagne if we get Eberhardt off his back."

"Will you get me my stuff or not?" asked Isabella, looking from one to the other.

Bucky waved an arm at the empty table. "You going to apologize to me for spoiling my game? I was winning, for Christ's sake."

"I'm sorry, Bucky, dear sweet brother."

"You know, Sis," Leo said deliberately, "we bailed you out. Broke into the guy's safe, did a hauling job for you we'd have charged a client a couple thousand bucks for. Because you're our baby sister and we hate Eberhardt's guts. But you can't expect us to do it twice."

"It won't hurt you to do it again."

"No," said Leo.

"You knew, didn't you, I was going to give you a share of that fifty thousand."

"Now you tell us." Bucky laughed. "Easy for you when you don't have fifty thousand to give us a share of."

Leo said, "How large a share were you planning to give us, Sis?"

Isabella looked from one to the other.

"There's your answer, Leo. Yeah, sure, 'I was planning to give you half of the loot,' " Bucky said in a baby-girl falsetto.

"It was money I earned!" said Isabella.

"Whoring," said Bucky and laughed.

"Cut it out," Leo snapped. Then to Isabella, "Give us a figure you agree to pay us to get your stuff back, and we'll consider it."

"Get it in writing," said Bucky. "And get it notarized."

"You just said you'd charge a couple of thousand to do the same job, what about four thousand?"

"Four thousand!" said Bucky getting up from his chair. "The money, the jewelry, the furs, and stuff, comes to more than a hundred thousand, and you're offering four? Don't make me laugh."

"Okay, make it ten thousand," said Isabella.

"Here's what," said Leo. "Bucky's right, that stuff is worth a lot more than a hundred thousand. Closer to a hundred fifty. What say you give us half of the fifty thousand, and we'll call it a deal."

"Half!" Isabella shrieked. "That's twenty-five thousand dollars."

"The girl can count," said Bucky.

"That's our offer."

"No," said Isabella.

"Okay, leave, so we can get back to our game," said Bucky.

"Wait a minute." Isabella combed her long

hair with her fingers. "This negotiating stuff is new to me."

"That's for sure," said Bucky.

"What about somewhere between ten and twenty-five thousand?"

Leo shook his head. "No."

"Twenty-five thousand is a lot of money."

"So, you'll end up with a lot of money plus fifty thousand in jewelry plus who knows what in clothes," said Leo.

"I'll have to check with Tank."

"What does he have to do with this?" said Bucky. "Since when did you marry the guy? He own you? Thought you was the independent woman."

"Go home," said Leo. "We can all forget about it."

"What about half of the money you recover, in case he's moved some of it someplace else?"

"No," said Leo. "A deal is a deal. Twenty-five or forget it."

"She better give us a paper with her signature," said Bucky.

"She'll pay," said Leo.

CHAPTER 28

As they often did on Mondays, Isabella and Sarah Germain were having lunch together at the Aquinnah Shop, which was perched high up on the colorful Gay Head cliffs. The shop was actually a sit-down restaurant run by Wampanoags, with about fifteen tables and souvenirs for sale as one entered. The food was good, the chowder was rated best on the Island, and the view was definitely five-star.

From the windows and an outdoor deck patrons had a 180-degree vista of Vineyard Sound far below them with the Elizabeth Islands a tantalizing green stripe in the distance. Fishing boats, sailboats, power-boats, and ferries constantly moved on the ever-changing panorama of the Sound. The heavy surf that pounded the shore far below looked like a delicate lace ruffle. A huge flock of eiders were tiny points just past the breaker line.

Isabella and Sarah each ordered a salad and a cup of quahog chowder. Isabella was describing in detail, between mouthfuls of greens, how Bruno Eberhardt had conned ChiefVanDyke into stealing her possessions. She didn't mention the money.

"My clothes. He stole my clothes. Why?" She dug her fork into her salad. "What's he going to do with my clothes, you know? He's not going to, like, wear my stuff, is he? He can hardly give it to some woman. I wouldn't think of wearing some other female's clothes, would you?"

Sarah had just dipped her spoon into the creamy chowder and was about to raise it to her mouth. "No way." She slipped the chowder into her mouth.

"I mean, you should have seen my outfits. I mean, dresses for everyday, cocktail dresses, evening dresses, slacks and blouses and shorts, bathing suits." She forked more salad into her mouth and chewed.

"That's really rough," said Sarah, who was wearing her T-shirt printed with TWO BRAVE HAULERS.

Isabella pointed her fork at her friend's shirt. "My brothers' outfit, you know?"

"Course I know," said Sarah. "Everybody on the Island knows Leo and Bucky. They gave me this shirt."

Isabella stuck her fork into her salad again and lifted a mass of greenery. She held it suspended between plate and mouth while she continued. "I had outfits for every season. You should have seen some of my clothes. I was setting out my fall outfits when I decided it was time to leave that crummy bastard."

"Fall outfits?" asked Sarah, whose entire wardrobe consisted of jeans and T-shirts in warm weather, jeans and sweatshirts in cold weather.

"Oh, my God! I had a black velvet suit with a long, slit skirt to die for."

"Where would you wear something like that?" asked Sarah.

"You know, a dinner party, theater."

"Here, on the Vineyard?"

"Well, the Boston Symphony. The opera."

"You like that stuff?" asked Sarah.

"I like the clothes," said Isabella. "Or I liked them." She sighed and popped the greenery, which had stopped dripping dressing, into her mouth and chewed.

They were both silent for a few minutes while they ate.

A gull alighted on the deck outside, snatched up some dropped morsel, and soared off.

Sarah finished her chowder, pushed the

cup to one side, and started in on her salad.

"And you should have seen the most beautiful silk suit I had," said Isabella. "Beige with a sort of raw silk nubble to it, you know?" She left the remains of her salad and moved on to her chowder. "And the most gorgeous corduroy pantsuit, gold, and so soft it was like velvet." She stroked the front of her shirt, a stained T-shirt borrowed from Tank. "The jacket had, like, real leather buttons, you know, and leather patches on the sleeves the same color as the suit. It even had a belt on the back of the jacket." She opened the cellophane packet of chowder crackers and shook them into her soup. "It was something you could wear to the races, you know? I mean, if you went to the Kentucky Derby or England or wherever. You could even wear it someplace like this without feeling overdressed. Real class."

At that point Sarah looked up from her salad. "Sort of like the outfit that woman who just came in is wearing?"

Isabella looked up. "What woman?"

"Behind you. Don't turn around. She's heading toward that empty table," Sarah nodded in the direction. "There's some big guy with her."

A tall well-built woman strode past their table, and when Isabella saw her, she dropped her spoon with a clatter. Chowder splashed onto Tank's shirt. "That's it! That's my suit!" She pushed herself back from the table.

"Hey," said Sarah. "What are you doing?"

"Finding out how come she's got my suit." Isabella stood.

"It can't be yours. There are probably a dozen suits exactly like it on the Island."

"No way. I know that suit. It's mine." Isabella crumpled up her paper napkin and threw it onto the table. She caught up with the woman. "Miss!"

The woman turned. She was about the same height as Isabella and about the same weight, had blond hair done up in an elaborate twist, and was smiling when she turned. However, the moment she saw Isabella's expression, the smile faded.

"Yes?" she asked.

"Where did you get that suit?" demanded Isabella.

"I beg your pardon," the woman said.

"It's mine," said Isabella.

The woman looked Isabella up and down, at the stained shirt and soiled jeans, and backed away with a look of distaste. The jeans were the same ones Isabella had worn for the past two days.

Isabella said more loudly, "I said, where

did you get that suit?"

"Really, it's none of your business where I get my clothes."

Isabella reached out a hand to pluck the sleeve of the gold jacket with leather patches. At that, the woman's male companion stepped out from behind her. He was taller than she, was a good fifty pounds heavier, and was wearing a tan V-necked sweater with a tiny animal of some sort embroidered on the left breast.

"You better go back to your table, lady, before I have you thrown out of this joint." He seemed to swell as he stared at Isabella. He had longish black hair, a curl of which fell onto his forehead, thick black eyebrows, and black eyes that glittered with annoyance. The woman turned her back on the encounter and settled herself in a chair at the empty table.

Isabella said again, "It's mine. I'd recognize it anywhere. It's mine, I tell you!"

"You better leave," said the man, clenching his fists.

By now, other patrons were turning in their chairs to watch, and the restaurant was silent. Sarah got up from her seat.

The waitress, a member of the tribe and a friend of both Sarah's and Isabella's, came up to Sarah and whispered, "Lunch is on the house, Sarah. Better get Isabella to leave before this guy causes any trouble."

"I'm not leaving until I know where she got . . ." said Isabella, still facing the man.

"Thanks, Joanne," said Sarah. "I have to get back to work, and Isabella's giving me a ride to headquarters." She turned to Isabella, who was glaring up into the stormy face of the man. "Come on, Izzy. I don't want to be late." She grabbed the back of Isabella's borrowed shirt and tugged her away.

Isabella turned and grudgingly let Sarah tow her out of the restaurant.

"It's my suit, damn it. I know every stitch in that suit. Where did she get it, anyway?"

"We'll never know," said Sarah. "Just forget about it."

Joanne Homlish, the waitress/cook at the Aquinnah Shop, hurried over to the woman in the gold pantsuit as soon as Isabella and Sarah left.

"I want to apologize for that unpleasantness," said Joanne. "It was uncalled for. I hope you won't think that happens often."

The woman looked up at Joanne. "Thank you. By the way, I'm Katherine Poss. I'm sure you've seen me on television. The poor girl was upset about something unrelated to me."

"Lunch is on the house, Ms. Poss," said Joanne, taking her pad out of her jeans pocket. "For both of you."

"Thanks," said the male companion, who'd seated himself across from Katherine. "It's really not necessary, but we appreciate it."

"I'm afraid it put a damper on your nice outing." Joanne turned to the woman and said, "I wanted to tell you I think your suit is just beautiful, Ms. Poss, and it looks lovely on you."

"Thank you." Katherine Poss looked down at the gold material stretched over her thighs. "You know, I would have told her where I got it if only she'd asked nicely."

"Did you get it here on the Island?" asked Joanne, with some hesitation, not wanting a repeat performance.

"Yes, I did. There's a wonderful place in West Tisbury."

"West Tisbury?" asked Joanne, puzzled. "I'm not sure I know the shop."

"Oh, it's not a shop," said Katherine. "It's a place with the most amazing assortment of clothing and other things."

Her companion nodded. "Beats the old-time general store."

"They had dresses and slacks and other clothes that were in my size, and I'm hard to fit. And of a really superior quality."

"Well, it's just beautiful," said Joanne, taking her pencil out from behind her ear. "There's something special about new clothes."

"This suit is supposedly recycled, but it's like new." Katherine held up an arm so Joanne could inspect the leather patch on the sleeve. "See?" She patted the collar and ran her hand down the velvety gold corduroy. "Honestly, you wouldn't believe the things they have there."

"I didn't get where you said the place is," said Joanne, thinking she might be referring to Alley's general store, but still puzzled.

"Oh. I guess I didn't say. It's almost like a department store, a place called the Dumptique. They have the most amazing selection of stuff, all free. You just help yourself and carry it away. It's the recycling building at the West Tisbury dump."

"We better order now," said the man, glancing at his watch. He looked up at Joanne. "Thanks for the free lunch."

Elizabeth returned home from work on Monday to find a frustrated Victoria seated at the cookroom table with notes in her loopy backhand writing spread out in front of her.

"I feel as though I'm putting out unnecessary fires when I need to work at something that will get us somewhere," said Victoria.

"After Saturday night, I hesitate to volunteer to help," said Elizabeth. "I guess that was one of your unnecessary fires?"

"No, that had to be taken care of. You did an admirable job of letting me know in time to join Mr. Eberhardt's meeting with the sheriff. The sheriff is alerted now, and Mr. Eberhardt will have to come up with another plan. It can no longer involve releasing Zack from jail."

Elizabeth sat down next to her grandmother. "What are your plans now?"

"I need to find the source of the leaves covering Samantha's body. So far the three people I've spoken to all have easy access to piles of last fall's maple leaves." Victoria checked her notes. "Is it possible that I'm on the wrong track, following the wrong lead?"

Elizabeth shrugged. "You think the killer is one of the parents?"

"I haven't ruled out anyone."

Elizabeth looked at the scattering of notes. "Who are you talking to next?"

"Dana Putnam."

"I don't recognize the name."

"He's a nurse at the hospital and is fairly new to the Island," said Victoria. "According to Joe the plumber, he has a daughter Emily, who had some dealings with Samantha."

"Does he have a wife?"

"They're divorced. He has custody of Emily." Victoria gathered up the notes and went through them again. "Interesting. All the teens involved with Samantha are children of single parents. Lincoln, Connie Burrowes, Anderson Jones, Dana Putnam. And all are only children."

"The kids were probably looking for a parent substitute. You have that thoughtful look, Gram. What are you thinking?"

"Another lead. I keep wondering about the dump truck that must have dropped off Samantha's body along with the leaves."

"There must be at least a hundred dump trucks on this Island. Couldn't it have been a pickup?"

"I'm going to call my friend, Bill O'Malley. He owns a dump truck and he may have some thoughts on owners."

O'Malley answered on the first ring. "Mrs. Trumbull! If you're calling for a ride, my truck is in the shop."

"I don't need a ride. I'm trying to track

down someone who dumped a load of leaves on the bicycle path about a week ago."

"In West Tisbury?"

"Yes."

Bill laughed. "And you're calling me because I own a dump truck."

"Well, yes."

"It wasn't me." He laughed again. "Mrs. Trumbull, there are at least a hundred landscapers on this Island, and most of them own dump trucks. In addition, builders must account for another hundred. Why did they dump leaves on the bike path?"

"I don't know why they dumped them there. That's a question I need to answer."

"Why are you interested?"

"There was a body in among the leaves."

"Oh." Long silence. "So somebody needed to get rid of the body in a hurry. They had no time to get to a more secluded spot?"

"That's my guess. What happened to your truck?"

"Nothing. Just in for maintenance."

"How would I go about identifying the owners?"

"My guess would be go to the Motor Vehicles Department. It's probably not restricted information, but you'd have to have a good reason to get a list of owners. How do you intend to narrow it down?"

"By town and by recognizing a name."

"Suppose, Mrs. Trumbull, someone at the garage where they're working on my truck, decided to borrow my truck for the nefarious purpose of transporting a dead body."

"I suppose I'd ask you if someone at the mechanic's used your truck during the week it's been at the garage."

"You know what the mechanic would say? That a bunch of guys took my truck out for test drives. Brakes. Acceleration. Gear shift. All gotta be checked, and every one of the kids who works there is crying to drive my dump truck past his girlfriend's house. A macho guy thing. Forget that angle, Mrs. Trumbull. Besides, could be a pickup we're talking about, right?"

"I suppose so," Victoria admitted.

After another long silence Bill said, "You're one determined lady. I'll ask around for you."

CHAPTER 29

Early Tuesday morning Sheriff Norton strolled down to the end cell, the one called the Pink Room, and rattled the cell door.

Zack woke with a start. "What time is it?"

"Six a.m. Time to get dressed."

Zack sat up in his lower bunk, hitting his head on the bunk above. "Ouch." He rubbed his head and looked down at his clothing. "I guess I'm dressed already." He was wearing orange prison-issued cotton pajamas.

"Here are your very own clothes." The sheriff unlocked the cell door. "They're nicely washed and ironed."

"Well. Gee. Thanks," said Zack. "What's the occasion?"

"You're released on bail. Your lawyer, Miranda Smith, worked it out."

"Really? I didn't think she liked me."

"She doesn't."

"Oh."

"She said, and I quote, 'Whether he did it or not, she deserved what she got.' You have any idea what she's talking about?"

Zack, baffled by everything that was swirling around him, shook his head.

"She convinced the judge you were not likely to jump bail." The sheriff handed the neat bundle of clothing to Zack, who got up from his bunk to take it.

"So I'm free?" Zack smoothed his hand over his clean clothes.

"Not exactly." The sheriff was standing in the hall outside the cell, holding one of the iron bars in the open door. "There's still that charge of attempted poisoning." He paused, thought a moment, then added, "You could still be charged with murder. You're just getting bail. Charges haven't been dropped."

"Yeah, well, I guess that's right," said Zack.

"Until then, we're releasing you to the custody of Mrs. Trumbull."

"Mrs. Trumbull? She's taking me back?"

"She called and offered to house you."

"But that means I'm free."

The sheriff sighed. "That means you're under house arrest until your trial. You'll be required to wear a tracking device on your leg until then."

"But I have a job. I have to get to my job."

"Where is it?"

"Chilmark. The Beetlebung Café. I'm a dishwasher there."

"I'll call them and make arrangements for you to go back to work. You won't be using your car. You can take the bus." The sheriff let go of the bar he'd been holding and re-locked the cell. "Get dressed."

"I can get some meals at work. What about my other meals?"

"Mrs. Trumbull said she'd take care of your breakfast."

"The food here at the jail is pretty good."

The sheriff, usually the epitome of patience, was getting testy. "What do you want, take-out? Mrs. Trumbull agreed to feed you breakfast. Baked beans, most likely."

"Can I get my car and drive there?"

"No."

"How do I get to Mrs. Trumbull's?"

"Jared will drive you there."

"But I need to get to work."

"As I said, you take the bus."

"What about my car?"

The sheriff turned away. "It's still at the Park and Ride where you left it. Also where we store abandoned or unclaimed cars."

Zack set his clean clothes on his bunk and

went up to the locked cell door. He held on to the bars with both hands. "I hope nobody steals it," he called out to the sheriff's retreating form.

The sheriff, who was some distance from the pink cell, called back over his shoulder, "If they do, we'll let them have your cell."

About the same time Zack was being released on bail, Leo and Bucky drove their van up the dirt road next to Eberhardt's drive, parked, and sat where they had a good view of his house and garage.

"Know anything about the people who live here?" asked Bucky, pointing his thumb at the enormous house whose drive they were parked on.

"Some dot-com guy," said Leo. "Spends two weeks in August here. One of our cops caretakes the place, so not to worry about him showing up."

"No sign of Eberhardt's Jaguar," said Bucky. "Could be he's off-Island. Think we're okay to go on in?"

"Not yet," said Leo.

Bucky yawned and stretched. "What've we got to eat today?"

Leo reached for the small cooler and lifted the lid. "Ham and cheese. Chips. Apples. O'Doul's." He lifted up the items. "Blueberry pie."

"Can't fault the lunch she packs," said Bucky, prying off the cap on one of the near beers.

They spent the afternoon watching Eberhardt's house. The UPS truck arrived. The driver parked in the area below the house, walked up the path to the house, and left packages on the porch. A black Subaru came. The driver went up onto the porch and knocked, then peered into the windows, then returned to his car and left. The FedEx truck came and the driver left a box on the porch next to two packages the UPS driver had delivered.

"He sure buys a lot of stuff," whispered Bucky.

"Money," said Leo.

Around four o'clock a gray Suzuki pulled in and a small woman with dark hair got out carrying a shopping bag. She went into the house, as though she was familiar with it.

Bucky sat up straight. "What do you make of that?"

"Housekeeper," said Leo.

The woman stayed in the house for two hours. She came out, shut the door behind her, walked down the path, this time with both the shopping bag and a mop, got back in her car, and left.

"Cleaning woman," said Bucky.

"Yeah," said Leo. "What I told you."

Just before sunset, a light-colored pickup pulled up to Eberhardt's. The driver went up to the house, knocked once and waited, knocked again, waited, then came back down the steps.

"Eberhardt didn't answer, that's for sure," said Leo.

"He's not home," said Bucky.

"You think?"

The driver got back into the truck and left.

It was dark now and lights flicked on in the house.

"He's home," said Bucky. "Let's get outta here!"

"The lights are on a timer, dummy, can't you tell? They went on all at once."

"He's away for sure, then," whispered Bucky. "Time to get to work?"

Leo thought for a few moments. "I reckon."

"Same drill as before?"

Leo thought some more. "He's probably replaced the safe. If I was him I'd have an alarm on it this time."

"No problem," said Bucky, no longer whispering. "Bet he's off-Island."

Leo nodded. "Could be."

"Well, then, let's go," said Bucky, opening the van's door. "What's holding you up?"

"I don't like the feel of it, that's what," said Leo.

"So he comes, our van is parked in front of his house, we're loading baby sister's stuff into it. What's he going to do?"

Leo sighed. "Get back in. We'll do it."

Bucky thrust a fist into the air. "Right on. Good to go."

They drove back to the main road and turned onto the dirt road to Eberhardt's, with the bright green grass in the middle. A rabbit was nibbling on the tender grass and hopped out of the way when their headlights flicked on him.

"Shoulda hit him," said Bucky. "Love a nice rabbit stew. Get Izzy to cook it for us."

"Tularemia," muttered Leo. "Two days and you're dead."

"What's the matter with you? Never seen you so negative."

"Things stink," said Leo.

"No they don't. We get Izzy's jewelry that she owns, her clothes that she owns. Nobody can say we're stealing anything."

"Breaking and entering," said Leo.

Bucky shook his head. "Can't touch us. We open the safe and take out the fifty grand —"

"If he put the money in a new safe."

"He figures he's safe — get it, new safe?" Bucky chortled.

"Very funny," snapped Leo.

"C'mon, lighten up, Lee. Eberhardt has Chief VanDyke on his side. He wants to show the world he can put his money where he wants."

"We'll find her jewelry and clothes, but I'll give you ten to one we don't find the money."

"No bet, Lee. Be stealing *your* money. We'll get the dough."

Leo parked the van at the foot of the path and they walked up to the porch steps, onto the porch, and to the front door. Leo lifted the whale-shaped bronze door knocker and slammed it down a couple of times.

They waited.

No answer.

Knocked again.

No answer.

"Okay?" asked Bucky.

"Yeah." Leo tested the door handle, as though he expected the door to be locked, but it opened.

"That's the Vineyard." Bucky was whispering again. "So we're not breaking and entering. We're neighbors dropping off a pie."

Leo turned on him. "Where's your god-damned pie, shithead? Keep your damned mouth shut, will you?"

"Okay, okay. I already ate the pie."

"We get the clothes and jewelry first, then open the safe last, in case it's alarmed."

"Guess if someone was about to dynamite me I'd be alarmed, too," cackled Bucky.

"Shut. Up."

They went into the house and tiptoed up the front stairs to Izzy's former room, opened the closet door, and . . . no clothes. Nothing but the same empty hangers they'd left on the floor. They checked drawers and cabinets, went into other rooms on the second floor.

Nothing.

"Well, we shouldn't've expected to see he'd hung them back up," said Bucky.

"You're right, for once," said Leo. "The cops brought the stuff back." He thrust both hands into his pockets and thought. "If I was the cops, I'd have laid hanging stuff on the dining room table, left boxes of other stuff on the floor."

"Let's go, then."

They went back downstairs, across the hall, through the great room, and into the dining room. The floor was littered with empty cardboard boxes. A dozen hangers were scattered on the table. More on the floor.

They stood and surveyed the mess. "How come the cleaning woman didn't clean in here?" asked Bucky.

"Who knows," said Leo. "She obviously didn't."

"What in hell did he do with all her stuff?" asked Bucky.

"Probably called the Good Riddance Girls. They hauled it off."

"He gave away fifty grand of jewelry?"

Leo thought. "He's not that dumb."

"Let's open the safe."

"You know, Bucky, this is not a good idea. Let's get outta here. We've done nothing they can get us for. Door was unlocked, we just stopped by. Neighborly visit to the grieving father, you know."

"I keep thinking of that safe."

"Just keep thinking about it. I'm gone," said Leo.

"I wanna see if he installed a new safe."

"You look. See you back at the ranch."

"Wait a sec, will you? I'll just look in the study."

"Okay, okay," said Leo,

"If he did, we could come back later . . ."

"Don't even think about it. Hurry up, will you?"

Leo headed for the front door while Bucky headed for the study door. He turned the knob. The door opened inward. He pushed it slowly away from him. The study was dark. It smelled kind of rusty. He reached for the light switch and flipped it up. The desk light went on and he saw the source of the smell. A man lay behind Eberhardt's desk, his head resting in a pool of congealed blood.

Bucky backed away, slammed the door shut, and yelled out, "Lee! C'mere, quick!"

"Now what, for Christ's sake," said Leo. "We gotta get out of here, Bucky."

"We got a problem, Lee."

Leo strode over to the study door and Bucky turned the knob and pushed it open again. The desk light was still on, illuminating the man behind the desk. The man was lying facedown. The short white hair on the back of his head was covered with black blood.

"Is it Eberhardt, Lee? What are we gonna do? He's dead, isn't he?"

"We leave. Now," said Leo. "Did you turn on that light?"

"Yeah, I did."

"Turn it off. You got something to wipe it off with?"

"The light switch?"

"What d'ya think I meant, the body?" said Leo. "Fingerprints, dummy."

"Don't get funny with me," said Bucky. "I don't feel so hot."

"You better not throw up. Wipe off that light switch."

"I don't have anything to wipe it off with."

"Your shirt. Use that. Hurry up, will you?"

Bucky stretched the bottom of his T-shirt up to the light switch.

"Take off your shirt. We got to erase everything we touched," said Leo. "Come on, get to work."

They backed out of the study, leaving the door open, and for the next ten minutes Bucky wiped everything they recalled touching with his T-shirt, and Leo followed with a used paper towel he had in his pocket.

"Okay, we get outta here," said Leo.

The two went down the path and got into their van with its bright scarlet logo in sixteen-inch-high letters and headed for their garage.

"Who do you think whacked him?" asked Bucky.

"How am I supposed to know?"

"You suppose it was the guy in the pickup?"

"Same answer," said Leo. "The pickup guy didn't even go in the house, stupid."

"Would you have taken him out?" asked Bucky.

Leo glanced at his younger brother. "Are you kidding?"

"No. I mean it. I would have done it, Lee."

"Yeah, sure, you hothead."

"I mean it, Lee. What he did to Izzy . . ."

"He didn't do a thing to Izzy she didn't deserve."

"Someone didn't like him," said Bucky.

"That's for sure."

"Do you think we should've called the cops?"

"Surely you jest," said Leo.

Their headlights picked up an occasional pair of bright eyes reflecting the light, peering out from the verge. Only a couple of cars passed them coming the other way.

"Pretty creepy at night," said Bucky. "Expect to see more cars this time of year."

"Tourists aren't driving around this time of day," said Leo. "They're out to dinner, the show, whatever."

"Who do you suppose whacked Eberhardt? It is Eberhardt, isn't it?"

Leo said nothing.

They drove in silence for several minutes. The stone walls on either side were unreal, two-dimensional, something you'd see on TV. Hundreds of years earlier farmers had fenced in their sheep with sturdy walls of stones they'd cleared from their fields. The scent of the sea wafted in through their open windows.

"Getting close to home," said Bucky. "Wonder what Izzy will have to say about us not getting her stuff." He glanced over at his older brother.

"Her problem, not ours. We did what we could."

"Should we tell her we took care of her problem?"

"Keep your mouth shut, Bucky. Don't tell her a thing about the body. Leave it, will you? Be glad we only have to deal with the fallout when she hears we didn't get her stuff."

"You'd have killed him, wouldn't you?"

"If I had to. Sure," said Leo. "I didn't have to. You didn't have to. Be thankful, will you? And just shut up."

CHAPTER 30

Isabella waited for her brothers to return from staking out Bruno Eberhardt's place.

When they'd moved her out of Bruno's house and into Tank's, they had packed up everything she owned plus a few things she thought she should own, which included her entire wardrobe, the most beautiful, expensive clothes. She might never have an occasion to wear the silks and velvets and linens, but it was the idea of seeing pretty things hanging in the closet with a perfumed sachet keeping them fresh.

Now that Chief VanDyke and his cronies had raided Tank's place and stole everything she owned, the only clothing she possessed was what she'd worn when she left Eberhardt's place. All her pretty things were gone.

Her brothers would get it all back.

Tank had gone to Oak Bluffs with his buddies. She didn't care how late it was when he came home.

It was boring waiting for her brothers. She busied herself around the place, straightening up messes of Tank's that were driving her crazy. Tank told her to leave them alone and she'd sworn she wouldn't touch them. After that, she turned on the TV and channel surfed, but reception was lousy and there was nothing worth watching anyway.

She made herself tuna fish salad for supper, put it on a paper plate, and set it up nicely on a tray with some chips, a glass of orange juice, and a paper napkin. She took her supper and a folding chair to the big front window where she could watch for her brothers. The window faced the road that ran through tribal housing. She'd recognize the sound of the van's engine and would see the lights before it reached the house.

She'd hinted to them that they might take care of Bruno. Perhaps they had. It couldn't be that difficult to kill someone. Hints didn't always work their way through her brothers' thick heads, though.

It was fully dark now. What was taking them so long?

She finished her tuna, took the tray into the kitchen area, and dropped the paper plate into the trash. Then she washed and dried her hands. While she was doing that, she heard the distinctive rumble of their van approaching. She went to the door, but the van, instead of stopping, passed by, heading toward the garage.

Stinkers, she thought. Now I'll have to carry all my things back here, getting them all dusty.

No, I'll make them drive back here with everything.

She slipped on her shoes and threw a sweatshirt of Tank's over her shoulders.

She walked to the Brave Haulers' garage, savoring what it would be like to get her stuff back. It will be worth twenty-five grand to have everything back again. She could live with only half the fifty thousand.

By the time Isabella reached her brothers' garage, they had parked the van off to one side of the garage. Bucky was unloading paper bags of something from the back.

"Hi, guys," said Isabella. "Where's my stuff?"

"You tell her, Lee," said Bucky.

"We didn't get your stuff." Leo took one of the heavy bags from Bucky and carried it to the office side of the garage.

"Are you going back tomorrow to get it?"

"No," said Leo, returning to the van.

"You better tell her, Lee," said Bucky.

"Keep your mouth shut," said Leo.

"What's with you? I want my clothes. Where are they?"

"We don't know where your clothes are," said Leo.

"What do you mean?" Isabella stamped her foot. "I waited all day. I want my things."

Leo carried another bag to the office side and returned. He jabbed a finger at his sister. "We've had a day from hell and we don't know where your stuff is, understand? It's gone. Vamoosed."

Isabella leaned against the side of the van. "What do you have in those bags?"

"Groceries. We wasted a whole day out of our lives to not get your stuff."

"We looked upstairs in your room," said Bucky. "We even looked in the closets and drawers and in the other upstairs rooms. Nothing there."

Isabella opened the van door and sat on the passenger's seat, facing out toward her brothers.

Bucky went on, "Then we came downstairs —"

"Watch it," cautioned Leo.

Bucky turned to him. "I'm just telling her what we saw."

"Well, watch it."

"Downstairs —"

"I'll tell her," said Leo. "In the dining room was where the cops took everything they got from here, because there were empty boxes, hangers, paper, all over the place, so we came home."

"My jewelry?"

"No sign of it."

"Did you check the safe? Surely he'd have put the money in the safe. He probably got a new safe to keep the money in."

Bucky said, "Yeah, we —"

"Shut up," said Leo.

"But . . . ?"

"I said, shut up."

"What's going on?" said Isabella. "They must have taken my clothes somewhere."

"We don't know, and you don't want to know," said Leo. "Now will you let us get some shut-eye? We're beat. We tried. We didn't succeed."

"What am I going to do?" asked Isabella.

"That's your problem, little sister," said Leo.

The dirty dishes from luncheon were piling up in the sink at the Beetlebung Café along with all the luncheon pots and pans. Will Osborne's hands were deep in soapy water in the sink, and he was scrubbing a lasagna pan. The sauce was baked on, of course. He removed his hands from the tepid water and shook off the greasy suds.

He turned to Phil Smith, owner and manager. "You know, Mr. Smith, now Zack's gone, I need help. I can only handle one more day of this shit." He nodded at the stack of soaking lasagna pans. "And that's with you helping, which I don't see you doing a lot of." He faced the sink again and turned on the hot water faucet full blast. "I have to tell you, this is getting old. One more day and I'm outta here."

"Right," said Phil, who was sitting at the prep table. "I hear you. Looks like it'll be a while before Zack is back on the dishes. He's a good worker." He studied the handful of reservations he was holding. "We need to hire a new waitress."

"A replacement for Samantha?" Will smirked. "Been a while."

"Don't mention that name to me." Phil went back to the reservation forms.

"What about a replacement for Zack?" asked Will.

"You know of anyone who needs a job washing dishes?"

"Nope, and I'm not willing to do it much longer."

"I'll put an ad in the *Enquirer,* 'waitress, dishwasher needed.' "

"How much are you offering for the dish-washing job?"

"Eight dollars an hour."

Will shook his head. "That's what you're paying me after working for six months. Raise me to nine-fifty before you offer a newbie eight. What were you paying Zack?"

Phil hesitated for a moment before answering. "Eight-fifty."

"Christ! And I been here longer than him. And he's in jail."

Phil continued to check the reservations.

Will stared at his boss. "You got nothing to say?" He wiped his hands on a dish towel and tossed the towel at the prep table. It slid onto the floor. He unwound his apron string, pulled the damp apron off, and tossed that onto the floor next to the dish towel.

"I quit."

He turned away from the sink and headed toward the door. "So long, Phil, you cheapskate sleaze."

"Hey, wait a minute," said Phil. "You can't just walk out."

"Oh no? Who's stopping me?"

Phil pointed to the pots and pans lined up beside the sink. "We need those for dinner and I've got to start cooking pretty soon."

"Wash 'em your damn self," said Will, taking a few steps closer to the door.

Phil stood. "Wait!"

Will stopped. "Wait for what?"

"Eight-fifty."

Will laughed. "I did say nine-fifty, didn't I? Well, it's ten now. Minimum wage is ten, right? *Ten,*" he repeated. "I can't wait to contact the whatever board that fines cheaters like you." He moved several steps closer to the door.

"Stop, will you? I can't afford to pay ten. You know what business is like."

"Yeah, poor you, just barely scraping out a living. Tough supporting that BMW of yours."

"I'll pay you nine-fifty an hour."

"Ten," said Will, turning to face his boss. "I'm thinking 'minimum wage.' Ten."

Phil plopped back onto his chair and tossed the reservation forms onto the prep table. "Okay. You got me. Ten."

"I want it in writing."

"Okay, okay."

"Before I go back to those freaking lasagna pans."

"Okay."

Will waited. "Well?"

"I'll write it out," said Phil.

Will picked up one of the reservation forms and turned it over. "Write it on the back of this." He handed the form to Phil. "And, if you want those pots washed for dinner, you're gonna have to get your hands dirty, too."

"Okay. Sure. Yeah," said Phil. He scribbled a note, handed it to Will, then got to his feet. He picked the apron up off the floor. "I'll get a clean one."

"Make it two."

For the next hour they worked silently, Will scrubbing the pots, Phil rinsing them, wiping them dry, and putting them away.

They were near the end when Phil said, "No hard feelings?"

"Who, me?" said Will. "Long as you stick by the agreement." He looked over his shoulder. "Someone's at the door."

Phil slung his dish towel over his shoulder, peered at the indistinct image in the frosted glass of the door, and unlocked it. Without really looking at the tall, well-built woman who stood in the dim light, he said, "Sorry, miss, we're not open for dinner yet."

"I'm not planning to have dinner here, I'm applying for your waitress position."

Phil looked up at her. Stared at her. "Isabella Minnowfish?"

"Yeah, that's me," said Isabella.

"Waitress job?"

"Yes," said Isabella. "You do need a waitress, don't you?"

"I didn't recognize you."

"Because I'm wearing jeans?"

"I mean, I didn't think you patronized places like this."

"I don't," said Isabella. "I'm looking for a job, and someone said you might need a waitress. Island grapevine at work, you know."

"Well, yeah, we do."

"Here I am."

Phil cleared his throat. "Excuse me for asking, but do you have any experience?"

"Experience!" said Isabella, with a laugh. "How many names do you want me to give you?"

Phil flushed. "I mean restaurants."

"I know what you meant. Do you supply uniforms?"

"We're not exactly a uniform-wearing res- taurant."

"Jeans?"

"Jeans are fine."

"What do you pay?"

Phil paused a long moment before he said, "Three-fifty an hour plus tips."

"Three-fifty? You must be joking."

"Tips should bring it up to ten. If not, I'll make it up."

"Okay," she said. "When do you want me to start?"

Phil cleared his throat again. "Tomorrow?"

"I'll be here." With that she turned and started to walk away.

"Hey, wait!" said Phil. "I need to show you the ropes."

"I know all about ropes," said Isabella, shifting her weight slightly. "You want me here about five or so?"

"The Senior Sunset Discount is five-thirty to six. Five is good."

"That will give me time to check *your* ropes," said Isabella with a smile and left.

Phil, slightly stunned, went back to Will and the last few pots.

"What's she doing here?" Will looked up from the latest pot.

"Our new waitress." said Phil, taking the dish towel off his shoulder. He picked up a pan, patted it dry, and hung it on a hook over the prep table.

"You're shitting me. What's Mr. Eberhardt got to say about this?"

"Maybe she's slumming." Phil picked up another pan.

"Princess Isabella?" Will rinsed the pot and set it on the drain board. "I'll bet ten to one Eberhardt's ditched her without giving her a dime. Looks like she's gonna have to support herself now."

"You know anything about her waitressing background?" asked Phil.

"Sure. Before Eberhardt decided she was hot stuff she waitressed in just about every eating place on the Island."

"How come?"

"How come what?"

"Job hopping," said Phil.

"No one ever fired her, I don't think. Better pay at the next new place, better tips, better working conditions. I think a couple times she was tired of the boss hitting on her."

"I can see why," said Phil. "How do you know about her?"

"We dishwashers get around," said Will. "Better pay, better working conditions . . ."

"Yeah, yeah," said Phil. "Wonder what happened?"

"You mean, Eberhardt and her?" Will picked up the last pan and submerged it in the sink water. It sank to the bottom with a gurgle. "My guess is your friend, Samantha, had something to do with it." He looked over at Phil, who at the mention of Samantha's name assumed an expression of distaste. "You never did tell me what happened between you and Samantha."

"You don't want to know." Phil tossed his dish towel onto the drain board and stalked away, ignoring the remaining pots.

"Hey," said Will. "Finish the damn dishes."

"Go to hell," said Phil.

CHAPTER 31

The unidentified injured man who'd been
wheeled into the hospital's emergency room
in critical condition on Tuesday night, hung
on, hour after hour, with no change. He'd
been examined, cleaned up, taken to the
intensive care unit, and hooked up to a battery of life-saving machines and fluids.
There was no sign of approaching death,
but no sign of improving life either.

Sergeant Smalley of the state police had
been called in late Tuesday evening as soon
as Doc Jeffers, who was on duty at the time,
determined that the man had suffered injury
at the hands of party or parties unknown.

"Hey, Doc." Smalley offered Jeffers his
hand. Doc Jeffers gave it a slap.

The doc was wearing a green cotton scrub
suit. A tuft of white hair showed in the V of
the neck. He peered at Smalley over the top
of his half-frame glasses. "Glad you could
make it. Come on into my office."

"Wouldn't have missed it. Always enjoy your late-night parties." Smalley was in full uniform, his black boots highly polished as usual.

They went into the office. Doc Jeffers sat behind his desk and Smalley took the guest chair facing it.

"Okay, Doc, who was he?"

"Bruno Eberhardt."

Smalley leaned back in his chair and whistled. "Is that right!"

"He'd not dead yet," said Doc Jeffers.

"Is he going to make it?"

Doc Jeffers shrugged. "Who knows?"

"Who found him?" asked Smalley.

"His Brazilian housekeeper, Maria Lima. She cleans three days a week."

Smalley leaned forward. "She call 911?"

The doc nodded. "She did all the right things. Called 911, didn't touch a thing, didn't try to doctor him and make things worse, laid a light blanket over him, stuck around waiting for the ambulance, and answered all our questions."

"Where was he when she found him?"

"In his study."

"Door closed?"

"The door was open," said Doc Jeffers. "That's what alerted her. His study was off limits to her cleaning. He always kept the door shut." Doc Jeffers opened a drawer, took out a tissue, removed his glasses, and polished the lenses. "So when she cleaned this afternoon she didn't go into the study." He put his glasses back on. "As usual the door was shut."

"But she found him this evening," said Smalley, still leaning forward. "And she'd cleaned this afternoon?"

"This afternoon she saw a van with red letters on the side, the next drive over. She thought that was odd since the house next door wasn't occupied." He dropped the tissue he'd used on his glasses into the wastepaper basket and shut his desk drawer. "She'd forgotten to water the plants, so she decided to use that as an excuse to return and see if the van was still there. She passed it on the road heading toward Aquinnah."

"Did she notice any identifying features about the van?"

Doc Jeffers laughed. "Bright red letters. A foot and a half tall. 'Two Brave Haulers.'"

"Leo and Bucky Minnowfish," said Smalley.

"You got it."

Smalley made a note. "Guess I need to talk to them."

Doc Jeffers continued, "So she went into the house, saw the study door open, and you know the rest."

"Was the front door locked?"

"Of course not."

Smalley looked up from his note taking. "Was that customary for him? He's wealthy. A lot to protect."

"Yes," said the doc. "Arrogant SOB. Maria wasn't sure a key to the front door even existed."

Smalley snorted. "This damned Island and its security."

Doc Jeffers nodded. "Lack thereof."

"What are the chances he'll make it?" asked Smalley.

"He's in bad shape. He'd been lying there at least a full day before Maria found him. A wonder he's alive." Doc Jeffers stood, pulled up the waist of his scrub pants and retied the cloth tape belt. "We're doing all we can. Some of the best physicians in the Northeast work here."

"Anything else you can tell me?"

"Not that I can think of," said the doc. He reseated himself on the corner of his desk. "Have you had any progress in finding his daughter's killer?"

"None," said Smalley. "Same modus for father and daughter. Both hit on the back of the head. Any idea what object would do it?"

"Something thin and heavy, same in both attacks. Tire iron, golf club, poker. Something like that."

"Would it take much strength to inflict that kind of damage?"

"Yes and no. If the assailant is close and can't get momentum into his swing, he'll need strength. Back up a little where he can give it a good, long swing, not much strength at all. A slight woman could have done it."

"Call if anything changes, will you? Whether he dies or looks like he'll recover. Any time. Day or night." Smalley snapped his notebook shut and stood. "Good luck."

"We need more than luck," said the doc. "We're with him twenty-four hours a day." He rose from his seat on the desktop. "Is it likely the assailant knows he's still alive?"

"No way of knowing. Half the people on this Island have scanners. Someone for sure heard the EMTs picked up a critically injured male at the Eberhardt residence."

"Do we need to request a police guard?"

"I was hoping you wouldn't ask. We are seriously shorthanded. I took my team off that parsonage fire and death investigation to work another case."

"I'll let you know if there's any change."

"If you have to cut the twenty-four/seven

watch for whatever reason, call me." Smalley started to walk away, but turned. "The housekeeper, Maria Lima. You have a number for her?"

"I'll get it for you." Doc Jeffers went to his desk, opened a drawer, and pulled out an address book. He peered through the bottom half of his glasses, scribbled a number on a scrap of paper, and handed it to Smalley.

"Thanks, Doc," said Smalley. "Have a good night, what's left of it."

Early the next morning Bucky and Leo were hosing down their van when Chief VanDyke showed up. They were working in the shade of the large maple in front of their garage. Sunlight filtered through the leaves making a pattern of sun dots on the ground. A mourning dove cooed.

Leo was crouched next to the van, washing one of the wheel wells. Bucky was leaning against the doorframe, eating an apple.

"Morning, boys. Nice day."

"Howdy, Chief," said Leo.

"See you're hard at work, there. Mind if I sit and watch?"

Leo glanced up. "Bucky, get the chief a chair." He continued to scrub the wheel well.

Bucky tossed the apple core aside, brought out one of the folding chairs, and opened it up. The chief straddled it and set his arms on the back.

"I hear you had quite a time yesterday," he said.

Bucky looked at Leo. Leo continued to wipe the wheel well.

"Getting that pretty clean, I see," said the chief.

"We didn't do anything," said Bucky. "We were just . . ." his voice trailed off. Leo was glaring at him.

"Let me get right down to business," said the chief. "Someone spotted you at Eberhardt's place yesterday. Care to explain?"

"We just wanted to get . . ." Bucky glanced again at Leo.

The chief turned to Leo. "Maybe you'd better explain. You were staking out Eberhardt's place. You can take it from there." He paused briefly. "Might just as well tell the truth. It's easier in the end."

Leo stood and threw down the rag he'd been using. "We wanted to get Izzy's stuff back. So we watched his place. Didn't see his car. Figured he was off-Island and went in."

"You didn't find Isabella's belongings, did you?"

Leo shook his head. "Empty boxes."

"The ones I had my men pack up here."

Bucky was standing a couple of feet from the chief to one side of the garage door. "Where is Izzy's stuff?"

Chief VanDyke laughed. "Eberhardt took it to the West Tisbury dump."

"All her clothes?" Bucky sounded aghast. "The dump? He just threw them away? Like thousands of dollars of clothes?"

"The recycling shed," said the chief. "Bunch of ladies Isabella's size going through old clothes are now wearing designer dresses." He smiled. "But we digress."

Bucky moved over to where Leo stood on the far side of the van.

"Spit it out, Chief," said Leo.

"Eberhardt was there, wasn't he. You found him."

"We didn't kill him," protested Bucky. "We was —"

"Watch it, Bucky," said Leo.

"Nothing to watch," said the chief. "You could have killed him. Next time you do a stakeout — if there ever is a next time — better not use a vehicle everyone on this Island recognizes."

"We had nothing to do with it," said Leo. "So what do you want from us?"

"Nothing, at the moment. At some point

I'll be taking you in to talk to the state police."

"They can't touch us," said Leo.

"For murder?" The chief laughed. "Oh yes they can. Rules have changed, sonny."

After Doc Jeffers left, Sergeant Smalley called the tribal police chief. "Got a delicate situation here, Josephus. You available if I come up to tribal headquarters in about an hour?"

"Of course," said the chief. "What's up, John?"

"I'd just as soon talk to you in person."

"I'll be here."

An hour later, Smalley showed up at tribal headquarters. He and Chief VanDyke went into the chief's office. A large map of Martha's Vineyard covered one wall. Most of the westernmost end of the Island was tinted a pale green.

Smalley went over to the map and examined it.

"Tribal lands are in green," said Josephus. "By the way, that was an interesting meeting of the Island police chiefs the other day." He indicated a chair beside his desk for Smalley. "What can I do for you, John?" The chief sat behind his desk.

Smalley, too, sat. "Has to do with the

question you asked about jurisdiction."

"You mean about tribal members and homicide?" The chief set his forearms on the table.

"Right. I want to ask you, off the record, was it the Minnowfish brothers you were referring to?"

"Their van was identified as being at the scene of the murder," said VanDyke.

"Have they been in trouble before?"

The chief lifted an arm and waggled his hand, palm down. "When Isabella left Bruno Eberhardt, her brothers cleared out not only all of her clothing from Eberhardt's house, but broke into Eberhardt's safe as well. They stole fifty thousand dollars in cash, as well as jewelry Eberhardt had given Isabella worth an estimated fifty thousand more."

Smalley whistled. "Did you handle the situation in your inimitable way?"

"Nicely put," said the chief. "My men and I returned things to Mr. Eberhardt."

"Clothing, too?"

"Yes, indeed."

"Just out of curiosity, why the clothes?"

The chief shrugged. "Mr. Eberhardt, a generous man, felt that his generosity had been imposed upon when his safe was burgled." He shrugged again. "Retaliation?"

"Do you have a problem with us taking the Minnowfish boys in for questioning?"

"Not at all. I've already spoken to them."

"We'll handle this as discreetly as possible, so as not to trespass on your prerogatives."

"Much appreciated," said the chief. "Does that cover what you wanted to discuss with me?"

"Yes. I don't trust phones or electronic devices."

"Wise. Much too accessible to the public," the chief said. "Then, if business is over, can I offer you a cup of coffee?"

"Thanks, but I'd better get back." Smalley stood.

The chief stood, too. "Always good to work with you, John."

"You, too, Josephus."

As they walked to the door, the chief said, "Unfortunate about Eberhardt's death."

"You haven't heard?" said Smalley.

"Heard what?"

"Eberhardt just might pull through."

"Is that right," said Josephus. "I assumed he was dead."

"It's touch and go," said Smalley. "But we've got top medics here at the hospital, and they're giving him a fighting chance."

"Wonderful news," said the chief. "Is he conscious?"

"Hasn't regained consciousness yet. He had a serious, near-lethal head injury."

"Terrible, terrible," said the chief, shaking his head. "I assume he's being guarded?"

"The hospital has a twenty-four/seven watch on him, monitoring his signs. They expect him to regain consciousness any time now."

"Do you have police guards as well?"

"Not enough," said Smalley.

"I'll assign two of my men to help. In fact, I'll take a watch, too," said the chief. "I feel responsible since tribal members may be the culprits."

"Of course," said Smalley. "That would be a great help. You don't need written approval, but I'll let them know anyway."

"Thanks, John. Terrible that a thing like this could happen here on the Island."

Smalley nodded. "Both Eberhardt and his daughter, the same modus. Undoubtedly the same perp. Or perps, if it's the Minnowfish brothers. Wonder what they had against the daughter? Assuming they're the ones."

"From what I understood, Samantha Eberhardt was asking for trouble."

Smalley nodded. "I think every town on the Island felt the impact of her personality."

"That's for sure." Josephus held out his hand and they shook.

CHAPTER 32

One morning a week, Casey drove Victoria to the nursing home connected to the hospital where Victoria spent an hour or so reading to the patients she called "the elderly." Wednesday was her day to read. Casey pulled up in front of the entrance.

"I've got an Island police chiefs' meeting at eleven, Victoria, so I may be late."

Victoria had already made a date for lunch with Dana Putnam. "I'll have lunch in the cafeteria."

"The hospital's food is better than good," said Casey. "If I get through early, I'll join you."

Victoria walked slowly down the long corridor studying the artwork on the walls. The hospital was quite literally an art gallery. The walls in every corridor and every room of the hospital and nursing home were adorned with original Island art — oils, watercolors, photos, and sculptures.

She arrived early at the activity room, where several occupied wheelchairs were pulled up in a semicircle before an empty armchair. Three or four people were seated on couches or chairs. Victoria always felt a bit nervous before she read, as though she was onstage performing.

She sat in the armchair facing her audience and set her bag of poetry books on the floor.

"Good morning." She looked around at her group. As usual, only four or five of those present acknowledged her. Victoria had the feeling that most of them didn't care whether she read or not. They were here because it was a break in the monotony of their day.

She read a few of her own short poems, and then she read poems from A. A. Milne's *When We Were Very Young.* She liked the rhythm of his poetry and her audience responded better to his poems than to hers. She must remember to bring more short, spritely poems.

The hour passed. Those in wheelchairs were then wheeled away. Each week while she packed up her books, the same two women stayed a few minutes longer, one who was able to walk to the readings, the other who could wheel herself. Both wore bathrobes and slippers. Victoria's own grandmother would never have allowed her to wear nightclothes out of the bedroom. Certainly not in public.

"I love to hear you read, Mrs. Trumbull," said the walker. "I loved hiking the Island's trails, and you bring back to me the lovely places I used to walk . . ." her voice trailed off.

The woman in the wheelchair said, "I'm sorry the others don't seem to appreciate your work. But really, they do. They like to see you and hear your voice."

"Thank you," said Victoria, touched.

The cafeteria was only a short walk from the activity room, but Victoria was out of breath when she got there, so she sat at one of the tables to rest before buying her lunch.

Dana Putnam, the nurse who was new to the Island, was to meet her here.

She was resting, thinking about what she would like to eat, when the nurse showed up. He was wearing green hospital scrubs and had short dark hair and black-framed glasses that emphasized his bright blue eyes.

"Good afternoon," he said. "You must be Victoria Trumbull."

She started to rise.

"Don't get up." He had a pleasant, deep

voice. He offered her his hand and she shook it.

"And you are Dana Putnam."

He bowed slightly. "I haven't bought my lunch yet. May I pick up something for you?"

"Yes, thank you," said Victoria, reaching for her wallet.

"No, no, Mrs. Trumbull. This is on me. I get a discount."

"A cup of clam chowder, then," said Victoria, smiling up at him. A good large nose, not as large as her own, of course, clean shaven so she could see his strong chin.

"Would you like a small salad to go with the chowder? I'll split an egg salad sandwich with you."

"Both sound delicious."

"I'll be right back," he said. "Save my seat for me."

She was rearranging her books in her cloth bag when he returned with a loaded tray.

Victoria examined the dishes. "Can we eat all that?"

"I think so," he said. "I've worked up an appetite dealing with one emergency after another in the ER, and you've earned your lunch."

He set the food out and they ate, talking in between mouthfuls about the hospital, the art, the food, the views from the windows.

He laid down his fork and wiped his hands on his napkin. "I know you'd like to talk to me about Emily and Samantha Eberhardt."

"If it's not too painful."

"It's painful, all right," he said, "but I want to explain to the world what a stupid mistake I made."

Victoria picked up her spoon. It seemed unfitting, somehow, to dip it into her chowder while he was talking. She set the spoon down.

"I suppose you know I'm divorced. I was awarded custody of Emily."

"Your ex-wife? What about her?" asked Victoria, not sure that was the right question.

"We parted on civilized terms. She is bipolar and is hospitalized on occasion. She loves Emily desperately and agreed that Emily would have a more stable home with me." He was digging into his own cup of chowder between sentences. His appetite didn't seem to be impaired by talking about his troubles, so Victoria picked up her spoon again. "As it turned out, Emily would have been far better off with her bipolar mother."

"Is Emily all right now?"

"No." He shook his head. "Emily got

hooked on some drug Ms. Eberhardt had her clique obtain for her. She's now in a drug treatment center in Boston. It's expensive and I can see her only rarely. My ex-wife had a serious relapse and holds me responsible for that, and she holds me responsible for Emily's addiction. And I don't blame her."

Victoria said nothing.

"I've gotten to know some of the other parents," he continued. "We have a support group. Samantha Survivors." He paused. "All of us have our kids in expensive treatment. None of us can afford the treatment. As a group, we decided to contact her father, Bruno Eberhardt, who has more money than he knows what to do with. We figured he'd be sympathetic and might like the idea of doing something decent with his money, like funding scholarships for drug treatment."

"And what happened?"

"He refused to meet with us. Refused to believe his Samantha was involved with drugs. Brushed us off. Now, I understand, he's planning to sue the support group for defaming his daughter and has accused us of covering up for the killer. He assumes it's one of us." He looked over at Victoria with a smile. "Could be. Hard to know who to put money on. There's enough anger among us to float a battleship. Killing Samantha?" He made a sweeping gesture with his hand. "Nothing to it."

"Didn't any of you realize what was going on?"

He shook his head. "Samantha Eberhardt seemed a nice young woman. Attractive, well-spoken, just the older sister you'd like your kids to have. They flocked to her and they wanted to emulate her."

"Didn't your children show signs of addiction?"

"We parents talked about this. We didn't expect our kids to get involved in drugs. We're all single parents, no partner to give a second opinion. What we all noticed was our kids' grades dropping. We all attributed that to our kids missing their mom or dad, and we tried to make up for that by being more lenient than we would have been otherwise." He bit into his half-sandwich.

"Will Emily recover from the addiction?"

"I don't know." He set the sandwich down. "I don't know if anyone ever fully recovers from drug addiction. Find another addiction, like fishing, maybe, to substitute for the kick drugs give you."

"I can't imagine what it's like," said Victoria.

"It's hell," said Dana.

They were silent for a few moments.

Victoria asked, "Do you live near the hospital?"

"I live on Barnes Road, near the roundabout. It's only a fifteen-minute commute."

"That's a lovely area," said Victoria.

"I have an apartment on the second floor of a nice old house, built probably before the Second World War." He smiled. "I don't suppose that sounds old to you. My landlady's house is in a grove of big trees that shade my apartment." He stood. "Would you like dessert? I'm getting a dish of coffee ice cream."

"I'd like that."

Before Dana returned with the ice cream, Casey came into the lunchroom. She looked around, spotted Victoria, and made her way to the table. "Finished already, Victoria? We can leave unless you don't mind sitting through lunch while I eat."

She was about to head to the buffet table when Dana returned. Casey looked at him, then at Victoria. "I don't know how you do it, Victoria. You're a magnet for handsome men."

He laughed. "She's a magnet, all right. I'm Dana Putnam, a nurse here." He held out a hand. "And you're a police officer, I see."

"Casey McNeill," she said, shaking his hand.

"West Tisbury's chief of police," said Victoria, "I serve as her deputy."

"May I get you anything, Chief?" asked Dana.

"Thanks, but I want to look over the offerings."

"If you've got to be in a hospital, this is the place to be," he said. "I'm convinced the chefs are cordon bleu." He sat. "I'll join Mrs. Trumbull for dessert, then I have to get back to the ER."

"I heard you had a busy time last night," said Casey.

"That's for sure. Around eight last night they brought in an unconscious man with a head injury. He'd been hit on the back of the head."

"Will he be all right?" asked Victoria.

Dana shrugged. "He's not in great shape."

"Be right back," said Casey, and left.

"Do you know who he is?" asked Victoria.

Dana shook his head. "Privacy rules prevent me from giving out any information."

"Of course. I knew that. I shouldn't have asked."

They finished their ice cream, and Dana cleared the empty dishes away. "Sorry to leave, Mrs. Trumbull. I've got to get back to work."

After Dana left and while Casey was still getting her lunch, Victoria's grandniece Hope, the head nurse at the hospital, stopped by her table.

"Hi, Aunty Vic. I didn't expect to see you here. It's your day to read, isn't it?"

"Yes, and afterward I met with Dana Putnam for lunch."

"That's so sad about Emily."

"Dana is an emergency room nurse, isn't he?"

"He's one of us. We rotate in the ER."

"I understand a seriously wounded man was brought in last night. Dana had to leave to get back to monitoring him. Does it look as though the man will survive?"

"He's still alive, barely. But people can pull through the most awful injuries with help of machines and tubes. I can't tell you anything more about him, but talk to Sergeant Smalley. He can tell you stuff. Cop to cop, you know."

"Do you have time to sit?" asked Victoria.

Hope looked at her watch. "Afraid not, Auntie Vic. Gotta run."

■ ■ ■ ■

Casey returned after Hope left.

"You missed my grandniece," said Victoria.

"We said hi to each other when I was on line." Casey unloaded her tray and set it aside. "Nice of Dana to join you." Casey picked up her fork. "What did you talk about?"

"His daughter, Emily."

Casey ate a few mouthfuls, looking thoughtful. "Okay, now I get the connection. At the drug task force meeting a couple weeks ago we discussed Emily Putnam's case. It involved Samantha."

Victoria nodded.

"You're doing a bit of investigation?"

"Now that I've got free rein."

Casey dug her fork into her salad. "Sad," she said after a pause. "She was a beautiful girl, quiet. A top student. Not many friends yet. Samantha approached her, hooked her on one of the opioid drugs." Casey set her fork down and picked up two sugar packets. She tore the corners off both and poured the sugar into her iced tea. "Emily's grades dropped. She lost weight. Her dad figured she was missing her mom."

"You'd think a nurse would recognize drug abuse symptoms," said Victoria.

"You know the old story about the shoe-maker's kids going without shoes. I guess the same applies to a nurse's kids." She continued to stir her iced tea while she talked. "Emily dropped out of school."

"Her father said she is in a rehabilitation center near Boston."

"Costing her father more than he earns," said Casey. "Her mother tried to commit suicide and blames everything on the father."

Victoria smoothed out her paper napkin, folded it, and put it in her pocket.

"You know the way people think, 'You took my child away from me, and now look what you've done to her and to me.' Same old, same old." Casey worked on her salad some more. "What did you learn from Dana, Victoria?"

"Just what you've told me, only from his point of view."

"Which was that he hated Samantha's guts and would have killed her if someone else hadn't done it first?"

"He didn't say that, exactly. He indicated that he thought the parents are covering up for whoever killed her, assuming it's one of them. And the parents are almost equally upset by Bruno Eberhardt, who's filed or is filing suit against them." Victoria changed the subject. "How was the police chiefs' meeting?"

Casey took a sip of her iced tea. "I don't think I told you that at the last meeting Chief VanDyke from Aquinnah wanted to clarify whether the state could prosecute tribal members in homicide cases or whether they had immunity because of their sovereign nation status."

"What was the decision?" asked Victoria, interested.

"The consensus was that in cases of homicide the state takes over. This week he mentioned, just sort of offhand, that he was afraid two tribal members might be involved in a homicide case. He wasn't any more specific than that." Casey finished her salad, took a final sip of her iced tea, put the remains back on her tray, and stood. "I'll dispose of this and then we can head for home. I have a pile of paperwork to take care of."

"I'd like to stop in at the state police barracks," said Victoria. "I want to ask Sergeant Smalley about the patient who was brought in to the hospital last night."

"Good idea. I'll join you," said Casey.

■ ■ ■ ■

The hospital was on a hill overlooking the harbor. From the parking lot they could see a ferry coming around the jetty. A flock of seagulls trailed behind it.

"Drugs bring such ugliness to this beautiful Island," said Casey.

"Ugliness and trouble," said Victoria.

They climbed into the police cruiser, and Casey pulled away from the space. "I heard on the police scanner about the injured man being brought here to the hospital. Have they identified him yet?"

"I'm sure they have," said Victoria, "but with all the privacy rules, the hospital couldn't tell me anything. Hope suggested I talk to Sergeant Smalley, cop to cop."

Casey laughed. "You're truly one of us, aren't you?"

They parked behind the barracks and went up to the side door. Tried the door, but it was locked. Casey knocked.

"Notice," said Casey, "that they lock their doors."

"This is Oak Bluffs," said Victoria. "Not West Tisbury."

Sergeant Smalley answered their knock.

"Mrs. Trumbull, good to see you," he said.

"You too, Chief. Come in. Fresh coffee is on."

"We don't mean to stay long," said Victoria.

"Come on into the conference room anyway and have a cup," said Smalley.

They had just taken their seats when Trooper Tim appeared with a tray and three mugs of steaming coffee.

"Thank you," Victoria said, smiling up at him.

"No problem," said Tim, and left.

"What's on your mind, Chief?" Smalley asked.

"Victoria wanted to see you, John. I'm her chauffeur today."

He turned to Victoria.

"It's about the man who was injured last night. I was curious to know if he's involved in the Eberhardt case, but the hospital can't provide information. They suggested we talk to you."

Smalley nodded. "Bruno Eberhardt."

"Is he still alive?"

"Barely."

"Are there concerns about his staying alive?"

Smalley took a deep breath. "We should have someone guarding him twenty-four hours a day. We have no idea who attacked him or why." He lifted his coffee mug but didn't drink. "The problem is, the hospital doesn't have the staff to continue watching over him once he's out of medical danger, and we police are shorthanded. We'll have someone with him as long and often as possible, but we can't dedicate a police guard twenty-four/seven." He took a sip of coffee and set the mug down.

"What about police from the other towns?" asked Casey. "We're shorthanded, too, but we'll give you whatever assistance we can."

"Thanks, Chief. I've contacted all the town selectmen. All the police departments are equally shorthanded, but they'll help out as much as they can. We already have offers of assistance from Aquinnah." He turned his mug around absently. "It would save us a lot of trouble if we could nail the assailant." He looked at Victoria. "I don't know if that gives you the answers you need."

"I'm not sure either," said Victoria.

"I'd like to stop at Cronig's," said Victoria when they were on their way back to West Tisbury. "I need to pick up cat food. I can take the bus home."

"I'll wait for you, Victoria," said Casey.

"The longer I can put off working on that paperwork, the better."

Victoria was in the pet food aisle looking through rows of canned cat food to find a kind that McCavity would eat, when a familiar voice said, "They're hard to please, aren't they?"

Victoria looked up from her search. "Hello, Abilene."

"What does your cat like?"

"Only the best," replied Victoria. "Wild salmon from Alaska. He turns up his nose at anything else."

"Mehitabel's the same way," said Abilene. "She refuses to catch the mice that inhabit my studio."

"Speaking of your studio," said Victoria. "I'd like to see it sometime."

"Of course. I'm there almost every day. Call first to make sure I'm not out running errands." She rummaged through her shoulder bag and brought out a business card, which she gave to Victoria. "Here's my phone number."

Victoria checked the address. "I'm not familiar with Maple Lane."

"It's off Old County Road, a long dirt road that ends at the State Forest. They changed the name from Skunk Alley."

"Then I know where it is. Maple Lane

isn't as colorful a name." She spotted the cans of Alaskan salmon she was looking for, reached for one, and checked the label. "This looks good enough for my supper. I think I'll get an extra can, just in case."

"They make it sound delicious, but it's probably mostly the icky stuff cats love. Skin, bones, and innards." She located Mehitabel's preference and added several cans to her own cart. "Would you like to come by this afternoon? I'd be happy to pick you up. I have some paperwork I have to finish up first." She wrinkled her nose. "It'll be a nice break. I hate paperwork."

"You and Casey. That's what she just said."

CHAPTER 33

Victoria was waiting by the west step when Abilene drove up in her pickup and got out.

"I hope you haven't been waiting long." She opened the door for Victoria, who climbed up into the passenger seat.

"I've been looking forward to visiting your studio," said Victoria.

"It's an honor, Mrs. Trumbull."

They turned onto the unpaved road now called Maple Lane.

"You're close enough to be called a neighbor," said Victoria.

"Actually, Mrs. Trumbull, I live even closer to you in my family's old camp on Tisbury Great Pond."

"I know the area well," said Victoria. "I understand the pond setting has been discovered by people with more money than taste."

"You're so right. My little house is now sandwiched between two monster trophy houses."

"They're eyesores," said Victoria. "A terrible waste of resources just to show off one's wealth."

"The owners think my camp is the eyesore."

They passed several houses and Abilene slowed in front of a small shingled house to their left in a grove of young trees. The leaves were beginning to be touched with the distinctive gold of sugar maples.

"That's the home of the couple who planted the trees and renamed the road after them."

"It will be even more lovely in a week or so, especially if we have a cold snap," said Victoria. "Is your studio nearby?"

"Right next door," said Abilene. "My windows look out on the neighbor's trees. You'll see." She turned into the next drive, which ended in a rough circle. Three or four cars were parked to one side.

"Those are my clients' cars."

"I've taken you away from your work, I'm afraid."

"Not at all. My classes are in the mornings. Some of my advanced students like to stay later, doing their own thing."

The studio was a barn-like building off to one side of the circle. Three steps led up to the plain wood door. Inside there was a kind of vestibule with shoes lined up below a coat rack.

Abilene took off her shoes, and Victoria bent down, untied her own, and slipped them off too. The vestibule led into a large, airy room.

Victoria's first impression was of the silence. Then of the light that poured in through floor-to-ceiling windows on three sides. The polished wood floor, as smooth as glass, reflected the sky and the trees to her left.

Several people were sitting or lying or stretched out on mats on the floor. The silence was so total, she thought at first the people were dummies until one of the stretchers moved his leg. It would be an intrusion to speak. She felt as though a single word would shatter the stillness of the big room.

"Follow me," Abilene said in a quiet voice, and Victoria followed her to a small office with a door that opened off the fourth wall, the one with no windows. They entered, and she closed the door.

A wooden desk with only a few items on it faced them. To their left a love seat and a rocking chair took up a corner of the room and to their right a large window gave the office a feeling of being almost out of doors.

Victoria sat in the rocker. "A beautiful setting for your yoga classes. It's peaceful."

"I do have to share the studio." Abilene took a seat behind her desk. "I couldn't afford to rent it full time, although I wish I could."

Outside, the maple leaves, barely tinged with early color, were quivering in a light breeze.

"Tell me more about your house on the pond. It was originally a hunting camp, wasn't it?" asked Victoria.

Abilene nodded. "My great-great-grandfather built it more than a hundred years ago. My grandmother used to tell me stories about him. He loved duck hunting."

"I haven't walked along the pond's edge for a long time. As I recall, your camp was right on the shore with a view toward the ocean, the only building on the point."

"You should see it now," said Abilene. "It looks like an ad for a billionaires' colony, except my poor little house spoils the effect."

"And your neighbors, what are they like?"

"They come only for a few weeks during the summer, so I haven't gotten to know them. I don't really want to know them." She moved some papers on her desk and looked out the window. "They certainly don't want to know me or have anything to do with me."

"At least you see very little of them."

"That's true. But since they've sicced their attorneys on me I have to think about them every minute of every day. And I don't have the wherewithal to fight them."

"Their lawyers?" asked Victoria.

"My abutters have gotten together. First, they offered nicely to buy me out before they even built, and I refused. Then they upped the offer to an obscene amount, and I refused again. It's been family land for more than a hundred years. It's my home. It's where I want to live."

"I understand your feeling about family roots."

Abilene nodded. "When that didn't work they started threatening me with a lawsuit. I have a right to my property, I know. But I don't have the money to fight to protect my right."

Victoria said nothing.

"Samantha promised to support me in my fight to keep the camp and my land."

"She had access to great wealth, didn't she?"

"Her father gave her whatever she wanted. She'd ask him for a thousand dollars, and he'd peel off hundred-dollar bills and hand them to her." Abilene pushed her chair back slightly. "She knew how much my place meant to me. She kept telling me how much I meant to her, and she promised to back me all the way. Pay for the best lawyers, and fight the abutters on my behalf. In fact, she had already engaged the lawyers. They would be contacting me any day, she said."

"But they never did?"

Abilene's laugh was bitter. "They did. They presented me with their bill. A bill I can't pay." Abilene looked out the window toward the maple trees and their shimmering leaves. "She promised and promised and nothing ever came of her promises. And now I'm about to be evicted."

"How unfortunate that she was killed before she could help you."

Abilene stood. "She never intended to help me, Mrs. Trumbull."

Isabella reported for work at the Beetlebung Café wearing one of her brothers' T-shirts emblazoned with TWO BRAVE HAULERS.

Phil opened the door for her. "I like the shirt."

"Free advertising for my brothers."

"That'll do it," said Phil, looking it over with interest.

"Where do you want me to start?"

"Set up the tables."

"Cloth napkins?"

"Cloth napkins for dinner, at lunch we wrap the flatware in a paper napkin with a paper band around it. Come into my office and I'll show you how to do it."

They moved into his office off the dining room, and both sat, Phil behind his desk, Isabella on a captain's chair moved from the dining room.

"You don't need to show me anything," said Isabella. "I told you, I've been around."

"Your coming by last night was great timing," said Phil. "I was about to place an ad in the *Enquirer*."

"What happened to the server you had before?" asked Isabella.

"I had to fire the previous girl. She was getting a little too friendly, if you know what I mean." Phil leaned back.

"With customers?"

Phil pointed at his chest. "With me."

Isabella looked him up and down in return. "I can understand."

"Thanks. But there's friendly and then there's friendly."

"Put me to work," said Isabella, and stood.

Phil stood too. "First, meet Will Osborne, our chief dishwasher."

Isabella followed him through the swinging door, where Will was bent over the sink, immersed in soapy water up to his elbows. He stood, shook suds off his hands, and held one out to Isabella.

She looked at it with distaste.

"It's clean." Will picked up a dish towel and dried his hands.

She turned away.

Phil said, "We're all family here."

"Not much longer if you don't get me some help," said Will. "How are you at washing dishes, Izzy?"

"My name is Isabella."

Phil patted her on the back. "He's kidding, Isabella. We're advertising for a new dishwasher. We need you waiting tables."

The phone rang. "I'll get it," said Will. He picked it up. "Beetlebung Café. How may I help you?" A pause. "Who?" A longer pause. "He's what?" Another pause. "You better talk to Phil." He handed the phone to his boss.

"Who am I talking to?" Phil said into the phone. "Yeah, Sheriff, Zack Zeller worked here." Phil looked around the kitchen at the pile of dirty pots. "Sure, we'll take him back. Whatever rules you got, we're okay. He's a good worker." He handed the phone back to Will.

"We're rehiring Zack?" Will set the phone back in its dock.

"We never let him go," said Phil.

"So what's up?"

"He wears a tracking device on his ankle. He's allowed here and Victoria Trumbull's, where he's staying, and on the bus to bring him here." He thrust both hands into his pockets and rocked back and forth on his feet.

"Is that your new dishwasher?" asked Isabella.

"Zack Zeller. He worked here before."

"Isn't he the one who tried to poison Samantha with edible mushrooms?" She laughed and brushed the front of her T-shirt. "He's not the brightest star in the universe."

"None other," said Will. "I served booze at that dinner party of yours."

"I thought you looked familiar," she said.

"You slumming or something, working here?"

Isabella looked at her cell phone. "It's almost time for your Senior Sunset diners, Phil. I've got to get busy."

Zack took the bus to the Beetlebung Café and walked through the familiar door into the restaurant.

Phil greeted him. "Glad to have you

back." He offered Zack his hand.

Shaking it enthusiastically, Zack said, "Can't tell you how glad I am to be back."

"Let's see your ankle bracelet," said Will.

Zack lifted his jeans leg so they could admire it.

"Can you take it off?" asked Will.

"I think they welded it on."

"You better not take it off," said Phil. "We're supposed to be your wardens."

"You and Mrs. Trumbull," said Zack. "Can't begin to tell you how much I missed you guys."

"We been saving the dirty pots for you," Will said.

CHAPTER 34

Phil Smith and Isabella were having a celebratory drink after her first day of work. She, a Scotch, neat. He, bourbon on the rocks. They held up their glasses in a toast.

The sound of the dishwashing machine in the background was a pleasant obbligato. Will and Zack's voices were pure harmony.

Isabella was a born waitress. The Sunset patrons, usually not much for tipping, had opened their hearts and change purses. The later diners had opened their wallets.

This was a night to celebrate.

They were on their second drinks.

Zack came out of the kitchen. "Gotta catch that nine thirty bus, Mr. Smith."

Phil stood. "Can't begin to tell you how glad we are to have you back. Stay out of trouble, now, you hear?"

"Yes, sir," said Zack.

"Is that leg thing painful?" asked Isabella.

"No, ma'am, not really. Just a nuisance.

I'm so glad to be out of that jail I'd put up with a ball and chain like they used to do in the old days."

"Did you get dinner?" Phil asked.

"Yes, sir. Thank you. You should have tried the food at the jail."

"I hear it's good. Get me their recipes, next time you're there."

"Yes, sir," said Zack. "See you tomorrow for the lunch dishes."

After Zack left, Isabella passed her glass to Phil for a refill.

"You'll be okay driving?" asked Phil.

"No problem. I'm just up the road in Aquinnah. The Chilmark cops know me." She took a small sip. "Who was the waitress you fired?"

"You don't want to know. She's not around anymore."

"I do want to know. You seem like an easy boss to work for."

"Too easy, I guess."

"Come on. Tell me."

"The daughter of your friend, Bruno Eberhardt." He picked up his drink.

"Omigod!" Isabella sat back abruptly and some of her Scotch spilled. "Samantha worked here?"

"Yeah," said Phil. He reached for a bar

towel and wiped up the small puddle of whisky.

"I don't know what to say. What happened? You told me it was a long story. Well, we have time."

Phil took a deep breath. "I was married. Samantha came along."

"That figures," said Isabella. "Go on."

"Nice, clean-cut girl. Sweet. Innocent."

"I know it all," said Isabella.

"I got swept up by all that innocence, and the next thing I knew my wife left me."

"I don't blame her. What did Sammy, sweet Sammy do then?"

"She blackmailed me."

"What for?"

"I really don't want to say."

"Come on, Phil. We're all on the same page."

"Taxes."

"You mean, like, IRS audit? Did she report you?"

"She was about to. I can't afford an IRS audit. I'd go out of business if the IRS was on my back."

"So what did you do?"

"I upped her wages."

"How did you get away with firing her?"

"I told her if the IRS came after me anytime over the next five years, whether it was her fault or not, I would kill her. She knew I meant it."

"Wow," said Isabella, laughing. "But you didn't, because the IRS didn't audit you."

"I was ready to kill her anyway."

"You're too nice a guy."

"You think so?" asked Phil.

"Is your wife still on the Island?"

Phil nodded. "She's an attorney. Public defender. Name's Miranda."

Isabella, a comfortable two drinks fueling her, was so warmed by Phil's confession of his feelings for Samantha, that she decided she would confide in him.

"You know, Phil, I hated that little bitch from the moment I met her."

"Oh?" said Phil. "You were living with her father."

"That phony all-American girl was an act. I saw through it right away. She was a druggie."

"It wasn't obvious."

"Sure it was, if you knew what you were looking at. I had a good thing going with Bruno. I liked him okay. He gave me stuff, clothes, jewelry." She sighed. "He was planning to set up a bank account for me. Darling daughter stopped that. Now it's all gone, thanks to the bitch."

"What triggered it all?" asked Phil.

"I told Bruno she was on drugs and ought to get treatment. He told her. From then on she was out to get me. Nothing I said to him made any difference. He kept excusing her. She wasn't asking him for much money. She had lots of nice friends. Something wrong with me." Isabella was quiet for several moments. "I decided the world would be a better place without her. I didn't even know about the high school kids she was destroying. She wrecked Bruno's and my relationship and cheated me out of a soft life and a hundred and fifty grand." She paused again. "I planned exactly how to kill her, right down to the last detail."

"Tell me you didn't," said Phil.

"Someone beat me to it."

When Victoria answered the phone the following afternoon, a young-sounding female voice said, "Mrs. Trumbull? You don't know me, but can I come and talk to you?"

"Yes, of course," said Victoria. "May I ask who you are?"

"My name is Brooke Burrowes. I'm Connie Burrowes' daughter."

"I'm delighted to hear from you," said Victoria. "I met with your mother recently."

"She told me you talked to her and to

Benjy's dad."

"I understand you and Benjy are friends."

"Close friends, you know, I mean, not close close."

"You're welcome to come here whenever it's convenient for you."

"Would you mind if Benjy came too?"

"Isn't he off-Island?"

"He's here now, you know, visiting his dad. He's on a two-day leave from the drug center and he has to go back tomorrow."

"Then come this afternoon. Do you have transportation?"

"My mom will bring us after school, if that's okay with you."

Victoria prepared for the arrival of Brooke Burrowes and Benjy Jones with cookies and hot chocolate.

She didn't know what to expect from the visit of the two high school students who'd been swept up in Samantha Eberhardt's net.

Around three fifteen a car pulled up, and Connie Burrowes came to the door followed by two teenagers, a slim girl, her face concealed by a soft black hat with a wide brim, and a tall boy who looked very much like his father, Anderson Jones.

"Come in," said Victoria. "Would you like to stay, Connie?"

"No, thanks," said Connie. "I'm going to spend some time in the library. Brooke can call me and I'll pick them up." She kissed Brooke on the cheek, shook Benjy's hand, and left.

Both teens were wearing raggedy jeans. Benjy had on a gray V-neck sweater over a white T-shirt. Brooke, a blue denim shirt.

They sat around the cookroom table, Victoria in her usual chair.

"I know your father misses you, Benjy. I'm glad you're able to visit."

"Me, too." Benjy smiled, his teeth white against his dark skin.

"Benjy and I, and Emily Putnam?" Brooke looked questioningly at Victoria.

"I know who she is. I've talked with her father."

"Well, we all wanted to see you, but only Benjy and I could make it at the same time." She stopped and looked down at her hands, clasped in her lap. "Actually, Emily isn't allowed to visit her dad."

"Why not?" asked Victoria.

"Her mother got a lawyer to say her dad couldn't see Emily."

"That sounds harsh," said Victoria.

Brooke shrugged. "I guess."

"What we have to say is really hard," said Benjy. "We agreed we had to talk to someone, you know. We decided you were the best person to talk to."

"It helps to talk things out with someone," said Victoria, not sure where this conversation was headed.

Brooke removed her hat and set it on the chair next to her. Long blond hair tumbled out in a cascade that fell well below her shoulders. "You go ahead, Benjy. You tell Mrs. Trumbull."

"Well." He glanced first at Brooke, then at Victoria.

Victoria let the silence grow. A titmouse landed on the birdfeeder, poked his bill into the small hole, and grabbed a seed. A shower of seeds fell to the ground.

"Go on, Benjy. I can't," said Brooke. "I just can't."

Benjy nodded. "It's like this, Mrs. Trumbull." Benjy looked directly at her. "A bunch of us used to meet in the old parsonage?" He cleared his throat.

Victoria nodded.

"The town cops never checked it out. I mean, they drove by and looked, but there was nothing to see, you know. I mean, we weren't making noise or anything. And we didn't have any lights except flashlights and candles."

The titmouse left the feeder. A chickadee

landed, snatched a seed, and flew off. Three wild turkeys, a male and two females, wandered into the drive and were dining on seed Victoria had thrown out for the cardinals and doves.

Brooke helped herself to an Oreo, split it apart, and bit into the part that had no filling. That was the way Victoria, too, ate Oreos. Saving the part with filling for last.

Benjy took a deep breath. "We didn't plan to meet that night, but Emily, Brooke, and I were all on leave from the rehab center, and Samantha called everybody in the group to say we were going to have a reunion and also have some fun with Sebastian Sibert. She promised no drugs."

"She kept her promise," Brooke put in. "We all knew Sebastian had a big crush on Samantha and she was kind of, like, egging him on, and we thought it was funny. Sebastian was a lot younger than us, really shy and awkward and we laughed at him behind his back." She picked up her mug. "This is hard to talk about. After what's happened."

"I understand," said Victoria, still not sure where this was leading. "How many were involved in the group?"

"About eight altogether," said Brooke, "including Benjy, Emily, Sebastian, and me. Four others. Maybe five. Only us three showed up."

Benjy said, "Like Brooke said, three of us showed up. Me, Brooke, and Emily. There was an older friend of Samantha's. I don't remember her name."

"Abilene," said Brooke.

"Yeah. Abilene. Sebastian hadn't got there yet. Samantha said we should all hide except for Abilene, and she was to wait outside until after Sebastian came. So that's what we did."

Victoria had a feeling she wasn't going to like what was next.

"Sebastian came, all cleaned up, hair combed, he had a present all wrapped up in blue paper with a ribbon. He lit the candle in a bottle we keep on the table. We were hiding behind some old screens at the side of the room." Benjy leaned his forearms on the table.

Victoria was silent. So was Brooke.

"Then Abilene comes in, says hi to Sebastian and says, 'You have a present for Samantha. I'll take it.' Sebastian says, 'I'm giving it to her, not you.' Like that. Then Abilene says, 'Let me see it,' and he says, 'It's for Samantha. I love her and she loves me,' And then Samantha comes out from behind the screen yelling 'Surprise!' and we all come out." Benjy paused.

Victoria said, "I suppose Sebastian was embarrassed."

Benjy nodded. "He was. Samantha thought it was real funny and she was laughing. When I saw him all upset . . . well, it wasn't a good feeling."

"It was mean of Samantha," said Brooke. "We'd gone along with her, just following her like she said. Sebastian was a nice kid. He didn't deserve that from her. Or from us."

One of the turkeys made a gobbling sound. The other turkey joined in. Victoria heard them, the others didn't seem to notice.

"Then what?" she asked.

"I left. Emily and Brooke did too. The only people still there were Samantha, Abilene, and Sebastian."

"No one else?" asked Victoria.

Brooke and Benjy looked at each other. Benjy shook his head.

"Do you have any idea how the fire started?" asked Victoria.

"Benjy and I were talking about that. The only thing we can think of is the candle, but, you know, it would have burned down and gone out stuck in the bottle the way it was."

"Unless the bottle got knocked over," said

Victoria.

"I suppose that could have happened."

"Were there papers around?"

"Yeah," said Benjy, taking up the lead again. "A big stack of old newspapers on the floor, like they were going to the recycling center or something. They weren't anywhere near the candle. We'd been careful about that. An open flame in an old building wasn't a smart idea. We put the bottle on, like, a throwaway aluminum pan."

"That was it, Mrs. Trumbull," said Brooke. "We left. Samantha and Abilene were still laughing at Sebastian, and he was really, really upset. He started to come with us, and Samantha got real serious, told him she was sorry, said please don't go, so I guess he stayed."

"Do you have any idea how long they were there?"

Brooke and Benjy looked at each other and shook their heads.

"When did you hear about the fire?" asked Victoria.

"Not until the next day after school," said Brooke.

"I was home and heard on my dad's scanner there was a fire somewhere, but I never thought it was the parsonage."

"Did either of you see Samantha or Abilene after the fire?"

Brooke looked down at the table. "I don't really remember."

"Me neither," said Benjy.

CHAPTER 35

After she met with Benjy and Brooke, Victoria invited Abilene to tea. Herbal tea for Abilene, Earl Grey for Victoria. That done they went into the cookroom with their cups and saucers.

"I wanted to thank you for showing me your studio," Victoria said.

"It was a pleasure. I love showing it off," said Abilene. "But I think you had some special reason for inviting me, didn't you?"

"Yes," said Victoria. When they were seated she said, "I understand you and Samantha were in the parsonage the night it burned down."

Abilene set her teacup down gently. "What do you mean, Mrs. Trumbull?"

"I've been trying to reconstruct what happened the night Sebastian died. Sebastian had a wampum necklace he was going to give Samantha that night. There was a meeting of some of Samantha's group that same night."

"What are you saying, Mrs. Trumbull?"

"Abilene, I know you were there. I need to ask you about the night of the fire."

"It's too painful, Mrs. Trumbull." Abilene looked away from Victoria, out the window, focused on something far away. She said in a soft voice, "Yes, I was there."

"After the others left, you were there with Samantha and Sebastian."

"Is that what they're saying?"

"Abilene, I want to know what happened after the others left."

"I really, truly don't want to talk about it."

"You can talk to me, or you can talk to the arson investigator. What happened? Did Sebastian give Samantha the necklace?"

Abilene heaved a sigh. "I took the package from him and I unwrapped it. He tried to take it back." She stopped. "Mrs. Trumbull, I can't talk about it."

"After you unwrapped it, what happened?"

"Sebastian grabbed it back from me, leaned down, and laid it under a pile of newspapers that was on the floor. He said, 'She doesn't deserve it.' "

"Where was Samantha?"

"She was there. She said if he had a wampum necklace for her, it was hers and she wanted it, and she tried to get it out from under the newspapers. Then they got into a pushing and shoving argument."

"What were you doing?"

"I was standing back watching them."

"Did they come to blows?" asked Victoria.

"I can't tell you exactly what happened. But somehow he got hurt and was lying down trying to get up. She said, we're getting out of here, and we got out of there."

"And left an injured boy?"

"We didn't think he was hurt badly. I thought he was faking." Abilene was twisting her fingers in her lap. "Mrs. Trumbull, it was all wrong. I'm guilty. I can't justify what I did. Or didn't do."

"How did the fire start?"

"I don't know. I honestly don't know." Abilene shook her head. "We'd met in the parsonage a lot of times before. We were always careful with the candles. We didn't want the police to see the light. We'd put a stub in a bottle and when it burned down the stub just fell into the bottle."

"Are you thinking someone else set the fire that killed Sebastian?"

Abilene put her head in her hands and began to cry. "I don't know, Mrs. Trumbull.

I haven't been able to sleep since it happened. It keeps running through my mind. I wish I could go back to before we left Sebastian lying on the floor. I wish I could go back to when Samantha talked about playing a joke on Sebastian. I could have done the right thing then, and I didn't."

"Did you realize then that Samantha was just toying with you, too, the way she was with Sebastian?" asked Victoria.

"It opened my eyes, the way she treated him. And everyone else." Abilene was sobbing. Victoria handed her a paper towel.

"I don't know how the fire started." Her voice quavered. "We didn't set that fire, Mrs. Trumbull. We never, never, ever dreamed of . . . of . . . of . . . Even Samantha, she was not a killer. Not Sebastian."

"How did the fire start, then?" asked Victoria.

She got the answer shortly after Abilene left, still in tears. Victoria couldn't feel sorry for her. She thought of Sebastian, lying hurt on the parsonage floor, and Samantha and Abilene leaving him there to die in the fire that followed.

Drugs. Was that what was responsible for their failing to aid a boy in trouble?

The phone rang. It was Casey.

"What is it?" said Victoria, more sharply than she'd intended.

"Don't bite my head off, Victoria. What's going on over there?"

"I'm sorry. It's about drugs and I'm sick of it."

"I don't blame you. I just talked to the arson investigator. His name, by the way, is Ashley."

At that, Victoria smiled. "That's appropriate. Have they been able to find anything?"

"They found trace evidence of accelerants in several places around the perimeter of the parsonage."

"What kind of accelerants?"

"I don't know," said Casey. "And I don't know how they detect something that was just a faint trace. But they did."

"Then someone set the fire deliberately," said Victoria. "Why? And why at that particular time? Did the arsonist know someone was inside?"

"I don't have any answers," said Casey.

Victoria realized it was futile to search for the source of leaves that covered Samantha's body. She had never imagined there were so many maple trees on the Island. Every one of her suspects had access to piles of last year's fallen leaves.

And then Bill O'Malley reported back to her.

His truck had been cleaned until the blue finish shone.

"It looks lovely," said Victoria admiring it.

"The engine looks just as lovely," said O'Malley. "Anderson Jones, the guy who does my truck maintenance, says there's no way we can track down the movements of one dump truck between the night the body was dumped there and the morning you found it."

"Is this the Anderson Jones who has the moped rental place?"

"The same," said Bill.

"I didn't realize he did vehicle maintenance."

"He does specialized maintenance on expensive cars and trucks."

"Such as Jaguars?" asked Victoria.

"Bruno Eberhardt's green Jag is in Anderson's shop right now for its annual maintenance."

Victoria was not easily discouraged. However, the two leads that she'd felt sure would guide her to the killer, maple leaves and dump trucks, were not going to help. Not that they were poor leads, but there were too many sources of leaves and too many dump trucks.

"Don't give up, Victoria," said O'Malley.

"I don't know where to turn." She looked at her watch. She'd let the afternoon get away from her and hadn't picked up the mail. She'd been concentrating too hard on the two deaths, Sebastian's and Samantha's. Then trying to deflect Bruno Eberhardt from taking revenge on Zack, the innocent, and now puzzling over who had attempted to kill Eberhardt.

"Can I give you a ride anywhere?" asked Bill.

"Yes. Anywhere would be fine. Would you take me to Alley's? I'd like to pick up my mail. Perhaps there'll be a real letter today."

"Not likely. All catalogs. I'll write you a real one."

Victoria smiled. "I'd settle for a seed catalog."

"I have to go to Chilmark, so I'll drop you off at Alley's on my way and pick you up again in, say, a half-hour?"

"That's just what I need," said Victoria. "A nice break from everything."

He'd parked his dump truck in Victoria's drive. He brought out the milk crate step he kept for Victoria's use and helped her up into the high seat. She was already beginning to feel a little better. Something about his shiny new truck with its air conditioning, country music, and the passenger seat so high above all other vehicles made it seem as though she was seated on a throne viewing the world below her.

He stopped in front of Alley's, and she waited while he set down her milk crate and helped her out of the high seat.

Joe the plumber and Sarah Germain watched from their places on the porch, as Bill escorted her up the steps.

"You sure get around, Mrs. Trumbull," said Sarah.

"See you in about a half-hour," said Bill.

Victoria waved a hand at them and dismissed Bill as he drove off.

"I like your chauffeur, Mrs. Trumbull," said Sarah. "He has class."

"Have you hitched with one of the septic system tankers yet?" said Joe. "Nice smooth ride, I hear."

Victoria went inside to pick up her mail and came back out with a half-dozen catalogs and a copy of the *Island Enquirer.*

Sarah moved over. She was wearing a black T-shirt with crossed tomahawks in Day-Glo orange. "Have a seat, Mrs. Trumbull. Any nice gossip you can share?"

Victoria sat. "Lincoln and Casey seem to

be keeping company. They're very secretive about it."

"That's good. Patrick is a nice kid and needs a father figure. And Linc needs to be a father figure." Sarah brushed a speck off her T-shirt. "I guess Casey, being the town's police chief, feels she shouldn't appear to be too friendly with a murder suspect."

"I don't think he's a serious suspect," said Victoria.

"Can I get you a soda?" Sarah started to get up.

"No, thank you," said Victoria. "How are things at tribal headquarters?"

"You heard about Isabella Minnowfish, didn't you?"

"I'm not sure I've heard the latest," said Victoria.

Sarah told her the whole story behind Isabella's departure with the help of her two brothers and the chief's confiscation of all she'd taken.

"Why did Chief VanDyke go along with Mr. Eberhardt? As the tribe's head policeman I would think he'd have refused."

"That's easy. The chief is a gambler, and Bruno Eberhardt bailed him out of trouble a couple of years ago. The tribe's not happy about how cozy the chief is with Bruno, but there's not much they can do about it. You

400

probably haven't heard the latest."

"I'm afraid to ask," said Victoria.

Sarah told how Isabella conned her brothers into trying to get her stuff back again, but that it was gone, and they found a body instead.

"Oh, my!" said Victoria. "What happened to her jewelry and the money?"

"Nobody seems to know." Sarah paused for dramatic effect. "Chief VanDyke is going to take them to the state police to book them for murder."

CHAPTER 36

Doc Jeffers punched in the number for the state police.

The phone was picked up on the first ring. "Sergeant Smalley, here."

"Doc Jeffers, here. I'm calling about Eberhardt."

"What's up?" said Smalley.

"He's showing signs of life," said Doc Jeffers. "Not a lot, but it's within the realm of possibility that he may survive."

"Will he recover brain function?"

"We can't tell at this point."

"Do you still have a twenty-four-hour watch on him?"

"Yes, but we can't do it much longer. Other patients need attention."

"I'm concerned his assailant will show up to finish the job."

"We are too, but there's only so much we can do."

"I'll get one of my guys there right away

to spell your people."

"Make it soon."

The state police, using volunteers from the Island's six police departments, set up four-hour watches outside the second-floor Intensive Care Unit, where Bruno Eberhardt lay unconscious, hooked up to machines and tubes.

Victoria was determined to be involved. Her grandniece, Hope, was on duty in the ICU, so Victoria spent as much time as she could spare at the hospital, conversing with the guard on duty, working on her poetry, and catching sight of Hope as she went about her duties. There was a comfortable couch where she could sit. When she got tired of sitting she wandered out to the roof garden. From there she had a panoramic view of the harbor and the white houses of Vineyard Haven.

She had become accustomed to the steady beeps and chirps of the machines that monitored Eberhardt's life systems.

It was Friday afternoon, three days after Eberhardt had been admitted to the hospital. Tim Eldredge was on duty, checking his watch when Smalley came up the stairs.

"Still on duty, Mrs. Trumbull?"

"It's a pleasant place to sit and write,"

said Victoria. "I spell Tim when he needs a break. You know my grandniece, Hope, don't you?"

The steady beeps from Eberhardt's room faltered, and Hope dashed toward the room. By the time she got there, the beeps had resumed their steady rhythm. From where Victoria sat she could see Hope checking gauges, monitors, tubes, and wires. Hope wrote something on a clipboard and returned to the nurses' station across from his room.

"That was fast," said Smalley. "Doesn't that noise from the monitors bother you, Mrs. Trumbull?"

"I've gotten accustomed to it. I wouldn't know what to do if it should change rhythm, but I'd know to call the nurses if they hadn't already responded."

"Fortunately, we don't need to concern ourselves with the medical end of this," said Smalley. "Our role is to make sure no unauthorized person has access to Eberhardt or the stuff that's keeping him alive."

"I don't see how anyone can gain unauthorized access with a nurse on duty all the time and a police guard as well."

"That's why I'm here, Mrs. Trumbull. The police guard duty. How would you feel about taking over for a couple of hours?"

"I'd be delighted."

"Tim has a family emergency and Chief VanDyke won't be here until five o'clock, which leaves two unguarded hours."

"I'll sit at the guard post right now," said Victoria, gathering up her papers in preparation of the move across the hall.

"You understand our function?" said Smalley. "No unauthorized person anywhere near the patient. Only the medical staff. No one is to enter his room, whether they're friends or not."

"I understand," said Victoria.

"The nursing and medical staff is all checked out," said Smalley. "Since the maternity ward is on this floor, there are going to be visitors. Also, the inpatient rooms are over there." He pointed to the hallway behind them. "They'll have visitors, too. But no one, and I mean no one, is to go into his room. No one — only authorized hospital staff."

"I understand," said Victoria again.

"I can't think of anyone I'd trust more with this guard job than you," said Smalley and left.

Tim placed a bookmark in his book and closed it. "Appreciate this, Mrs. Trumbull."

"I'm sorry about your emergency," said Victoria.

"It's not a big deal," said Tim. "The engine on my brother's lobster boat cut out and he needs my help getting it going again."

Victoria laughed. "A better emergency than someone falling and breaking something."

"You sure you'll be okay?"

"Of course. I've been observing you for the past two hours, and my grandniece is on duty," said Victoria. "Furthermore there certainly are a lot of visitors to keep me entertained."

"Sure are. Well, thanks, Mrs. T."

After he left, Hope moved Victoria's armchair closer to Eberhardt's door, where Tim had been sitting, and Victoria sat

"It's a wonder he survived," said Hope. "He'd been lying there for at least a full day before his cleaning woman found him."

"A full day?" asked Victoria. "The Minnowfish brothers couldn't have killed him, then."

"I don't understand," said Hope.

"They were there to get Isabella's clothing only minutes before Maria Lima found Bruno."

"I gotta get back to work," said Hope. "You'll figure it out."

Victoria could see Bruno Eberhardt

through the open door. His head was wrapped in bandages that looked like a Sikh's turban. His face was pasty white. A white hospital blanket was pulled up to his chest. Everything around him was white except for his hospital gown, which was light blue and printed with bright flowers and colorful toy animals, a small attempt at bringing cheer. Both of his arms were straight down beside him. Victoria could make out tubes and wires coming from everywhere — arms, nose, chest, and from under the blanket. A bottle of liquid hung from a stand and a tube led from that to his arm. There was a steady beeping, chirping, piping, humming, clicking from the various machines near his bed and the nurses' station.

Who could possibly interpret all the reports from those machines? What was going on inside that inert body?

"Hello, Mrs. Trumbull."

Victoria, surprised, looked away from the patient. "Good afternoon, Abilene. What are you doing here?"

"I was about to ask you the same, Mrs. Trumbull."

"I'm a police guard," said Victoria. "And you?" Early on, Victoria had considered Abilene a suspect in Samantha's death, and now it seemed likely she had made the attempt on Samantha's father. She was strong and had powerful motives for killing both of them.

Furthermore, the thought of Abilene leaving an injured Sebastian disturbed her. Someone had set that fire. Had she?

"I'm visiting a client who's here." Abilene held up a mason jar with a bouquet of wild flowers. "I'm taking her some flowers."

"I hope your friend is not seriously ill," said Victoria.

"I don't think she even needs to be hospitalized," Abilene replied. "But she had flu-like symptoms, and who knows what that means. Is Bruno in there?" She nodded toward the door.

"Yes," said Victoria.

"How is he?"

"I really don't know," said Victoria.

"Is he likely to recover?"

"He's quite fragile, I understand," said Victoria.

"I don't mean to wish him ill, but . . . Well, yes, I do wish him ill. Well, off to see my client." She went to the nurses' station and spoke to Hope, then returned to Victoria, still holding the bouquet in the mason jar. "They never admitted her. Here, you can have these." She put the jar down on the small table next to Victoria and left.

A few minutes later, Isabella Minnowfish came up the stairs and stopped in front of Victoria. She introduced herself. "I don't believe we've ever met formally," she said. "Of course I know who you are."

"I'm delighted to meet you," said Victoria. "Your great-grandmother was a friend of mine."

"I never knew her," said Isabella. "Is Bruno still alive?"

"He's very fragile," said Victoria.

"I don't suppose I can look in on him?"

"I'm afraid that's out of the question," said Victoria.

"Oh, well. I was just passing by and thought I'd check."

About an hour later, a big, pleasant-looking man, a bit overweight, came off the elevator.

"Mrs. Trumbull, I'm Phil Smith, Zack's boss at the café."

"Yes, of course," said Victoria. "Thank you for taking him back as dishwasher."

"Not at all. He's indispensable." He nodded toward the room where Bruno lay. "That our boy Eberhardt in there?"

Victoria nodded.

"Came to pay my respects. Okay to go on in?"

"Sorry," said Victoria. "No one but medical staff is allowed in."

"How's he doing?"

"I really can't say," said Victoria.

"If he should, by any chance, pull through, tell him I stopped by," said Phil. "That should give him a thrill." He grinned and left.

The two hours went by quickly, with several people Victoria knew visiting patients in rooms down the hall, and Victoria was pleasantly surprised when Chief Josephus VanDyke showed up. He was in full uniform, ruggedly handsome with a smile that created deep creases from nose to mouth on his leathery face.

"I'm here to relieve you, Mrs. Trumbull." He hiked up the trousers that were belted below his large stomach. "Appreciate your being part of the guard team."

"It's really quite enjoyable, Chief Van-Dyke," said Victoria. "I had no idea there were so many visitors to the hospital."

"Now I've relieved you, do you have someone to drive you home?"

"My granddaughter. She works at the Oak Bluffs Harbor."

"Just a hop, skip, and a jump from here," said the chief. "When does she get off duty?"

Victoria checked her watch. "Anytime now."

"I'll take over then. You can wait downstairs for her."

"Thank you." Victoria was glad to be relieved after the long day. She gathered up her papers and headed for the elevator. As she was waiting for it to come, a bell chimed, and Hope rushed past her to one of the rooms down the hall. The elevator arrived. Just as Victoria was about to step aboard, it occurred to her that with Hope tending a patient, Chief VanDyke should have someone there with him. The elevator door closed without her and she turned. The chief was not at the guard chair. He had entered Eberhardt's room.

No one was to enter that room. Victoria called out to him.

"Chief VanDyke!"

He immediately appeared.

Victoria blurted, "Only medical staff are allowed in that room."

"I was checking on him," said the chief.

"I apologize for even questioning you, but Sergeant Smalley was adamant."

"Rightly so," said the chief.

Hope returned from the room down the hall. "The patient's water pitcher was empty," she said. "Is everything all right here?"

"Definitely," said the chief.

"I should mention that Chief VanDyke went into Mr. Eberhardt's room," said Victoria.

"I'd better check him again." Hope went into the room and was there for several minutes. When she came out again she was flustered. "One of the tubes was out. I've replaced it."

Victoria glanced at the chief.

"I saw that it was," he said. "I was about to call you."

"Sir, you were not to enter his room," said Hope.

"I'm a police officer," said the chief. "My duty is to ensure his safety, and I did just that. One of the tubes was out."

"Why didn't the monitors sound the alarm?" asked Victoria.

"The alarm goes off when the fluid level is low," said Hope. "I check every ten minutes or so, but ten minutes could be too late."

"I believe I'll wait for Elizabeth here," said Victoria, returning to her chair.

Elizabeth came up the stairs to the second floor and saw a stern-faced Victoria sitting on her chair, her papers on the side table, her arms crossed. Chief Josephus VanDyke was sitting in the guard chair, his arms crossed, too, glaring straight ahead at nothing.

She looked from one stony face to the other. "Ready to go, Gram?"

"I'll be staying for the four-hour watch to keep Chief VanDyke company," said Victoria. "Would you mind getting me something to eat?"

"Sure, be glad to," said Elizabeth.

Victoria reached for her papers, scribbled a quick note, and handed it to Elizabeth.

The note said, "Get Smalley here NOW." Elizabeth nodded, looked up from the note and said brightly, "Can I get you something to eat, too, Chief VanDyke?"

He took his wallet out of his back pocket and checked inside. "I guess not. Thank you, though."

"I'll be right back, Gram. Something to drink, too?"

"Cranberry juice," said Victoria.

Elizabeth went down to the lobby and called the state police number. Smalley answered.

"Come to the hospital immediately," Elizabeth said. "My grandmother and Chief VanDyke look like a tornado is brewing."

"Be there in ten minutes or less," said Smalley.

"I'm taking up some food to camouflage whatever is going on," said Elizabeth.

She made a quick trip to the cafeteria, grabbed a ready-made salad and a bottle of cranberry juice, handed the woman at the checkout a ten-dollar bill and left.

"Your change!" the woman called out.

"Keep it," said Elizabeth, and dashed up the stairs.

After Elizabeth left, the chief rose from his seat. "Mrs. Trumbull," he said, taking a deep breath. "It's commendable that you alerted the nurse to the fact that a person had entered Mr. Eberhardt's room. However, you are completely out of line to question me. Or the fact that I entered that room. I am a police officer." He patted his chest. "I am a chief of police." He stepped toward her. "I volunteered my time to guard that room. And that's what I intend to do."

"No one," Victoria slapped a hand on the arm of her chair, "no one, absolutely no one except medical staff, was to enter that room."

"As a police officer, I am an exception, Mrs. Trumbull." He moved closer to her. "Surely you understand that." He smiled.

"We appreciate your efforts to guard Mr. Eberhardt's room." Then he pointed a finger at her and said, quite firmly, "However," he paused. "You have no experience. You have no training. Do not interfere with police work, Mrs. Trumbull. Spend more time with your grandchildren, your great-grandchildren. Bake them cookies. Read to them." He smiled again. "I'm afraid your great age has warped your judgment."

Victoria, her face a bright pink, rose from her seat. "Don't you dare question my experience, Chief VanDyke." She stepped toward him and shook her fist at him. "I was guarding precious people before you were born." Her eyes glittered. "How dare you speak to me like that!" She took another step toward him. "*You* detached that tube, didn't you? You had every reason to kill Mr. Eberhardt, and you almost succeeded."

At that VanDyke drew his gun. "You've lost your mind, Mrs. Trumbull. Don't come another step toward me, or I'll shoot."

When Elizabeth reached the second floor, she saw the chief pointing his gun at Victoria, who was standing stock still. Hope was cowering behind the nurses' station.

"Here's the food!" shouted Elizabeth.

The chief glanced over at her.

At the momentary distraction, Elizabeth threw the cranberry juice bottle as hard as she could at the chief's head. It hit with a solid thwack and the gun dropped. Hope came out from behind the desk and kicked the fallen gun across the hall.

There was a moment's stunned silence. The chief put a hand up to his head. "You don't realize what you've just done, foolish girl."

"You were about to shoot my grandmother," Elizabeth said.

"I was not about to shoot anybody," said the chief, with indignation. "I had no other course but to draw my weapon. Your grandmother was out of control."

"That's my grandmother," said Elizabeth.

"Furthermore," said the chief, pointing at Elizabeth with the hand not holding his head, "I am charging you with assaulting a police officer and interfering with me in the course of doing my job."

Victoria had returned to her seat. "Are the state police on their way?" she asked Elizabeth.

"I look forward to their arrival," said the chief.

Elizabeth went over and picked up the gun.

Chief VanDyke took a blue-bordered

handkerchief out of his pants pocket and wiped his forehead.

"Everybody sit still until the police arrive," said Elizabeth. "They can sort things out."

Smalley arrived in less than ten minutes accompanied by Tim, who'd apparently repaired his brother's boat engine in record time.

Elizabeth was leaning against the counter that surrounded the nurses' station, still holding the gun. Hope was in Eberhardt's room checking everything for the third time.

"What's up, Josephus?" said Smalley.

"You can see what's up," said the chief. "Mrs. Trumbull's granddaughter is holding my gun and I am charging her with assault."

Victoria stood. "Chief VanDyke attempted to kill Bruno Eberhardt."

The chief laughed. "John, that is absurd."

"Mrs. Trumbull?" said Smalley.

"Chief VanDyke disconnected one of the tubes keeping Mr. Eberhardt alive," said Victoria.

Hope came out of Eberhardt's room and stood off to one side.

"It's fortunate I went into his room," said the chief. "When I checked the wires and tubes I found that one had become dislodged. I was about to call the nurse when

Mrs. Trumbull became upset about my entering his room." He smacked his right fist into the palm of his left hand. "I undoubtedly saved his life."

"The tube could never have come loose by accident," said Hope.

"You're mistaken," said the chief.

"I am a nurse," said Hope, stretching up to her full height, almost as tall as her great-aunt. "I repeat, the tube could not have come loose by accident. I checked everything a few minutes before Chief VanDyke entered the room. Everything was in order then."

"You checked it because a monitor stopped beeping," said VanDyke. "It was undoubtedly loose."

Victoria said again to Smalley, "Chief Josephus VanDyke attempted to murder Bruno Eberhardt."

Josephus laughed. "John, this is outrageous."

"Furthermore," said Victoria, "I believe you will find that he stole fifty thousand dollars in cash that belongs to Mr. Eberhardt."

"Just a moment, Mrs. Trumbull . . . !" said the chief.

"Hold on," said Smalley lifting up a hand. "Calm down, everyone." Smalley looked from one to another. "Be careful who you accuse, Mrs. Trumbull. Chief VanDyke is the tribal chief of police."

"I think if you look in the chief's wallet you may find two or three of the hundred-dollar bills he stole. Mr. Eberhardt had listed the numbers of all five hundred of the bills."

"We can check that easily enough," said Smalley. "Shall we go back to the barracks and discuss this?"

"I'd like to have my gun back," said the chief holding out his hand to Elizabeth.

"I'll take it," said Smalley.

"Shouldn't you put him in handcuffs?" asked Elizabeth, as she handed him the gun.

"He's not a suspect," said Smalley. "Tensions are running high, right now. I'll hold on to your gun, Josephus, until all this is sorted out." He turned to Tim. "Take over the watch."

"Yes, sir," said Tim, and saluted.

CHAPTER 37

Back at the barracks Victoria and Elizabeth, Sergeant John Smalley, and Chief Josephus VanDyke seated themselves around the conference table in an uncomfortable silence.

Smalley spoke. "I think we can solve this easily." He leaned back in his chair. "For some reason, Eberhardt faxed the numbers for those hundred-dollar bills to us at the state police barracks. Paranoid guy. What about it, Josephus, you got any hundreds in your wallet?"

"No. I don't." The chief folded his arms across his chest.

"We have no right to search you, and furthermore, I don't believe that's necessary," said Smalley. "Mind taking out your wallet and showing us what's in there?"

"Not at all." The chief reached into his back pocket, took out a well-worn black leather wallet, opened it, and fanned out the bills. A ten and several ones.

"There's your answer, Mrs. Trumbull," said Smalley.

Victoria wrinkled up her face, said "Ahh!" a couple of times and sneezed, then sneezed again. Elizabeth looked at her in astonishment. Victoria sneezed a third time and held a hand up to her great nose. She sneezed once again and apologized.

"I'm afraid I don't have a handkerchief. Chief VanDyke," she continued to hold her hand to her nose, "may I borrow yours?"

"Certainly, Mrs. Trumbull." He reached into his right-hand trousers pocket and brought out his blue-bordered white handkerchief.

Along with the handkerchief, several crumpled bills dropped to the floor. He bent over to pick them up, but Elizabeth reached them first.

She smoothed them out. "Hundred-dollar bills," she said.

The chief reached for them. "Thank you, I'll just put those back in my pocket."

"Let me have them, Elizabeth," said Smalley. "I'll check the numbers and that should clear things up." He took the bills from her. "Sorry we're putting you through this, Josephus, but I'm sure you want this cleared up as much as I do. We do," he corrected himself.

Victoria returned the handkerchief, unused, to Chief VanDyke. "Thank you," she said.

With a wry smile he said, "You're welcome."

Smalley returned with several faxed pages and the hundred-dollar bills. "Fortunately, Eberhardt listed them in order so it won't take a minute."

"Never mind, John," said Josephus. "You'll find a match."

"I believe we could use some coffee about now," said Smalley. "Trooper Ben made a fresh pot. We might as well be civilized about this whole thing."

Ben brought in the coffee and poured it into four mugs.

"You want to say anything, Josephus," said Smalley, "or would you prefer to have Mrs. Trumbull do the talking. I don't think we need to Mirandize you."

"I'd like to hear what Mrs. Trumbull has to say," said the chief. He turned to her. "Why me, Mrs. Trumbull? I would have named a half dozen suspects before considering me." He paused, then that wry smile again. "Me, the chief of police."

"I was told you are a gambler, Chief Van-Dyke."

He nodded. "An unfortunate addiction."

"And I was told that you owe much too much to Bruno Eberhardt."

"Both money and favors."

Smalley began to doodle on the yellow pad in front of him.

Victoria continued. "After he bailed you out, your gambling debts mounted again, didn't they?"

"Luck of the draw, I'm afraid."

"When Mr. Eberhardt asked you to collect Isabella's clothing, her jewelry, and fifty thousand dollars in cash, how did you explain to him that you had kept the money?"

The chief wrapped his hands around his coffee mug as though to warm them. "I told him Isabella and Tank had stashed the money in a safe place and I would get it to him later. He said he would withhold the generous bonus he'd promised to pay me until I recovered the money."

Smalley tossed his pencil down. "Did you think you'd win this time?"

"Yes," said the chief. "I put down only half. Twenty-five thousand. Had I won, I would have doubled it. Fifty thousand. I planned to turn over his fifty thousand to him and I would have twenty-five thousand in addition to the bonus he would give me."

"But you lost, of course," said Smalley. "And when you lost, you had no excuse to give Bruno Eberhardt. Did you kill him when he threatened to expose you?"

"Yes. There was a thoroughly unpleasant argument that ended when I struck him."

"The weapon, Josephus. What did you use?" asked Smalley.

"The fireplace poker in his study," said the chief.

Smalley said, "All right, Mrs. Trumbull. Tell us about your sneezing fit."

"I saw that Chief VanDyke had a handkerchief in his pocket. He's a courteous man and I was sure he would let me borrow it if I needed it."

Chief VanDyke made a slight bow in her direction.

"And?" said Smalley.

"On the way here from the hospital he put something in his pocket. I didn't think much of it at the time." Victoria turned back to the chief. "But I recalled that when Elizabeth offered to get us food, you opened your wallet and I saw a number of hundred-dollar bills in it. At the time I wondered if they were part of Mr. Eberhardt's fifty thousand dollars."

Josephus nodded. "You're too observant, Mrs. Trumbull. I underestimated you."

"Did you kill Samantha, too?" asked Victoria.

Chief VanDyke turned to Sergeant Smalley. "I assume none of this is being taped, John?"

Smalley nodded.

"And I assume this is all quite informal?"

Smalley nodded again.

"I'll take my chances at trial."

"You did kill Samantha," said Victoria.

"Yes, Mrs. Trumbull. I did."

"Why?"

The chief lifted his coffee mug in a kind of salute to all. "I met Samantha through my dealings with Bruno. I was attracted to her. My vital juices flowed again. I was in love."

"What about your wife?" asked Smalley.

"The same sorry and tiresome story. A husband cheating on a wife who didn't deserve to be cheated on."

"That foggy night a couple of weeks ago, was that when you killed her?" asked Victoria.

"Yes." He leaned back and crossed his arms over his chest. "I was driving from Aquinnah that night and almost hit a small car that had skidded on the slick road into my path. Shortly after, I realized it was Samantha's car. I'd come close to killing her." He looked up, and again the wry smile. "Ironic, isn't it." He sat forward and took a sip of his coffee. "I doubled back to her place to see if she was okay. I thought I was in love with her, you know."

Victoria nodded.

"We had a glass of wine at her cottage, then I suggested we go back to my place. She took her car."

"Where was your wife?" asked Smalley.

"Off-Island, visiting her mother in Albuquerque."

"So you went back to your place," prompted Victoria.

"One thing led to another. I was as randy as a teenager. Things seemed to be going fine until the third or fourth glass of wine took effect and she started bragging about her conquests." He rubbed his forehead. "Then teasing me about my performance. She went on and on and on. I couldn't stop her. I couldn't stand it. I don't know what got into me. I could see only glaring red light flashing before my eyes. I grabbed my rifle, which I keep on a shelf above my bedroom door, and smacked her on the back of the head with the butt end."

"Killed her," said Smalley.

He nodded. "I knew right away I'd killed her. I got cold sober in a hurry. I knew I had to take her body as far from Aquinnah as possible and decided to drop her off the municipal pier in Edgartown. Let the tide carry her out to Nantucket Sound and the creatures that feed on carrion. It was late at night and I could hardly see."

Ben came in with a fresh pot of coffee, looked at the sober faces, and left without pouring. The ferry whistle sounded. A car passed in front of the barracks. A second car passed.

"I loaded her body into my pickup," the chief continued. "Then saw she was too obvious. I park my truck beside the Brave Haulers garage where there's a big tree. Wind had piled up leaves behind the garage. I didn't have a tarp to cover the back of my truck, so instead I scooped up leaves and heaped them on top of her body to conceal it."

"Why dump her body on the bicycle path?" asked Victoria.

"A mistake." He shook his head. "The night was calm. But halfway to Edgartown the wind came up. Leaves started blowing off. I had to get rid of her before she was uncovered and a passing vehicle saw her. When I came to that small valley on the Edgartown Road, I backed in and unloaded her. Covered her with leaves and left." He shrugged. "I smoothed out the tire tracks with a branch."

"We found the tracks, but you did a good job of obliterating the identifying prints," said Smalley. "Mrs. Trumbull, anything else?"

She turned to Josephus. "You set fire to the parsonage. Why?"

"I had no idea the boy was in there. I regret that."

"Why did you burn the parsonage?" said Victoria.

"The building was a gathering place for Samantha and her friends. I suspected drugs were involved. The building was old, derelict, and unsafe. The current owners had abandoned it. I thought to purify the site." He smiled. "An ancient Indian site. I had followed Samantha and waited until I saw her and her followers leave." He looked up.

"The boy never should have died." He looked away again. "I poured paint thinner around the foundations and lit a match." He held out his hands, palms up. "You can arrest me now, John."

Smalley took a card out of his wallet. "Your Miranda rights, Josephus. You have the right to remain silent. Anything you say can be used against you in court . . ."

CHAPTER 38

Several days later, Victoria, Elizabeth, and Zack were eating breakfast together, blueberry muffins, bacon, and eggs.

"What have they decided to charge you with, Zack?" asked Elizabeth.

"Miranda Smith, my lawyer, told the judge there was nothing in the books to justify charging me with anything. She said thinking about making someone sick and not following through with it was not a crime." He helped himself to a second blueberry muffin. "But the judge ordered me to do fifty hours of community service anyway."

"What will you do?" asked Elizabeth.

"Help maintain trails at Sachem's Rock."

"Don't pick any mushrooms," said Victoria.

"No, ma'am," said Zack. "My boss has invited you to a party he's throwing this afternoon to celebrate my freedom."

430

So when Elizabeth came home from the harbor that afternoon, they got into her convertible and headed toward Chilmark. The late afternoon light was golden and mellow. Splashes of scarlet marked poison ivy twining around fence-posts. The Norway maples were a bright yellow against the deep blue sky. They passed Doane's hayfield, where a flock of Canada geese was browsing on the stubble. They passed the tiny police station and the Mill Pond, where the swans sailed with their nearly grown cygnets. They waved at the regulars sitting on the porch at Alley's Store and continued past the gas station and crossed the town line into Chilmark. The road now was bounded by the stone walls of Chilmark, each new stretch of wall was a distinctive piece of art that showed the builder's creativity. They passed the Allen sheep farm with its spectacular view of the Atlantic beyond the rolling meadow where sheep grazed, and came to the crossroads where the beetlebung trees had turned their distinctive dark maroon.

They were met at the Beetlebung Café by Phil Smith and a woman with long, sleek, black hair.

"Mrs. Trumbull, this is my wife, Miranda," said Phil, his arm around her shoulder.

"Thank you for acting on behalf of Zack," said Victoria.

"I'd have gotten him off even if he had killed her," said Miranda.

"Here's Isabella," said Phil, as she came into the dining room carrying a tray loaded with hors d'oeuvres. "She's been bringing in so much business, I'm expanding."

"You know what he's paying me?" said Isabella. "Three-fifty an hour."

"Plus tips," said Phil. "Her tips have rocketed it up to close to twenty an hour."

Victoria helped herself to a crab cake. "How are your brothers?" she asked.

"Same old," said Isabella. "They'll never change."

"Does anyone know how Bruno is doing?" asked Phil.

"It looks as though he may recover fully," said Victoria. "I've been going to see him at the hospital, and over the last couple of days he's agreed, after much consideration, to fund several scholarships at the drug treatment center. Brooke, Benjy, and Emily have all qualified."

Will brought out a chilled bottle of Champagne. Phil eased out the cork and poured it into flutes for all. He held up his own glass. "A toast to Victoria Trumbull, and another case solved."

ABOUT THE AUTHOR

Cynthia Riggs is the author of more than a dozen books in the Martha's Vineyard mystery series featuring 92-year-old poet, Victoria Trumbull, a guidebook called *Victoria Trumbull's Martha's Vineyard,* and the first book of a new series set in Washington, DC. She was born on Martha's Vineyard and is the eight generation to live in her family homestead which she runs as a bed and breakfast catering to poets, writers, and other creative people. She lives in West Tisbury, Massachusetts.

The employees of Thorndike Press hope you have enjoyed this Large Print book. All our Thorndike, Wheeler, and Kennebec Large Print titles are designed for easy reading, and all our books are made to last. Other Thorndike Press Large Print books are available at your library, through selected bookstores, or directly from us.

For information about titles, please call:
  (800) 223-1244

or visit our website at:
  gale.com/thorndike

To share your comments, please write:
  Publisher
  Thorndike Press
  10 Water St., Suite 310
  Waterville, ME 04901